Someone is watching them ... waiting ...

edge of
time

Susan M. MacDonald

www.breakwaterbooks.com

Breakwater Books is committed to choosing papers and
materials for our books that help to protect our environment.
To this end, this book is printed on a recycled paper that is
certified by the Forest Stewardship Council®.

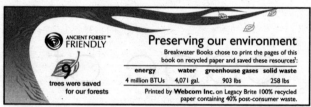

Preserving our environment

Breakwater Books chose to print the pages of this
book on recycled paper and saved these resources[1]:

	energy	water	greenhouse gases	solid waste
	4 million BTUs	4,071 gal.	903 lbs	258 lbs

Printed by **Webcom Inc.** on Legacy Brite 100% recycled
paper containing 40% post-consumer waste.

ANCIENT FOREST™ FRIENDLY

9 trees were saved
for our forests

[1]Estimates were made using the Environmental Defense Paper Calculator.

ISBN 978-1-55081-357-9
A CIP catalogue record for this book
is available from Library Archives Canada.

© 2011 Susan M. MacDonald
Cover Photo: Pritesh Gandhi, Ambient Devices

 Canada Council   Conseil des Arts
for the Arts   du Canada   Canada   Newfoundland
Labrador

We acknowledge the support of the Canada Council for the Arts which
last year invested $20.1 million in writing and publishing throughout Canada,
the Government of Canada through the Canada Book Fund and the
Government of Newfoundland and Labrador through the department of
Tourism, Culture and Recreation for our publishing activities.

Printed in Canada.

For Christopher, Caileigh, Jamieson and
my mum, Margot, for constantly believing I could.

This novel is dedicated to my father, Wilson.

The Writer's Alliance of Newfoundland and
Labrador's Mentorship program was valuable
in helping this novel reach publishable form.

Nothing like a little shoplifting to get the blood pumping, Alec thought as he tucked the DVD down the front of his jeans. He picked up another from the display and pretended to be absorbed in the story outline. Sure it was a stupid thing to do and his father would kill him if he found out, but only losers backed out of a bet at the last minute. And besides, he *really* needed the money.

The music store was packed with kids on summer vacation. Overhead, coloured lights flashed with the heavy bass rhythm that throbbed through the soles of Alec's feet. Someone jostled him from behind as they pushed through the crowd. Stevie and Chin were waiting behind the rack of discounted television series, neither looking at him. He meandered in their direction, playing it cool, but it felt like everyone was watching him. Was that a plain-clothes security guard lounging by Heavy Metal? Alec halted and feigned a sudden interest in the CDs on the shelf next to him. Grabbing three, he held them up to his face to hide his gaze.

For several long moments the suspected cop did nothing, then headed off to the cashiers. Alec tossed the CDs back.

The DVD slipped slightly with every step. Any minute it was going to fall right down onto the floor. Alec shoved his hands into his front pockets and tried to unobtrusively grasp the edge of the case with a couple of fingers, keenly aware of how it looked. Time to change plans and just get out of

1

there. The mall entrance was almost closer than Stevie and Chin anyway and there was no way the fat security guard lounging at the entrance would be able to catch him.

He turned to give Chin the signal he was leaving and caught a glimpse of the man out of the side of his eye. His heart gave a funny jump. There, behind Stevie. He glanced again, taking his time to make sure without being obvious.

He wasn't mistaken. It was the same guy. He'd noticed him outside his high school, at the park, and twice at soccer practice over the last few weeks. At least ten years older than Alec, of medium height and slim build, he didn't *look* like a cop, but that didn't mean anything. Something in the way he always seemed to be watching made Alec feel uneasy. Scarborough was a huge sprawl of cement and humanity. You hardly ever saw the same people day after day unless they worked or went to school with you, and even then you could easily miss someone. Was this guy following him?

Deliberately turning his eyes away, Alec put the stranger out of his mind. He had forty bucks to win. He glanced towards the mall. Twenty metres to the concourse. The DVD slipped even farther. He had to get out of there. Now.

Suddenly a most peculiar feeling slipped over his skin. Like the first icy touch of winter, raising the hair on his arms and neck with the slightest chill. Alec stopped walking. He looked up.

A punk with oversize jeans falling off his narrow hips and a hood flung up over his Blue Jays cap was slouching up the aisle towards him. His eyes were totally blank yet staring directly at Alec. The punk said nothing and no one around even seemed to notice him. Alec couldn't tear his eyes away. There was something odd here, something he should be ...

When he was about three metres away, the punk stopped. He pulled his right hand from the pocket of his hoodie and slowly raised it. He pointed a small gun straight at Alec.

What the hell?

Part of Alec's mind screamed, *run*, but he couldn't move. He couldn't even open his mouth to shout for help. It was like something out of a zombie horror movie – too bizarre to even contemplate as real.

The punk's trigger knuckle tightened in slow motion.

Suddenly Alec was tackled from behind. He hit the tiles with a thud that knocked the air out of his lungs. His chin glanced painfully off the dirty floor. A terrific *bang* thundered above, momentarily deafening him. Acrid gunpowder smoke filled the air. Somewhere someone screamed. It might have been him.

Strong hands pinned him. Alec squirmed helplessly. He couldn't even turn his head to get a clear view of his rescuer, but he knew with sudden overwhelming conviction that it was the guy who'd been following him around over the last few weeks.

"Hold still," the stranger hissed as he shifted slightly. His free hand shot out past Alec's nose. Alec saw a glass ball, the size of a small orange, which glowed with an almost blinding blue-white light, clasped in his fist.

There wasn't time to think about what his rescuer was doing. The punk wouldn't miss such an easy target again. This was it. Alec squeezed his eyes shut and held his breath. What a stupid way to die.

A brilliant white flash ripped under his eyelids the same instant the roaring blast thundered above him. His protector jerked spasmodically with a grunt but didn't lessen his grip on Alec's neck. It was all Alec could do not to scream. The rolling echo of the gunshot reverberated through the store. There were more shrieks above the blasting music, and several steps away, a dull thud as something heavy fell to the floor.

Alec opened his eyes, almost too afraid to see the blood and devastation. His rescuer scrambled sideways, easing himself off Alec's prostrate form. He slipped the glowing

9

ball into his pocket, murmuring directly into Alec's ear in a soft Irish lilt, "Next time, Alec, they won't miss." Before Alec could open his mouth to reply, the man disappeared into the gathering crowd.

Alec scrambled to his knees. Hang on a minute. There was *no way* the punk could have missed. He looked down at himself. No blood.

Still shaking, he climbed to his feet. His heart, which only a moment before had taken up lodging in his throat, returned to its normal position and slammed against his ribs. He felt dazed and slightly ill. Where had his rescuer gone? Was he hurt? *And how did he know his name?*

Alec barely noticed the points and stares. He shuffled over and stood right above the sprawled form of his assailant. A crimson stain had blossomed through the thicker fabric of the punk's hoodie. Glazed eyes stared upward. The beginnings of a ratty moustache fuzzed over thin lips that would never speak again. The gun was still loosely clasped in his hand.

Bile rose unbidden in Alec's throat. There wasn't any air. He couldn't breathe. Without heeding the shout of the security guard, Alec bolted.

He raced past the electronic boutique and the lingerie store. Skidding around the corner of his favourite clothing store, his stomach heaved when he caught the eye of a mannequin in the store window wearing the same jacket as the dead guy. He slammed his hands down on the bar that released the glass exit doors and shoved so hard they smacked against the doorstops. He stumbled outside into the stifling heat of the parking lot.

A crowd of shoppers milled at the entrance, several watching as a mall security guard, walkie-talkie held to his mouth, waved at a rapidly approaching fire truck.

Alec skidded to a stop, dropped his hands to his knees and gasped for breath. His stomach surged in revolt.

Hold it together, he admonished himself. It's over.

Too late.

Nearly two hours later, Alec eased open the door to his apartment and ducked inside the living room gloom.

His father was barely visible in the grey recliner, just the top of his balding head showing over the back of the headrest. Only the bluish flickering of the television set lighted the room. The news. His father only watched the news, and lately, it was all bad.

A pale yellow light shone from under the door of the galley kitchen and the comforting smells of allspice and coconut indicated his mother was in the final stages of dinner preparations. Pots clattered for a second. His father reached forward and thumbed the remote.

The large sliding doors were partly open and the floor-length curtains were not drawn against the early twilight. On the narrow balcony, his older brother, Peter, was curled up on a battered lounge chair, an ever-present book in his hand.

Alec stood silently. He tried to take some deep and calming breaths, but his chest felt constricted, like someone was squeezing him, and his legs still felt like jelly. If Chin hadn't walked him home, he doubted he would have made it.

The next news story flashed on the television screen. Between the fire engines, the doors of the mall winked into view. A reporter, her eyes wide with salacious glee, raised a microphone to her lips and began to speak. "For the fourth time this week, area residents have witnessed senseless violence ..."

Alec dashed across the living room and past the kitchen door. He had almost made it into the bedroom hallway when the light spilled out behind him and he heard his mother's voice.

"Alec, is that you?"

He stopped in his tracks and carefully modulated his tone. "Yeah." Sassing his mother twice in one day would have his father out of his chair so fast his head would spin.

"I asked you to be back by five." His mother wiped her hands on a dishtowel and leaned one weary shoulder against the kitchen doorjamb. She was shorter than Alec by several inches now, but it was kind of like seeing a female version of himself. The same dark curls, the same chocolate eyes.

Alec scuffed his toe on the scratched linoleum. "I got sick at the mall. Ask Chin. I threw up all over the sidewalk."

His mother frowned. Her hand whipped out and before he could back away, felt his forehead in the manner of concerned mothers the world over.

"You're a bit clammy. What did you eat?"

Alec shrugged. "I dunno."

"Better lie down. I'll keep your supper warm, in case you feel hungry later." She dismissed him without another glance and disappeared into the kitchen. Behind him, the television droned. He could feel his father's eyes on the back of his neck.

Peter hadn't turned on the light and their room was bathed in the pale blue of the street lamp directly outside. Alec crossed the floor in three strides and yanked the curtains shut. He pulled the DVD from his waistband and tossed it onto the cluttered dresser. He climbed the rungs to the top bunk, shoving the pile of freshly folded laundry off the end of his mattress with his foot, before flopping down on top of the comforter. Clasping the back of his head, he stared at the ceiling.

He'd seen a guy get shot. Not a movie or a cartoon or his video games. But real and right in front of him. And the guy, whoever he was, had been aiming right at him.

He knew he'd never seen the punk before. The guy had been too old to still be in high school and he certainly didn't play against him in any sport. The creep looked like he'd get winded climbing a flight of stairs. So why did he try to kill him? And maybe more importantly, why did that guy who pinned him to the ground say what he said?

Next time, they won't miss.

What on earth did *that* mean? Who were *they*? Were they really after *him*?

And if someone did have it out for him, what was he going to do?

"Your mother wants to know if you want anything to eat."

His father's voice from the doorway was an almost welcome disruption to Alec's unpleasant dream. He blinked several times and sat partway up. He checked his watch. Just after nine.

"Yeah. I guess so." Alec swung his legs over the side of the bunk and slid down onto the floor. He brushed past his father, avoiding his gaze, and headed down the hall.

"What's this?" his father asked.

Alec composed his face. "What?"

His father was holding the DVD aloft, waving it back and forth. He wasn't smiling. "Where did you get this?"

"Stevie. He got it for me."

"Uh-huh."

"I got sick. He thought it would make me feel better."

His father walked towards him. In another year, Alec would be taller, but now his father had the advantage of height as well as years of authority. He poked Alec in the chest with the corner of the movie case. "Since when does Stevie buy you anything?"

"I dunno. It was a buy-one-get-one-free deal. He got something for himself first."

"If I find out you're stealing, Alec, the provincial tournament is off. Do you hear me? You'll spend the rest of the summer grounded." His father thrust the DVD into Alec's hand and headed to the living room.

2

Alec kept his eyes glued to the floor and bit back the profanity. He counted to ten as slowly as he could.

His mother poked her head out of the kitchen. "Come and have your supper," she said before disappearing.

If he missed the meal his mom would have a thermometer stuck under his tongue and an herbal tonic down his throat before he could blink. Barely controlling the urge to kick something, he pushed the door open and dragged a chair out from under the table. He pushed her papers away from his spot. His mother placed a plate heaped with macaroni and cheese and jerk chicken in front of him and passed him the ketchup. She sat down with a quiet sigh and picked up a pen.

Bills again.

Alec speared a stack of cheesy pasta tubes, dipped it in a mound of ketchup and tried not to watch as his mother ran the pen tip down a row of numbers. The pen was shaking.

"How bad is it?" he asked.

"Bad enough," she replied without looking up. She shuffled some papers and began scanning more numbers. Alec could read the letterhead upside down. Those were the figures for the provincial soccer association. He'd been thrilled to make the team again this year until he learned that the final tournament would be held in Prince Edward Island. The airfare alone was way too much.

"I put in an application at McDonald's and Wendy's. They're both hiring. They said they'd call."

"That's good," his mother said, nodding. She lifted another sheet of paper and placed it on top. Her pen underlined a couple of lines. "What was your father mad about?"

Alec shovelled another forkful into his mouth. "What's he *not* mad about." He chewed for a moment then swallowed. "He doesn't trust me."

"He has good reason. No man likes to hear the school principal list why his son is suspended. No mother, either."

"I told you. They swung first."

"That's not what the principal said." His mother dropped

the pen to the table and looked at him directly. She looked exhausted and her Jamaican accent was stronger than usual, indicating the depth of her fatigue and frustration. "Did we raise you this way? To use other kids as punching bags? To steal? How can we believe you when you've let us down like this? Trust takes time to rebuild."

"Yeah, it works both ways."

"He apologized. I've forgiven him."

"I haven't."

"I've always forgiven you, when you messed up, Alec. Isn't that what families do? Love you despite yourself?"

Alec's cheeks burned. His mother could wound him so easily. He dropped his eyes to the pile of bills that got bigger every month.

"Nothing I ever do is right," Alec muttered.

"Look. You know as well as I do that your father's not coping with being unemployed. The new medication hasn't started to work yet, either. He feels like he's failing us. So cut him some slack, Alec."

"He should cut *me* some. Nothing I do ever makes him happy. He wants me to be Peter, and I'm not." Alec pushed the plate away.

"He wants you to be yourself. The man he knows you can be. That *we* know you can be. You're better than this, Alec. You're smarter and kinder and have too much going for you to throw it all away with lousy grades and petty crimes. Neither of us wants you working in a fast food joint for the rest of your life."

"Yeah, whatever." Alec got up and scraped his plate into the garbage. He dumped the cutlery and the plate into the dishwasher and shoved the door closed with his hip. He eased past his mother's chair. As almost an afterthought, he bent down and dropped a quick kiss on the top of her head.

There wasn't anyplace he could go except the living room or back to his bedroom. The apartment was far smaller than their house had been, but that, like his father's good mood, had disappeared a long time ago.

His father was clicking his way through television channels and shaking his head at the repeated scenes of police and fighting. Peter was sprawled on the couch, a paperback between his hands, ignoring his father's repeated "will you look at that" remarks.

It was too late to go out and hang with the guys. His dad would have a fit if he tried to leave, even though it wasn't a school night or anything. Hanging out on the street corner was apparently the first step to a life of illicit drugs and organized crime. There was nothing else to do but go to bed. Alec headed to the bathroom to brush his teeth. In a couple of minutes he was back in his room and tossing his tee shirt into the laundry bin in the corner. The door opened.

"I'm going to bed. Keep the light off," he barked.

"I'm just getting another book." Peter walked past him to the desk by the window and pulled his bulging knapsack towards him.

Alec tossed his jeans on top of the shirt. He swung himself onto the upper bunk. Peter still had his back to him.

"Heard you went to the mall today." Peter shuffled through the pile of paperbacks.

"So?" Alec stared at the ceiling.

"Heard there was a bit of excitement," Peter continued.

"What if?"

"Heard you were right in the middle of it."

Alec sat bolt upright, remembering to crouch at the last minute so he wouldn't hit his head on the ceiling. "Who said?"

"Mrs. Lee and Chin. Met them at the bus stop. Chin couldn't keep a secret if you gagged him."

Damn. Alec flopped back down on the bed. If Peter said anything to their father …

"Keep your mouth shut," Alec hissed. "You owe me."

"Chin said you saw a guy get shot. It was on the news tonight."

Alec ground his teeth together.

"Well." Peter turned around. "Did you?"

"Bite yourself."

"When Dad finds out, you are gonna be in such trouble. Honestly, don't you ever think?"

"Stop bossing me around."

"Stop being such an idiot and I won't have to."

Alec vaulted over the side of the bed and landed at Peter's feet. He straightened up. Peter might have eleven months on him, might have a straight A average, might never cause his parents a moment of worry, but Alec had a good inch of height. Ever since Christmas. He leaned forward, breathing heavily. "I mean it. Leave. Me. Alone."

"Or what?" Peter answered. His brown eyes were narrowed with dislike.

"Take a guess."

"You wouldn't. You promised." Peter deliberately turned his back and continued to search. Pulling out a paperback, he laid it on the desk and zippered up the knapsack. The edge of the curtain caught in the zipper and the movement pulled the curtain open. The outside street lamp, only two stories below, flooded the room with its eerie hue.

"Yeah, well, if keeping your secrets gets me into any more trouble, you can just kiss my promise goodbye." Alec crossed his arms. "Think about *that* before you go running to Dad. Or the next time you get surrounded and can't fight back."

"I was totally outnumbered. You know it. And I'm not saying anything. Yet," Peter said as he leaned forward to tug the drape closed. "What the hell …"

"What is it?"

"Stand back. Turn off the overhead light."

"Turn it off yourself," Alec snapped.

"Do it. Before he sees us."

Something in Peter's voice galvanized Alec and before he could argue he had crossed the few feet to the light switch and flipped the toggle. The room became dark again, except for the street lamp.

"What?" Alec returned to Peter's side.

"See that guy? Standing under the light? He's been following me for weeks."

Alec peered downward. In the cold pool of lamplight, a young man leaned against the lamp pole. He was wearing a light summer jacket and jeans. He had short, dark blond hair. Alec couldn't see his face but a creepy feeling started to ooze around his stomach.

"What does he want?" Alec asked quietly. *Turn around,* he thought towards the man, *look up for a second.*

"I dunno. But he's everywhere I go. He was at school before the end of the year. I saw him a couple of times in the cafeteria. And he comes into the bookstore all the time. He never says anything."

"How do you know he's following you?"

"Look, I just do." Peter yanked the curtain shut. "Leave it alone. And stay away from him."

"Why?"

"Because I said so." Peter grabbed his book and stalked to the door. "He's weird. So stay away from him." The door slammed shut behind him.

Alec stood by the desk. He couldn't remember seeing Peter so angry or so off balance. It was just one guy, not the crowd from school again. Alec pulled back the curtain just enough to see through and looked down. The man hadn't moved. Maybe the guy had a crush on Peter and was working up the nerve to ask him out?

He was about to drop the curtain when the man turned around. He raised his head and stared straight up. Alec felt himself go cold. His stomach hit the floor. He stepped quickly back into the darkness, out of sight.

It was the guy from the music store. The one who'd saved his life.

R iley Cohen stepped down from the VIA train onto the crowded platform at Toronto's Union station. Heaving her heavy backpack more firmly onto her thin shoulders, she followed the streaming crowd. She ignored the jostling, self-absorbed passengers, intent on keeping the exit sign in sight.

The crowd bottlenecked through the exit hallway and emptied into the larger terminal where a milling throng stared intently at the constantly updating information boards. Unable to see over those ahead, Riley squeezed her way to the front and craned her neck upward. Her eyes scanned the schedule. There it was. Her next train wasn't leaving for another four hours. Track seven.

Great. Was nothing on time?

Riley let the knapsack fall to the ground with relief while she considered what to do. She pulled a battered map and guidebook from the back pocket of her black jeans, and thumbed through the creased pages until she found what she was looking for. The tourist highlights were listed in italic font. Four hours wasn't long enough to really go anywhere interesting or see anything major. The CN tower wasn't too far away, at least looking at the map, but was out of the question with the heavy bag.

She shoved a lock of black hair off her forehead and looked around for a sign indicating facilities for checking luggage. Unfortunately, all she could see were other passengers. With an impatient grunt, she grabbed the straps of the knapsack and swung it back over her shoulders and headed away from the throng.

"May I help you?"

Riley stopped abruptly as a young man stepped in front of her and blocked her path. He was of medium height and slim build. His jeans and windbreaker had seen better days but he wore them with a certain style. He was gorgeous, like something out of her sister Deborah's Italian *Vogue*, all lips and carved cheekbones. Dirty blond hair and eyes the colour of the Tahitian sea. *Wow*.

"Nope. I don't think so." Riley directed her comment to the young man's throat and began to walk around him. They were probably contact lenses.

"Are you sure?" The man sidestepped to block her path. "That bag is far too heavy."

"I'm able to carry my own stuff." Maybe *some* women couldn't think their way out of a paper bag and needed some guy to open their doors and carry their luggage, like her sister, but she certainly didn't.

The man's lips began to curl into a grin. "I was just trying to be polite."

"Yeah, well, thanks but no thanks." The smile she returned was patently false. She heaved at the knapsack strap, which was slipping down one shoulder, and walked around him with a brisk stride.

With a frustrated sigh, she battled against the tide of humanity, figuring that an information booth was likely to be closer to the entrance of the station than her present location. She had almost completely forgotten the handsome man, until he spoke again a few minutes later directly behind her.

"If you're looking for something, maybe I can help."

Man, this guy was persistent. Fifteen minutes off the train that was going to take her to Vancouver and her sister's apartment, and some loser was attaching himself to her like a leech. Riley stopped so abruptly the young man

21

bumped into her. She nearly fell over. He grabbed her arm just in time.

"That bag is far too heavy. You nearly fell."

"Hate to burst your bubble, pal, but the bag isn't the problem. It's you. You nearly knocked me over," Riley snorted.

The man smiled. He almost glowed with pleasure.

Riley barely stopped the twitch of her own lips. If she'd ever seen a more attractive male, she couldn't remember it, and the smile seemed infectious, despite her annoyance. Which was quickly draining away, and why, she didn't know.

"Look," the man said, squaring his shoulders and letting go of her arm. "I didn't mean to make you angry. I just want to help. See, I have this assignment for my philosophy course and I really have to get it done today. And I thought you looked like a friendly girl who might help me out."

Friendly? How on earth had he interpreted her new Goth-styled makeup, black clothing and several piercings as friendly? He must be a bit stunned. No, she didn't want to encourage any guy right now; she was leaving town in a couple of hours. And, no, she also couldn't be bothered to help with some stupid assignment. She had enough on her mind. But he *was* very attractive and the longer she stood there the more she felt her resolve slipping. She bit her lip. Walk away, she thought.

"What assignment?" she heard herself say.

The man pulled out a battered roll of foolscap papers from his back pocket and waved it vaguely. "It takes about six minutes to answer," he said with a pleading look. He glanced around quickly then back to her. "I'll loan you the pen. I'll even buy the coffee."

Riley sighed. Why did she allow herself to do these things? Helping anyone always bit you in the bum later. Ignore him and walk away.

"I take cream and sugar," she said.

"There's a snack bar just down in the commuter rail section. I'll carry your bag."

Riley didn't refuse. The words were on her lips but wouldn't come out. He pulled the strap deftly off her shoulder and hoisted it over his own. She didn't even want to stop him. "Wow, you must be strong," he said, before turning quickly and heading off.

Riley stifled down the little flip of pleasure and followed as he wove his way through the crowd. She tried to generate a measure of annoyance and focused on the highhanded manner in which he'd pried her backpack from her. Her purse was in that satchel. If he chose to run off with all her worldly possessions, she'd never be able to stop him. The last month would seem like a day in the park compared to being stranded in Toronto without any money, identification or change of clothes. Why wasn't she more concerned? She reached out and snatched one of the straps.

"Here we are," the young man said as he veered into a cluster of plastic tables and chairs of a small café next to an emergency exit. He dropped her bag on an empty chair and called over his shoulder. "Want anything to eat?"

Riley shook her head and sat down slowly. She pulled her knapsack onto her lap. What on earth was she doing?

The man was back in a moment carrying two Styrofoam cups. He placed one in front of her, sat down and pried the lid off his own. His eyes closed with pleasure as he took a long sip. "I love this stuff," he said unnecessarily.

Riley left the lid on hers. Women got drugged and kidnapped all the time in big cities. He didn't look like the type but one could never be too careful.

"My name is Darius Finn." The young man stretched his hand out to shake hers.

She swallowed the sigh as she clasped his hand briefly. "So what's this questionnaire you want me to answer?"

Darius smoothed the pages out on the stained table, seemingly oblivious to the crumbs and coffee stains. He took another mouthful of coffee before giving her a look that made her toes curl. "I'll read them out to you. Okay? Ready? Number one: Have you ever been the victim of attempted murder?"

Riley shot to her feet. Her heart zoomed up into her throat. She backed away, knocking over the chair with a clatter. Several patrons turned to stare.

"How did you know?" she breathed. She looked around quickly. She hadn't told *anyone*. "How did you—"

"I know who you are, Riley." Darius' voice dropped. The aquamarine eyes bore into her like lasers. "I know what happened. I'm here to warn you. They won't miss again."

"No, no …" Riley turned. The world was closing in on her. It felt like she couldn't breathe. She backed away another few steps, then turned, grabbed her bag and ran.

Darius shouted. Riley didn't hear the exact words but she felt an inexplicable mental tug. She ignored the compulsion to go back. All that was important now was getting away. Again.

Holding her bag tightly in her arms, she ran through the commuters, dodging and darting, without once looking behind. Forget the CN tower. Where the hell was Track seven?

He was behind her, catching up quickly with his much longer legs. She heard him call her name.

Run, she admonished herself. A stitch caught in her side. She gasped with pain but didn't slow down. There were too many people and she couldn't see the signs for the track she wanted. She'd have to disappear instead.

As if her prayers were answered, the crowd around her parted for a second and revealed the subway entrance. Decision instantaneously made, she turned and dove through the doors, across the outside corridor and down the stairs. She nearly collapsed at the tollbooth. Panting, she struggled to balance her knapsack on the turnstile while she rummaged in the front pocket of her jeans for a couple of toonies. Never had she cursed the tightness of her jeans, as she did now.

The coins slipped into her shaking fingers. She dumped them on the little tray. "Keep the change," she directed the clerk before shoving the turnstile forward and entering the subway.

She permitted herself a glance behind.

Darius Finn was taking the steps two at a time. He was staring right at her. He nearly knocked over a teenage boy who was shuffling up the steps. The boy turned and shouted "Hey!" before a look of incredulity crossed his face. Then the crowd swallowed him up and he was lost to Riley's view.

She didn't bother to hang around. She ran down the escalator, pushing past people with no regard for their disgruntled comments, and entered the platform. There was no train.

Crap.

There weren't many people and all of them seemed to be intently reading the newspaper and frowning. The wide platform stretched ahead, but other than a couple of graffiti-covered pillars, there was nothing to hide behind. She knew that running down the tracks was a very stupid idea. There didn't seem to be another exit.

A tall, well-dressed woman stepped out from the cluster of commuters facing the open track. She turned and stared at Riley with dead eyes. The hair rose on Riley's arms and on the back of her neck as if an icy breeze had sprung up all around her. *Oh no. Not again.*

The woman began to walk towards her, the high heels clicking hollowly on the tiled floor. Time seemed to slow down.

It was just like at home. The woman, the concert, the panic. All over again. Riley shook her head and backed away. Her damp palms clutched the knapsack to her chest like a talisman.

The woman opened her designer purse and pulled out a tiny gun.

Riley's breath caught in her chest. She couldn't wrench her eyes away from the silver weapon.

Darius grabbed her from behind. She screamed.

Riley struggled but Darius' arms were like steel bands around her. "Stop fighting me, you fool. I'm here to help you," he muttered as he practically lifted her off her feet. He yelled at the woman. "Give it up. She's mine."

No one else on the platform seemed to notice what was going on. It was like one of those weird dreams, where everyone goes about their business while something terrible is happening.

"Ow! Riley, cut it out." Darius twisted her to the side so that he could face the woman unobstructed as Riley's heel connected sharply with his shin. He was trying to reach something in his pocket but Riley's hip was in the way. "Keep your distance," he shouted at the advancing assailant.

"I don't fear you, Guardian." The woman spoke in a heavy, low voice that didn't suit her. "The Potential is mine." She didn't stop walking. There were only a few metres between them.

Riley twisted desperately. Her heart was pounding so hard in her ears she could barely hear what Darius and the woman were saying. A slight breeze brushed her bangs off her forehead: a subway train was approaching. Darius managed to pull something out of his pocket that Riley couldn't see.

"Hey!"

Riley glanced back at the shout. Running down the stairs was the gangly teenager Darius nearly knocked over entering the subway station. He was pointing right at Darius. "Hey, I want to talk to you."

The woman was almost within touching distance but she had stopped and was staring up the stairs, a look of pure malevolent cunning upon her face. The overhead lights glinted off the silver of the gun. "Two for one," she said.

Darius twisted around, thrusting Riley almost in the other direction. He swore.

A blast of cool air whipped up debris and dust.

The boy leaped the last few steps and landed breathless beside them.

Something white flashed from Darius' hand towards the woman. The woman cried out and stumbled backwards.

Darius didn't hesitate. He lunged towards the boy, grabbed him around the waist, knocking him off his feet.

The woman regained her balance and, snarling, raised her gun.

Darius, carrying both Riley and the teenage boy, dashed across the several paces of platform and jumped into the train track chasm.

Riley was too shocked to even yell. They hit the ground with a thud then rolled in a heap against the wall next to an outside rail. Riley was momentarily winded. Darius and the boy fell against her. Panicked that she might touch the live middle rail of the subway, she pulled her feet up as fast as she could. There was no time to worry about anything else as her attention was diverted the moment she looked upwards.

The bright light of the subway train was hurtling towards her. She was seconds away from certain death.

A jagged, tingling sensation ran through her body, starting where Darius held her and spreading outwards. There was a sharp tug, as if she were jerked by invisible hands.

Then everything around her disappeared.

Riley tumbled to her knees and fell over. It took several seconds before her mind started working again. The first thing she noticed was that her hand was wet. She blinked several times to clear the fog. Her hand was in a puddle of water. Carefully, she raised it to eye level. Not blood. She looked around.

Darius was sitting behind her. His head rested on his upturned knees. The boy that had followed them down into the subway was lying on his side a short distance away and curled into a fetal position. His eyes were tightly shut.

They weren't in the subway any longer.

The corrugated metal ceiling of the empty warehouse stretched high above. There were no windows in the dingy metal walls, yet there was enough light to see. The concrete floor was dirty, and here and there small puddles had formed in the depressions. The air smelled of cold metal and something unfamiliar. A small group of people walked quickly towards them.

Riley struggled to her feet. She swayed for a moment until her legs found their strength. A cold shiver ran down her spine.

A young woman approached, followed by several teenagers. She was tall and slim with white-blonde hair pulled severely back in a tight ponytail. It flipped from side to side with each step. She was quite pretty in a cool, understated way and wore dark, form-fitting trousers, a white tee shirt and

4

running shoes. Around her neck a silver chain winked in the half-light above her collar. She wasn't smiling. In fact, she looked downright annoyed.

Of the five teenagers behind her, three were boys. All were wearing jeans, tees and hooded jackets. All had looks of intense interest.

The woman stopped two paces away from Riley. She looked her up and down silently as if examining a specimen on a slide. Then she turned her gaze to Darius. "I assume you have a good explanation for this."

Darius didn't lift his head. His voice was muffled and tired. "I'm thinking of one as we speak."

"Not surprising." The woman turned her frosty gaze towards Riley. "What happened? Were you cornered?"

The snooty tone of voice had to go. Riley pointed at Darius. "He threw me in front of a train."

Several of the onlookers raised their eyebrows but no one spoke.

"A train?" The woman raised one finely groomed eyebrow before turning her gaze back to Darius.

Riley raised her voice. "A subway train. As if that matters. How did I get here? Who are you? And where am I anyway? I've got a VIA train to catch."

The woman shrugged. "You *had* a train to catch. Not now. Grab your bag." She turned to the tallest boy on her right. "Gino, help Alec to his feet, will you?"

A skinny boy with ringlets to his shoulders and far too many pimples nodded as he walked over to the boy on the ground and shook his shoulder. Riley couldn't hear what he said but it didn't matter. That kid was not her concern. Darius was not her concern. Getting back to Union Station was.

"Whatever," Riley said curtly. "Just point me in the direction of downtown, lady, and I'll get out of your hair." She swung her knapsack up and over her shoulder. She adjusted the straps. Her knees wobbled.

The blonde didn't reply. Behind her, Darius was slowly getting to his feet.

She was not going to waste another minute with these weird people. Without a word she strode towards the far wall. The blonde was talking again, but her voice was indistinct in the cavernous building the farther Riley walked. Riley heard Darius reply, "Anna, listen. I'm not."

There was no door. Riley stopped and bit her lower lip. She was sure she'd seen one. She blinked several times. With an impatient sigh, she turned and inspected the walls on either side. Nothing. She turned on her heel and squinted at the farthest wall. Angrily she headed back. She refused to look at the woman, the teenagers or Darius as she stalked past.

There was no door at the far wall, either. Riley's heart gave a little jolt as she came to an abrupt halt. Who built a warehouse with no door? She spun around. Someone was yanking her chain and she *so* did not like that.

Darius' smile slipped away as she approached. He spoke before she could. "You can't get out. Sorry."

Riley dropped her bag at her feet. Her nostrils flared. "And just why not? I want to leave. Now." She stopped herself from stamping her foot, just in time. "What kind of idiot builds a warehouse without a door, for heaven's sake?"

Darius held up a hand. "I can explain everything. But it'll be a lot safer if we go down to do it."

The boy who had been thrown in front of the subway train with her shuffled forward and touched Darius on the arm. "Why was she going to shoot me?" he asked.

"Hey, bucko, stop interrupting," Riley snapped, her eyes narrowing.

"Shoot both of you," Darius corrected, speaking to the boy first. "She was after Riley as much as she was after you, Alec."

So his name was Alec. Riley stared at him as he stared back. He was tall and thin, and probably younger than her. He had that gawky look of someone who had grown a lot in a short time but he moved with athletic grace. His hair needed cutting. He had dark brown eyes with long lashes and dark fuzz over his upper lip. Someday, he was going to be very handsome. Right now, there was mostly potential.

Riley shifted her gaze back to Darius. "Just who are you, anyway? Why did that woman want to kill us? Why isn't there a door?"

The woman Darius called Anna interrupted. "Protocol states the Potentials need to be informed within one hour of contact. I assume from their lack of knowledge that you were wasting time roleplaying again." She pulled out a glass ball, slightly larger than a golf ball, from her pants' pocket. She stared intently at it for a moment and then looked up. "They're on their way. Several. We need to move."

"What the hell is going on?" Riley demanded. Everyone looked very serious all of a sudden.

Darius grabbed Riley's knapsack and walked several steps away before she could even think to reach for it. Everyone followed, except for Alec who stood still and pale as if rooted to the spot. He glanced over at Riley as if for instructions, but she paid him no attention.

"That's my bag," she shouted at Darius. "Give it back." Furious, Riley reached him quickly and grabbed at her bag, tugging it impotently. Darius didn't even break his stride.

"I mean it. Leggo." Riley yanked again but Darius was extraordinarily strong. He didn't even look at her. With his free hand he reached into his jeans pocket. He pulled out a glass ball similar to the one that Anna had looked at a moment ago. Riley had only a moment to notice his focused attention on the glass before she fell to the ground. Darius had let go of the bag at the same time she tugged and the force of her pull knocked her off balance. She landed on her butt with an "oof."

Suddenly the floor beneath her began to move.

31

"You might want to get behind me," Darius murmured, with a nod at the cement floor, which had developed several seams and was now pulling apart like an aperture of an old-fashioned camera lens.

Riley scuttled backwards. Her eyes widened with disbelief.

A gaping round hole now existed in the middle of the warehouse floor, and inside it, a long set of polished stairs led downwards. Riley leaned over the edge for a better view. The stairs, fashioned out of some kind of dark metal, seemed to glow. The base of the stairwell was shrouded in shadow.

The teenagers streamed around her and quickly descended the stairs, their heads disappearing downwards. No one spoke. Alec appeared with Anna at his side. He balked at the top.

"Where does this go?" he asked in a shaky voice.

"Down to our quarters, Alec. Anna will show you the way. There's nothing to be frightened of," Darius answered.

Alec flushed to the roots of his hair. "I'm not scared," he muttered. As if to prove it, he almost ran down the stairs. Anna exchanged a quick look with Darius before she followed.

Darius swung Riley's knapsack over his shoulder and stepped down to the first tread. He raised one eyebrow. "In less than one minute, several Emissaries are going to show up, just outside of this compound. They are all after you. My job, Riley, is to protect you. And I would very much prefer if I'm not killed because you are too stubborn to save yourself."

Someone began pounding on the outside warehouse wall. Darius' gaze never left her face. "You know that I speak the truth. You can feel it, in the same way you've known when you were a target. You don't know why yet. But you know you're in danger. Trust your instincts, Riley.

They saved you in Yarmouth and in Halifax. They'll save you now."

Riley swallowed convulsively. Darius, whoever he was, was right about one thing. She had known she was in trouble both times in the last month. Instinct, superstition, gut reaction – whatever you want to call it. The back of her mind had screamed in fear and she'd run.

But, now, the threat she could feel inching up the back of her spine was less clearly defined. Did it come from the gorgeous man in front of her, or from outside the warehouse?

The pounding got louder.

Trust this guy or wait to see who was trying to get in?

Something heavy rammed up against the wall with a resounding crack. A second later, it happened again.

Her mouth was dry, her heart pounding.

Another crash. Louder.

Riley raced down the steps, Darius right behind her. The aperture closed above, encasing them in darkness.

Alec looked around with a mixture of curiosity, fear and forced bravado. The stairwell stopped after nearly thirty precipitous steps at a small landing. He stepped through a narrow doorway into a rather large, rectangular room constructed entirely from the same metal as the stairwell. A huge table, surrounded by chairs, dominated the centre of the room. There were several metal bunk beds, two low sofas and two desks. There were two other doors but both were closed.

The other teenagers were settling themselves around the table silently. Several gave him appraising looks but Alec pretended to ignore them. There'd better be answers about what had happened. He'd landed almost underneath Darius and had the breath knocked out of him. He'd heard the scream of the train's wheels and felt the rush of air signalling sudden death. Then, before he could even think, they were somewhere else. It defied belief.

Anna touched his shoulder. He turned. "Have a seat. As soon as Riley arrives, we'll begin."

"Riley?" Alec asked.

"Your companion. The dark-haired girl with the metallic pin in her eyebrow."

"I never met her before—" Alec began, but Darius and Riley's arrival interrupted. The door slid shut behind them as they entered the room.

"Let's get right to it, shall we?" Darius said. He pointed to the table. "Take a seat, Alec. You too, Riley."

"I'm not sitting anywhere." Riley was standing with her back against the wall, where only a moment ago there had been a door. Her arms were crossed and her eyes were narrowed.

Alec tried not to appear to be giving her the once over, but he couldn't quite drag his eyes away from the tiny Goth girl. Her black hair was cut into a wild geometric design and striped with fuchsia and blue. Her black jeans fit like a second skin and the heavy studded belt slung low over her hips emphasized the fact she was definitely female. Indigo eyes stared out from beneath her fringe with the kind of glance that cut boys into ribbons. She was hot, no doubt about it, and really pissed.

Anna crossed the room and took Riley's arm. She pulled her to the edge of the table, yanked out an empty chair with her free hand and shoved Riley into it. "Sit down before you fall down," she advised, placing both her hands on Riley's slim shoulders to prevent her getting up again.

"I'm—" Riley sputtered as she squirmed.

"About to feel the effects of teleportation," Darius interrupted smoothly as he pulled out a chair, swung it around and straddled it backwards. "And, when you do, your legs will turn to jelly and you'll get the shakes. Falling down is the usual response. Gino, please get our newest companions some juice." He smiled at Alec. "The sugar in the juice counteracts the effects. You'll feel better after you drink it."

Alec was already feeling shaky and it was a relief to know that it wasn't his nerve deserting him.

Darius leaned his elbows on the table and smiled. "Welcome to Tyon Training Station Number Seven. Most of what I'm going to tell you won't make sense yet. Anna and I know that this will take time to comprehend. Unfortunately, time is something we don't have a lot of right now.

"Gino and Mary Beth have been here the longest, and

they'll help you settle in." He raised his hand at Riley's sudden inhalation. "Yes, you will be staying here. Nothing you say, nothing you do, will change our minds about this. Your safety, as I mentioned above, is our main priority."

The tallest boy carried two narrow, metallic beakers over to the table and placed one in front of Alec, the other at Riley's elbow. He gave Alec a quick smile, then took his seat at the other end of the table.

"As we speak, forces are attempting to end your lives," Anna said. "The one who tried to kill you over the last several weeks will not give up. He cannot be dissuaded. You have no other protection, but us."

"He? Who's he? I only saw some businesswoman with a seriously bad attitude. Unless she is a he?" Riley scoffed. She was very pale and her hands were trembling. She glanced towards Alec and shoved them under the table.

"Actually, we have no idea if Rhozan has a gender." Darius' eyebrows rose into his hair. He gave Anna a quizzical look. "We think he's male, but ..."

"Who's Rhozan?" Alec took a sip of his juice and swallowed. He looked from Anna's face to Darius, then back again. He avoided Riley's gaze and hoped he wasn't blushing.

Darius turned in his chair to face Alec. "The Tyon Collective, of which Anna and I are members, seek out and protect individuals who harbour a gift that was bred into your world several generations ago. It is just now, with your generation, that the gift has manifested itself. We are the harvesters of that initial dissemination."

"Huh?" said Alec. What gift? No one had given him any gift, except for his fifteenth birthday last September, and, of course, Christmas. And then all he'd gotten were new soccer cleats.

"Not a present, Alec, a gift. A special ability. Something you were born with."

Alec frowned. Why would someone want to kill him

because he was athletic?

Darius smiled. "Bear with me for a minute, okay. The Others – that's what we call them – figure they can take over anywhere they want, and armed with that idea, they travel around looking for new civilizations to conquer. The Tyon Collective was formed to deal with the problem."

"And you're part of the Tyon ... whatever it is." Alec raised a skeptical eyebrow. The whole thing sounded like something from one of Peter's sci-fi novels.

"Collective. Yes. We are. And soon, with a bit of training, you will be, too." Darius smiled.

"And this Rhozan guy?"

"Is one of the Others, yes." Darius replied.

If this Darius guy thought he was gullible enough to believe that crock of garbage, he had another thought coming. There had to be another explanation. Alec glanced over at Riley to assess her reaction. Her lips had thinned to a dark purple line. She wasn't drinking her juice. Maybe it was poisoned? His stomach dropped at the thought. How much had he drunk?

"There's nothing in the juice except juice. Don't worry." Anna must have noticed his expression. "Finish it and you'll feel better. You too, Riley."

Darius continued. "We tried to get here first, sow the seeds of resistance, so to speak. And, unfortunately for you, we were right. He's here."

"The woman in the red dress," Riley muttered almost to herself.

"Yes, in a manner of speaking. And this is where it gets a bit weird. The woman you met at the concert, and the other one at the drive-through, are puppets, a figment of Rhozan's will that manifests itself in innocent bystanders and is capable of killing."

"Hang on there a minute." Riley had pushed her juice to one side and was leaning over the table, peering at Darius with frank incredulity. "What do you mean, a puppet? She blackened my eye and broke two of my ribs. And who the hell is Rhozan?"

"Rhozan is the one who wants you dead," Darius said.

The room was completely silent.

"How long have you been off your meds?" Riley leaned back in her chair and folded her arms. With her eyebrow piercing she reminded Alec of a skeptical Vulcan.

"Rhozan is no joke. Sorry," said Darius.

"Oh, come on. This is ridiculous." Riley's voice rose. "I've never met anyone named Rhozan. There is no reason on Earth why he wants me dead."

"The reason isn't on Earth. That's what I've been trying to tell you." Darius sighed. He looked up at Anna. "You try."

Anna let go of Riley's shoulders and walked to the side of the table so that she could look both Riley and Alec in the eye. "The Tyon Collective is a secret intergalactic agency concerned with maintaining the balance between self-direction and interference. The Others, of whom Rhozan is a member, are pan-dimensional beings that feed off negative emotions, such as anger, despair and misery. They travel from place to place and devour weaker worlds. We try to stop them within the boundaries the Celestial Council permits.

"In simple terms, Riley, we're the good guys. Rhozan and the Others are the bad ones. And you and Alec, like the rest of the individuals here, are the rare humans with the inborn strength to fight his invasion. That's why he wants you dead. And that's why we need to protect and train you."

38   "Train me for what?" Alec interrupted. He was almost afraid to ask.

"To fight Rhozan and save your world," Darius said softly, "because you are the only ones who can."

Alec watched Darius rummage in the cupboard for a moment. He tossed a small glass ball from one hand to the other as he walked to Alec's side. He pitched the crystal and Alec caught it without thinking.

"You're going to need an orb," Darius said.

Alec rolled it around in the palm of his hand. The bluish glass was warm and it seemed to fit his palm as if made for it. Strangely, holding the orb made him feel better, calmer, as if the uncertainty of the last hour was melting away. Alec frowned.

"You're feeling the connection, aren't you?" Darius leaned in. This close, his eyes sparkled. "I felt it, too, the first time an Operative dropped one into my hand. Of course, I was younger than you."

"You were found by these guys, like me?" Alec asked. He didn't want to be interested in these people and he certainly wasn't going to help them out, but the words were out of his mouth before he could stop them.

"Sure. Recruited, trained and ready for action. The way you will be." Darius' grin was infectious. "You have no idea how interesting your life is going to get."

Anna arrived at Darius' elbow. Immediately the twinkle diminished and his face became more serious.

"I'm working with the other Potentials," said Anna. "While you're waiting for regen, Darius, start Alec on basic concentration and focus techniques."

6

"Sure," Darius replied.

"No chatter. Alec will learn about the training program all in good time."

"Agreed."

"Leave Riley to me. I'll start her with an orb as soon as she settles down. Hands off." Anna headed back to the other teens that were crowded together on the sofas and seemed to be in deep concentration.

Alec watched her walk away. Anna was very good looking in a cold, distant way, but there was something about her that made him slightly uncomfortable.

"There's a reason she affects you that way," Darius murmured, with a nod in Anna's direction. "Someday I'll tell you about it."

Alec said nothing. He dropped his eyes to the orb. It was freaky how Darius seemed to know what he was thinking. He'd have to control his facial expressions better. He glanced over at Riley. She was sitting on the farthest lower bunk and huddled against the wall, her knapsack held in front of her like a shield. What Alec knew about women could easily fit on the head of a pin, but even an idiot could read her mutinous expression a soccer pitch away.

Darius was staring at Riley, too. "I think Anna has her work cut out for her," he said. He turned back to Alec and winked. "Should be interesting to watch."

"Yeah, so?"

Darius gave a short laugh. "There isn't much Anna can't handle. That's why she was assigned here. She's one of the most capable officers I know."

"You guys are some kind of army?"

"Senior Field Officer, Tyon Collective. Outranks me big time." Darius shrugged. He gave Anna a covert look and dropped his voice lower. "But I'm stronger."

Alec smirked. "Well, duh. Men generally are. We studied it in Bio last fall. It's our testosterone and stuff."

Darius tapped his temple with a finger. "Stronger this

way," he said in a conspiratorial tone. "Power. Strongest Potential in the last three centuries."

"What's a Potential?"

"You are. Someone with the gift. You're not far behind me. That's how we picked you up so quickly. You shine like a beacon."

Alec found himself clasping the orb tightly and a tingling feeling shimmered up his arm and into his shoulder. It was always Peter getting the attention, the great grades, the accolades. Except on a soccer pitch. No one could touch him there. Was Darius trying to get him on his side with flattery? Did he really have special power? "Does my brother have it?"

"Peter's power is different from yours." Darius nodded at the other teens. "More like them. Trainable. Still a threat to Rhozan. Which is the main problem, of course."

"Because Rhozan will be looking for him, right?" Alec didn't want to believe this stuff but it was giving him goosebumps nonetheless. "This Rhozan dude is bad news?"

"Hold the orb lightly in your hands and close your eyes. Anna's watching." Darius dropped his voice even lower.

Alec found himself complying with Darius' request before he could even think about it. He tried to take a deep breath and unclench his fingers around the orb. Why was he obeying this guy?

"We don't know much about Rhozan," Darius continued. "We think he's a Field Marshall. You know, scopes out new worlds for the invading fleet, determines if conditions are right."

"Conditions?"

"Rips," Darius said, "in the time/space continuum. That's how the Others get into our dimension. We don't know how they find them, we only know what happens when they do."

"What happens?" Despite the fact this *could not be true*, Alec's heart had started pounding somewhere in the

41

vicinity of his Adam's apple.

"Trouble. Seriously awful trouble." Darius stood up. "Try and let your mind go blank. Let the orb do its thing. Don't force it. Just relax."

What exactly would the orb do? Alec wondered. And why on earth would he want to do it, whatever it was?

"You'll see." Darius answered his unspoken question before walking over to Anna's side.

Alec sat back and let the orb roll around in his hand. He watched Darius and Anna out of the corner of his eye while his brain leap-frogged from one subject to another. These guys were aliens. Darius had saved his life. Someone was really trying to kill him. Riley was pretty cute. He was kidnapped. He had some kind of power that other people wanted. Part of him was excited beyond belief, but another part of him wanted to tell Darius and Anna where they could stick their orbs and storm out because the whole thing was totally implausible.

Was it possible the subway train had killed him and this was some weird after-life experience? Was he having the kind of delusion you read about in grocery store tabloids?

Regardless, he had to go home. If he was late again, his father would kill him.

He looked around for the exit. He'd been so distracted when he entered, he hadn't kept track of the door's location. Now he couldn't see it.

Darius sat down at the end of the table and waved his orb in a complicated pattern. Directly in front of him, a type of screen winked into existence. Alec could see directly through it. A series of glowing symbols scrolled quickly across the perimeters of the screen. Whatever the language was, Darius was reading it and not liking what he saw. "There's more activity. Increased by thirty percent. I'll have to go now."

Anna leaned over his shoulder.

"I know what I'm doing," Darius said.

Anna pointed a finger at the screen. "Two more overnight. He's strengthening quickly. Better go now."

"That's what I said." Darius got up. "There's a second in the Beaches but I'll get Peter first."

Alec tried to suppress his astonishment. These guys had technology right out of one of his favourite video games. As far as he knew, no one had yet to develop that kind of stuff on earth, which meant ...

He *had* to get out of there. Darius and Anna might really be aliens. His hand tightened on the orb unconsciously. The minute the door opened ...

"Here, you're going to need an orb."

Riley jumped at Anna's voice. She had been so lost in her angry thoughts she'd missed the woman crossing the floor to stand at the end of the bunk. The small glass ball rolled along the blanket to rest at her knee.

"Doubt it." Riley examined her nail polish.

"An orb is your only weapon against Rhozan's Emissaries. You might want to learn how to use one." Anna headed back towards the teens on the sofas.

7

Riley snorted. As if. She didn't believe in aliens or flying saucers or invasions from outer space. She believed in science. And so far, no one had any proof of little green men from Alpha Centauri, bug-eyed monsters from Mars or UFOs in the skies overhead. But there wasn't any other answer she could come up with as to how she'd been transported across town in the blink of an eye, or the technology in this bunker, which was clearly advanced, and she was forced to accept that what Darius and Anna were saying could *possibly* be true. Maybe. But she did *not* like it.

Aliens or not, Riley wanted out. Now.

She pulled out her wallet and cellphone and stuck them into her jeans pockets. The bag would slow her down. The police would retrieve it for her later, because she was going to have Darius arrested and tossed into jail so fast he'd cut himself on his own cheekbones.

Where was the door they'd entered through? The two visible doors only opened into a cupboard and what looked like a bathroom. She picked up the ball that Anna called an orb and absently rolled it around in the palm of her hand while watching Darius root around in the cupboard. Any minute now he'd be leaving. She'd watch carefully and see what he did to find the exit.

Darius ruffled the hair of the smallest boy as he donned a jacket. "How's it coming, Jake?" he asked.

The skinny, red-headed kid, not much taller than Riley, shrugged. "Slow."

"Keep at it, kiddo. I'll give you a hand when I get back." Darius shoved something into his pocket. "Anything you want while I'm gone?" he asked Anna.

"Just do your job, Finn. No fooling around." Anna didn't raise her head to look at him.

"The manual says—"

"I don't care if assimilation into the surrounding society is required or not. The situation warrants quick and decisive action. Remove the older Anderson boy and the new Potential without preamble. Try not to be noticed."

Darius gave a mock salute but Anna wasn't looking. He glanced over at Riley and winked. "Guess we'll never finish that questionnaire now, huh?"

Riley pretended not to hear.

Darius stopped at the end of her bunk. "Join the others and figure out how to use the orb. It's your destiny and the faster you become proficient with it, the faster you can take care of yourself."

"I have no intention of learning to do anything with this marble." Riley dropped it on the blanket. "And I will remind you that I do not believe a single word you've told me since we met."

"You're in danger, Riley. Those attacks were not random. You were the target. You *are* the target. And until you are dead, you *will* be the target. Smarten up and get over it."

45

He turned and walked over to the farthest wall. He pulled out his orb and muttered something Riley couldn't quite hear. A door materialized and opened for him. The instant he was through, the door slid closed and blended into the wall.

"What the …" Riley gasped. She jumped off the bed and ran over to the exact spot where Darius had exited. There was absolutely no sign of a door. The metal was cool and revoltingly slippery.

"You need an orb to get out, Riley," Anna said. "The faster you learn to use one, the better."

Refusing to answer, Riley stalked back to the bed and plunked herself down with a snort. These idiots had another thing coming if they thought she was going to jump on their bandwagon that easily. If she could stand firm through two years of her soon-to-be-stepmother's constant criticism, she could resist anything.

Several long minutes passed. Riley picked up her orb and jammed it into the tight pocket of her jeans. She'd need it for police evidence. The room was almost eerily silent as none of the teenagers spoke while doing their exercises. Alec was staring at his orb, too, as if intent on learning its secrets. It was kind of a shame how quickly he joined up with these weirdos, but it didn't matter. Once she was gone she'd never see him again. Suddenly, goosebumps rose all over Riley's arms. Before she could wonder why, a blast of electricity ran through her, as if she'd stuck her finger in a socket.

Anna grabbed the edge of the table to prevent herself from falling. The other kids gasped collectively. In less than a second, Anna was across the room and at Alec's side. He was face-down on the table.

Anna flung him over her shoulder, carried him to the closest bunk and laid him down. Everyone crowded around.

"What's the matter with him?" the blonde girl asked as

she peered over Anna's shoulder.

"Did you feel that wave of power, Mary Beth?" Anna asked as she arranged a pillow under Alec's head. He was awfully pale and beads of sweat were forming on his forehead and his upper lip. His body gave a quick shake and then was very still. She pulled the orb from his clenched fingers. "That was Alec."

"What'd he do?" Gino leaned over to get a better look.

Anna didn't answer. Instead, she placed one hand on Alec's forehead and held her orb with the other. She closed her eyes.

Riley watched but said nothing. The very air was sharp with the scent of something odd, expectant. Alec shook again, gave a strangled gasp and then was deathly still. Mary Beth began to bite her nails.

Riley pushed herself closer, elbowing Gino out of the way. It was clear that Alec had suffered some sort of seizure and he needed his airway protected, if not medical attention. Anna didn't seem to know that.

"Move him onto his side, for Pete's sake." Riley grasped Alec's shoulder. She intended to pull him over partway, just enough to keep his airway clear, but the second she touched him, the electricity jolted right through her. Worse still, she fell into his mind.

Riley sprawled on the farthest bunk. She wasn't sure how she'd gotten there. One minute she was about to render first-aid, the next, the impressions, feelings, memories, tastes and emotions of someone else flooded her mind like a tidal wave. It had been awful. Now the room was spinning lazily and her stomach was threatening to turn inside out. Gino hovered at the end of her bunk, looking sheepish. Riley ignored him.

Mary Beth pulled a chair over to the side of Riley's bed. She cocked her head to one side and watched, reminding Riley of a plump pigeon. "How do you feel?"

"What's it to you?" Riley muttered.

"Nothing," Mary Beth replied. "But if you're going to puke all over my bunk, don't expect me to clean it up."

"Maybe you could cut her a bit of slack, M.B. I mean, she just got here and everything." Gino was flushing and rocking on the balls of his feet. He didn't look at either of them.

"Excuse me." Riley sat up. She swung her legs over the edge of the bed. The floor tilted dangerously for a second before settling down.

The door to the outside stairs opened and Darius tumbled in. He had his arm around a familiar-looking boy who was barely standing and bleeding from his forehead. Both were dishevelled. Darius' lip was cut. The door slid shut behind them and vanished.

"Arm it," Darius gasped. "They're right behind me."

Anna waved her orb and the lights of the bunker took on a reddish hue. The temperature dropped enough to be noticeable. Anna grasped the newcomer under his arms and she and Darius carried him over to the bunk next to Riley.

"What happened?" The boy was conscious but sounded weak. "Where am I?"

"Good question." Anna turned to Darius. "Where's the other?"

"Dead." Darius hit the brace of the bunk bed with a closed fist. "Missed him by minutes. Three Emissaries, all armed."

"Where are they getting the weapons?" Anna's hands gripped her hips. "I've never seen this before."

"Beats me," Darius replied.

"I wish you'd drop the annoying colloquial slang, Darius. It's wearing," Anna snapped.

"It's my home planet," Darius shrugged. "I think it suits me."

"It sounds childish. Peter, are you injured anywhere else?" Anna asked as she waved her orb over his torso.

So this was Alec's brother, Riley surmised. No wonder he looked familiar. A bit stockier, more rounded, with lighter hair and eyes and an incongruous earring in his left lobe, but similar enough.

"He took quite a punch to his stomach," Darius advised. "Rhozan had already taken over several people and was just waiting."

"How?"

"I have no idea. Unless it was Alec." Darius looked at the farthest bunk where Alec still lay. "They probably heard him in Africa."

"You felt it?" Anna asked, slipping the orb back into her pocket.

"Are you kidding?" Darius rubbed his jaw ruefully. "The kid's lightning. Are you okay?" He reached out and touched

Anna's shoulder for a second, before she pulled away.

She didn't look at him as she headed back to Alec's side. "I managed to get my shields up in time." She sat back down on the edge of Alec's bunk and brushed a lock of hair off his forehead. "I wasn't expecting it. What did you tell him to do?"

"Just the usual." Darius sighed. "I'm not sure how we'll get out. There were four of them inside the warehouse."

"Impossible. The shields haven't lessened. I've monitored it." As if to reassure herself, she created another screen in mid-air. "See, there, in place."

"Go and look for yourself, if you don't believe me." Darius dropped into a chair and closed his eyes.

"Are you all right?" Anna asked, the barest hint of warmth in her voice.

Darius smiled but didn't open his eyes. "Anytime you want to come over here and check me out is fine with me."

"What's going to happen? I mean, with the Emissaries upstairs? How will we get out?" Gino asked.

"Get Darius some juice, Mary Beth," Anna said briskly. "He needs to regen. Don't worry, Gino. They can't get in here."

"You said they can't get in the warehouse, but Darius said they had." Gino's Adam's apple bobbed up and down.

Riley watched with satisfaction. Anna's hold over this little party was weakening. She could feel the building anxiety. Any minute someone was going to try and leave. The only snag was the Emissaries waiting upstairs. If they were the same as the woman in the subway station or the others back home, she was in trouble. One had been bad enough, but four?

50

Peter sat up on the bunk beside Riley and looked around. "Where am I?" He caught sight of Alec. "Hey," he shouted, "what have you done to my brother?"

The lights went off.

"Nobody move!" Anna shouted. "Darius?"

The lights flickered for a moment before coming back on. Anna and Darius faced one another, their orbs held outwards, flashing a faint bluish lightning from one orb to the other.

Peter grasped the brace of the bunk bed and leaned forward. "What's going on?" he whispered.

"I dunno," Riley replied.

"Check the perimeters," Anna instructed.

Darius nodded briskly and traced a screen into the air with his orb. Immediately it filled with moving symbols.

Alec gave a pathetic moan. Riley crossed to his side. She dropped to the edge of his bed and grabbed his wrist. His pulse was strong and steady. Other than some slight static electricity, he seemed to be fine.

"What's the matter with him?" Peter leaned over her shoulder.

"He took some kind of seizure," Riley replied. "Does he have any medical problems that you know of?"

"Are you a nurse?" Peter asked.

"First year pre-med. This coming September," she added. "Answer my question."

"No. He never even gets a cold. It's ridiculous."

"I'm not sure what happened to him. Anna," Riley pointed out who was Anna, "found him unconscious. I think he was fooling around with one of these." She held up her orb.

"Did he swallow it?"

"Don't be an idiot," Riley scoffed. "He'd have choked."

The overhead light got redder.

"Look, what is this place? Why did that guy bring me here? Who were those nuts who tried to kill me? What's going on?"

"These people are aliens from another planet." Riley couldn't help but grimace as she heard herself speak. It sounded so crazy. "Anna and Darius have kidnapped all of us and brought us to train to fight the bad guys who are about to invade our planet." She waited for Peter's scathing response.

Peter leaned forward and lowered his voice. "I saw him lots of times. He was following me around for the last couple of weeks. I thought he …" Peter blushed. "I warned Alec to stay away from him, but Alec never does what he's told."

"Yeah, well, too late now." Riley dropped Alec's wrist back on the bed, suddenly aware that she'd been holding it far too long. She focused on a chip in her black nail polish.

"How do we get out of here?" Peter asked.

"The only door opens with this." Again she held up the orb. "I'm not sure exactly how it works. I've been waiting for a diversion so that I can slip out. Could be soon, too. Something's happening."

The lighting got redder.

"What's with the stupid lights?" Peter asked. He gave his brother a shake and jerked his hand back as if he'd been burned. "What's with him?"

"Alec seems to be filled with static electricity. Don't ask me how it happened. It won't hurt you." Riley neglected to mention anything about contacting Alec's mind because it hadn't happened. It had all been a figment of her imagination. "The lights are some kind of warning sign. Darius thinks those people who hurt you followed you here and that they're waiting outside."

Peter blanched. "There were four of them. I've never been so creeped out in my life."

"Like zombies?" Riley asked. "Just focused on you and nothing else. And no one else seems to notice, right?"

"How did you know?"

"It happened to me. Several times. I thought, at first, that it was, I dunno, weird. Like something out of a bad horror movie. But I shook them off. No problem."

Alec moaned and raised a shaky hand to his forehead. "What are you doing here?"

Peter shrugged. "What's it to you?"

Alec struggled to a sitting position.

"How do you feel?" Riley asked in her most professional manner.

"All right, I guess. Bit of a headache. What happened to me?"

"What do you remember?" asked Riley.

Alec's forehead wrinkled in concentration. "I guess I was holding the orb Darius gave me, and I …" He trailed off, a strange distant look sliding over his features. All of a sudden his eyes widened. He pointed at Riley. "You were there. In my head."

"No way." Riley started to get up.

"You were, I know it." Alec grabbed onto her arm and a trickle of electricity shot up into her shoulder and neck. "You're going to your sister's cuz you hate it at home. You think your new stepmom is a witch. You don't think you're pretty." Alec could barely get the words out fast enough.

"That's enough." Riley shoved at him. "Get away from me."

"What's going on?" Peter tried to wrest Riley's arm free.

Alec ignored him. "But you are pretty," he babbled. "Really hot, actually."

Suddenly he stopped and let go. Riley clasped her arms around herself and backed away. Alec panted slightly, watching her intently as a dull flush rose up his neck.

"Both of you are total idiots," Peter said.

Riley didn't answer. Alec didn't have a chance to speak. At that moment, the bunker was attacked.

9

The walls echoed with the sound of a thunderclap that shook the very air as huge cracks appeared on each of the four walls. Alec fell off the bunk and onto the floor and bashed his elbow on the bed frame. The floor tilted. Riley tumbled out of sight. Peter grabbed onto the brace of the upper bunk to prevent himself from falling.

The glow from Anna's orb mixed with Darius' and grew to dazzling brightness. Alec grabbed his own without thinking.

"Rips, underneath?" Anna shouted.

"Impossible. He can't make them appear," Darius gasped as he waved his hand furiously at the transparent screen.

"Doesn't matter now. We have to get everyone out."

"We can't transport them all," Darius shouted back above another hideous cracking.

The air in front of Alec began to shimmer. He squinted. The hazy air began to sparkle, expanding slowly and growing between himself and Peter. Mesmerized, Alec couldn't move.

Peter leaned over, holding onto the edge of the upper bunk to steady himself and swaying slightly. With his free hand, he pointed at the shimmer and mouthed something, but Alec couldn't hear it over the roaring that seemed to come from everywhere at once.

An odd feeling crept over his skin the more he looked. Something really bad would happen if the sparkles touched him. Alec slid onto his back, easing away without taking his eyes off the shimmering. He bumped into the bed. He glanced under the bunk as briefly as possible. Riley was on the floor on the other side. She was yelling something he couldn't hear and waggling her fingers, encouraging him to slide under the bunk towards her.

He didn't hesitate. He thrust out his arm to her.

The shimmering lights moved closer.

Alec's fingers touched Riley's and he clasped tightly.

He turned back just in time to see Peter's arm reach through the shimmering air.

"No!" Darius yelled as he ran towards them. He grabbed for Peter, but in the instant he did so, Peter disappeared *into* the sparkles like he was sucked down a drain.

Alec opened his mouth to scream but before he could draw breath, Darius threw himself down on top of him. There was a yank, a pull and then … nothing.

The bunker around them vanished.

Alec landed with a brain-jarring *thud*. Darius nearly flattened him as he winked into existence immediately after, and Riley, who was still holding his hand so tightly he'd lost all feeling in his fingers, landed farther away, nearly pulling his arm from its socket.

"Ow!" he screeched as he yanked his hand from Riley's.

Darius heaved himself off Alec and looked around with a darkening frown. He glanced up at the sky then back at Alec. "Did you mean to bring us here?"

"Err?" Alec tried to sit up but was immediately overcome by a very unpleasant wooziness. This was far worse than the teleporting from the subway station. The world tilted alarmingly to one side, then spun for a moment before righting itself. His stomach decided to move to a new location. Off to his left, Riley groaned.

10

Darius held his orb out in the palm of his hand like a water diviner. He bit his lip for a moment and then shoved the orb back into his pocket. Thunderclouds amassed across his face. At Riley's second groan he stepped over a pile of refuse and yanked her to her feet.

"Nice spot you've brought us to," he said sharply to Alec as he held onto Riley's shoulder with one hand and knocked a flattened cigarette box from her knee, along with other, unidentifiable rubbish. "Ten out of ten for getting us out of a tricky situation, but minus several million for moving us in time."

Alec blinked several times, trying to clear the fuzziness from his vision, while the world heaved itself to the left again. "*What?*"

"Time," Darius snapped. "The past, the present, the future. It's changed." He angrily pulled out his orb again.

"Alec can move time?" Riley wiped a shaky hand over her pale face and gave Alec a dark look. "That's stupid. No one can–"

"No." Darius grimaced. "Time doesn't move around. We did. He transported us back by several hours, if I calculated it correctly. And it's a serious problem."

Alec gave his head a shake to clear it but it didn't help. Darius wasn't making much sense and the sick feeling churning inside wasn't making paying attention any easier.

"Serious? Why?" Riley pulled her hand from Darius' grip. She warily took a step away from him and nearly toppled over.

"Reliving time you've already spent goes against all the laws of nature. You start all sorts of paths that go nowhere. It's a fundamental rule that cannot be broken. Ever." Darius turned to face Alec. The knuckles that gripped his orb were white. "I don't care how you did it, or why, Alec. But you can never do it again. There are rules that *cannot* be broken. The consequences are unimaginable. Promise me, never again."

Alec shrugged. He felt so awful that it didn't much matter what Darius was yakking on about. He'd just panicked in the bunker and for an instant desperately prayed to go anywhere, before this had all started. He hadn't actually *done* anything.

"Alec," Darius cut into his thoughts, "promise me."

"Yeah, whatever." Alec swallowed the bile at the back of his throat. He tried to take a deep breath but the alley's foul odour made him gag.

"We're in trouble, in case you need a reminder," Darius

57

continued. "The bunker was infiltrated, several of your fellow Potentials are probably dead, Anna is out of reach and Peter has been taken."

"Huh?" Alec raised his head. "Whaddya mean? Who's dead?"

"Jake and Mohammed."

"What about Mary Beth and the other girl?" Riley rubbed her hands over her arms and shivered as she took stock of their surroundings.

"Gone with Anna. I hope. Gino too." Darius walked down the alleyway, looking closely at the walls, the doors and the fire escape.

Alec thought back over the last harrowing moments in the bunker. Darius and Anna's increasing desperation. His feeling of uninformed helplessness. The glittering air that winked into existence right in front of him and his growing dread as it reached closer and closer. Peter had put his arm right through it.

"Where'd Peter go?" Alec gasped.

"Rhozan has him," Darius called from the farthest end of the alley.

The air whooshed out of Alec's lungs. "How?"

Darius strode back. "Rips are openings in the time/space continuum. A portal of some kind between our dimension and theirs. The Others can sense them. They wait for one to open and either empty their life force through into your world, manipulating the people they contact for their own pleasure, or they pull someone through. One opened up inside the bunker and Peter fell into it. Or was pulled."

Where on earth was a different dimension? How was he going to tell his mom? "How'll we get him back?"

"Good question." Darius ran his fingers through his hair. "No one's ever come back. I mean, we can sense them in there, we've just got no idea how to reach them."

Alec slowly pulled himself to his feet, careful not to

meet anyone's eyes. He leaned over, bracing his hands on his knees, and waited for the vertigo to pass, while Darius headed towards the street.

There was nothing else to do. Whatever idiocy Darius was saying would probably sort itself later. Right now he had to figure out where they were and get back home. Alec followed Darius' footsteps to the alley entrance. The road in front of him was completely unfamiliar. They were downtown somewhere, but the buildings were lower than those of inner-city Toronto and Alec had the impression that the ground was sloping away from him. A bike messenger whizzed by and two women, both pulling heavy carryalls, slowly meandered past. There was an unfamiliar tang in the air.

"No matter how far you run, you can never quite leave home," Riley said to no one in particular.

Darius sighed. "We're going to have to get something to eat and think about transportation."

"A bus is cheapest," Alec said before thinking. He blushed. Only losers took the bus.

"Do either of you have any money?" Darius asked.

Alec didn't have to check his pockets. "Five bucks. That's it."

Riley didn't answer.

"Riley?" Darius asked.

"You're the one who's organizing this picnic. You pay."

Darius gave a one-shoulder shrug. "Fine. Come on." He turned left and led them down to the end of the block. A blinking traffic light warned non-existent traffic. Darius stopped, looked both ways and stepped off the curb. Riley was already halfway across. Alec, still feeling muddled, trudged behind them. The road they crossed headed downward at a steep angle. There were several more streets parallel to the one he was walking along, a traffic light at each, and at the bottom, several blocks away, the tantalizing glimpse of water.

This was not Toronto.

Riley was speaking. Alec hurried to catch up with her but it was difficult on such wobbling legs.

"The airport is really far out of town. About forty kilometres from here. A taxi will cost a bomb."

"And the bus station?" asked Darius.

"Have no idea. I never take the bus. You can get the train, but it's pricey and will take awhile," Riley said.

"Airfare is out of the question," Darius sighed. "Guardians don't have unlimited monetary funds. And even if I did, I doubt Alec has identification on him sufficient for air travel. Wasn't there a tightening of restrictions several years ago? I had a memo on it."

"A memo." Riley smirked. "Alien invaders hand out memos. Puh-lease."

"Blending seamlessly into the surrounding environment is essential, hence the use of simulations and extensive investigation. Field agents are constantly updating cultural information."

"You have field agents here. In Halifax," Riley snorted, without breaking her stride.

"Well, not here exactly. But several in Canada. Wherever there's a Tyon training centre, there are field agents, gathering information, keeping our records up to date."

Alec startled. *Halifax*? That meant the water was the ocean. Cool. He loved the Pacific.

"Atlantic Ocean, Alec," Darius said, before turning his attention back to Riley. "Once a planet is deemed possible, the Collective establishes bases and operatives to collect information, introduce the resistor and monitor the situation."

60

"What's a resistor? What are you guys monitoring here, anyway?" Riley stopped walking and stood, feet wide apart. Her hands went to her hips. "Just what are you introducing to my planet?"

"We're monitoring for the Others."

"Uh-huh." Riley's eyes narrowed. "Right. You're here as protectors, keeping the intergalactic peace."

Darius beamed. "You catch on quick. Most struggle with this concept for several weeks."

Riley gave Darius a quick shove. "That was sarcasm, idiot."

Darius frowned. "I have trouble with sarcasm."

Alec was trying to follow the conversation, but there were so many questions. Did the Tyon Collective really travel around the galaxy and hide on unsuspecting worlds, keeping an eye out for trouble? Was that what Darius was going to train them for? And why wasn't Riley even a bit concerned that his brother had just been sucked into the enemy's whatever-it-was? He rubbed at a rapidly building ache across his forehead and prayed not to throw up.

"The resistor. What's that?" Riley called over her shoulder as she strode down the hill.

Darius set off behind her but he didn't answer the question immediately. Alec wasn't sure if he looked embarrassed or merely reluctant.

"The resistor is the genetic mutation that allows humans and humanoids to resist the mind control the Others employ. It's a natural genetic aberration on some planets, and has to be introduced into the humans on others."

Riley stopped again abruptly. Darius nearly walked into her. For a moment she looked puzzled, then her eyes blazed. "And just *how* is it introduced?"

Alec took a step backwards. Riley might be small, but the look she gave Darius could slice concrete into ribbons. Darius didn't seem to notice. Either that or he was completely oblivious for his personal safety. "Interbreeding," he said blithely.

Riley's nostrils flared. "Are you telling me that you aliens have bred with humans on this planet, just to insert some kind of *thing* into our genes?"

61

Darius nodded. "It takes several generations to disseminate and strengthen. We didn't know if we'd have enough time for maximum genetic penetration before the Others arrived. We figured they'd be interested in this world; it was only a matter of time. We'd hoped for enough time to protect you but it seems we miscalculated. It's too late."

Riley's heart was pounding so hard she could barely hear herself think. Of all the arrogant, high-handed, infuriatingly condescending things she'd ever heard, that one took the cake.

And now Darius had brought them back to Halifax, a city she'd only just escaped a few days ago. Alec of course hadn't done it. He was just a kid. A lanky, scruffy, kind of good-looking kid. That she did *not* find attractive.

Infuriated, she whirled on her heel, crossing the street without looking. This was *ridiculous*. She wouldn't believe a word of it. She was heading for the bookstore at the bottom of the road and she was going to walk in and bully Bjorn into letting her sit in the storeroom until her father came to get her. Darius and Alec could take a long walk off a short pier.

11

"You appear annoyed, and I grant that you may have reason, but–" Darius started. Riley didn't let him finish.

"Reason? I might have reason?" Her voice got higher with every word. "Look, buddy boy, you might think that you're God's gift to this planet, you and your alien friends, but I do not, I repeat, do not, like having my DNA fooled around with. Especially without my permission."

"What's he done with your DNA?" asked Alec, who was half-running to keep up with them.

"You'd be one of them, if we hadn't," Darius retorted. "And, I'm not an alien."

"Them?"

"Look around you, Riley. They're sheep, ready to be slaughtered. They can't stop him; they can't even put up a fight. You can. Is that what you want, to lie down and die, without even having a chance?"

Riley stomped around the corner onto the main street and headed straight for the first shop door, set back between two huge plate-glass windows filled to the brim with books. The door didn't budge when Riley grasped the brass door handle and yanked hard. She kicked the bottom of the door in frustration, but other than bruising her toe, nothing happened. She banged on the wooden rim of the door with her fist.

"It's closed," Alec offered.

"Yeah, good one, Sherlock," Riley snapped. She cupped her hands together on the glass and leaned in for a closer look.

Darius leaned against the doorjamb, one eyebrow raised and his arms crossed. He nodded towards the window display. "Got an overwhelming need to read about light-houses?"

"I have a friend here," Riley muttered, her voice muted from speaking against the glass.

The heavy door suddenly opened.

"I thought you'd left for Deborah's place?" The tall, bushy-eyebrowed man looked at Riley with mild interest. He had a clipped accent, bony wrists that protruded inches from the sleeves of his shirt and the fair, ruddy skin of someone from a very northern climate.

"I did." Riley barged into the warm, musty interior of the bookstore. The overpoweringly familiar scent nearly brought her to tears. "Can I use your phone, Bjorn?"

"Ya. If you can get the damn thing working. Nadine has done something with the answering machine again." Bjorn turned to her companions. "Aren't you going to introduce your friends?"

Riley had half a mind to tell her former boss that neither Darius nor Alec were friends in any way, shape or form, but the words never left her lips. Darius was staring at her, one eyebrow sardonically raised, almost daring her to denounce him, and Alec was still shuffling awkwardly on the sidewalk.

"Darius Finn and Alec Somebody-or-other. Just met them," Riley muttered. She took in a deep breath and plunked herself down on a small wooden chair sandwiched between two towering stacks of hard-covers.

Darius and Bjorn shook hands briefly. Alec slouched into the store and gave Bjorn a brief nod. Riley rolled her eyes.

"Want me to look at the answering machine?" she asked.

Bjorn shook his head. He sat down on the edge of a high wooden stool, his long legs crossed in front of him. He placed a pipe between his lips and surveyed his company with mild interest. "I took you to the train station. Changed your mind and want to go to the wedding after all?"

Riley shuddered. "Not in this lifetime."

"Then what happened?"

The words rushed into Riley's mouth but oddly she couldn't say them. She'd known Bjorn for years, ever since he'd hired her to stack shelves and answer the phone. Bjorn had been the silent, dependable rock in her stormy waters and she'd grown more fond of him than perhaps she'd thought. Still, would he believe a word about alien invasions and her new "special status"? Would anyone?

A high-pitched whine emanated from the back of the shop. Bjorn slid off his stool. "Got to get that fax. Be right back." He headed down an aisle of cluttered shelving.

Darius appeared at Riley's elbow. "So, you spent all your spare time in a bookstore. A life-changing pastime."

65

Riley bristled. "If there's anything more important in this world than books, I haven't heard about it."

"World peace?" Darius grinned. "Global warming?"

"Shut up," said Riley.

Darius meandered a short distance away, chuckling under

his breath. Bjorn returned with several papers in hand. He dropped them onto the counter by the cash register before strolling over to Darius' side.

"Interested in sailing?" Bjorn asked politely, eyeing the glossy coffee-table book, which Darius was slowly flipping through.

"You own a boat?" Darius asked casually.

"Motor," said Bjorn. "Gave up sailing years ago." He raised his shoulders in a fatalistic shrug. "Arthritis. Runs in the family. Still, gets me out on the water, ya?"

Darius put the book down. He reached into his jacket pocket with one hand and laid the other on Bjorn's long arm. "I would love to go out on your boat," he said.

Bjorn smiled. "I'd be happy to take you. Now if you wish."

Goosebumps sprang to life up and down Riley's neck. Bjorn *never* invited *anyone* onto his boat.

"Right now would be good. Maybe," Darius glanced over at Alec, "we could pick up some food. Have a picnic on board."

Bjorn headed back to the small office at the back of his store. His voice was muffled as he partially closed the door to reach his windbreaker. "There's a convenience store on the way."

Without another word he left the store. Alec fell in behind without a look at either at them.

Darius waited at the door. "Coming, Riley?"

"No, I'm not. I don't know how you managed to make him agree to take you on his boat, but I'm not going."

"Afraid, are you? I can easily use the same, er, influence on you as I did on him." His eyes narrowed. "Want to try it?"

"Go ahead." Riley crossed her arms. She was *so* not going.

Darius pulled out the orb from his jacket pocket and cradled it in the palm of his hand. Sunlight caught the inner refractions and danced within. Grinning, he held it out towards her. Riley's heart thudded but she didn't move an inch from the counter. Those glass balls had no power over her, no matter what he might think.

"Riley," Darius crooned, "come with us."

The words wrapped themselves around her. Stroked, caressed, tugged.

"You will come with us, Riley," Darius said, a bit louder, his smile more feral than pleasant.

Invisible coils tightened themselves around her, pulling her towards him. She tried to shake off the feeling, actually shaking physically to do it. It wouldn't budge. In fact, it was getting stronger.

"You want to." Darius took a step closer. The orb seemed to pulse with a faint radiance.

"I don't," Riley muttered. The glow got stronger. She couldn't tear her eyes away. This couldn't be happening.

"Oh, you do." Another step closer. "You will. The more you resist me, the stronger I'll make the command. Do you know what that means, Riley?" Another step. "Do you? You'll do everything I say. The control will be absolute."

Riley tried to pull her eyes from the unearthly light that enveloped her, mesmerizing her into inactivity. "Stop it, Darius," she whispered.

"Want to be under my complete and absolute power, sweet?" Darius was now close enough for her to count the freckles flung across his nose. He leaned forward and whispered in her ear. "Tell me to stop, Riley. Go on. I dare you."

It took all she had, but she managed to croak, "Stop."

Darius gave a cold little laugh. He stepped back and dropped the orb into his pocket. Riley's legs began to shake.

"The orb permits me to expand the scope of my desires," he said conversationally, as if the last few moments hadn't happened. "My will, subjugating yours. It's a neat trick. I can teach it to you if you want."

Riley shoved past him, darting out the door into the sun, where the world still spun on its normal axis and non-alien people were now wandering up and down a totally normal, non-alien street. She walked as fast as her legs would go. The heavy glass door shut firmly behind her and she knew that it was Darius' footsteps that were quickly catching up behind her, but she didn't turn to check. When Darius arrived at her side, she ignored him.

That had been truly frightening. She'd barely managed to hold onto her control. If he tried it again, could she resist him?

Most shops were still not open, but more cars had appeared, and delivery trucks, diesel engines belching fumes, idled here and there. She glanced at her watch, grimacing in annoyance. The digital readout was blank. She yanked her cellphone from her pocket and thumbed the on switch. Nothing.

"Electric things don't teleport well," Darius said.

She frowned but kept silent. He might think he'd won, the smug alien creep, but he hadn't. She was not going to get on Bjorn's boat. She was going to go home. She just needed change for a public telephone, if there were any anymore.

She ducked into the convenience store on the corner. It was more of a mini market than anything, she remembered, selling fruit and vegetables and cans of single-serving prepared foods for people who couldn't cook. Bjorn was already piling a hand-held basket with bread and cheese and fruit. Alec was loading up his arms with several jumbo bags of potato chips. He gave a sharp "hey" as Darius plucked all but one from him.

"Healthy food equals a healthy body," Darius said, dropping the chip bags onto a shelf before sweeping over to the dairy case.

68   Within minutes they were leaving, a veritable feast divided into three white plastic bags swinging from Alec's hands. Darius was holding his orb, Riley noted, as they turned towards the ocean and proceeded along the wooden boardwalk, away from the historic section of town. Just seeing him holding it made her uncomfortable.

She hadn't gotten change for the phone while in the store. She just couldn't seem to make herself go up to the counter and speak to the cashier. The female clerk watched Darius hungrily from the moment they entered the little store to the moment they left. She hadn't even noticed Alec swiping a chocolate bar. Darius, the swine, had encouraged her, grinning winsomely, winking and giving her the kind of long smoldering looks found in romance novels. Riley stalked out of the store, infuriated.

She still had her wallet, and there were a couple of credit cards her father had arranged for her, just before she left, as well as a few twenties and at least one loonie. She could grab a taxi, if she saw one, and get home. The housekeeper would let her in.

Darius was walking directly beside her, within arm's length, rolling his orb around carelessly in his hand, and staring with unabashed interest at the harbour. But his lack of attention towards her was a ruse. When she tripped slightly over an uneven boardwalk slat, his hand was at her elbow, gripping her almost before she'd even noticed she'd stumbled. And they both knew he was waiting for her to bolt.

Around them, seabirds cried and wheeled overhead. Joggers sweated past and a constant parade of mothers, babes in strollers, trundled by. The day was already warming, despite the early hour. It would be blisteringly hot in a few hours.

In front of her, Bjorn and Alec were chatting away about motors as if they'd known each other for years. She tuned the conversation out, concentrating instead on her plan. If she couldn't talk to anyone and get money for the phone because Darius had put some kind of weird voodoo hex on her, well then, she'd have to think of something else.

And soon. The marina was only a block away.

69

Alec pulled apart the sealed opening to a bag of all-dressed chips and helped himself to a mouthful of breakfast. Sure, it wasn't the sort of meal his mother would approve of, but he was starving. And besides, in Toronto, it was afternoon. Or at least it had been an hour ago.

Alec was still trying to get his head around everything. They'd been attacked, some kids had been killed and his own brother was now missing. In addition, he'd somehow brought everyone to Nova Scotia. And changed time. *Without even trying.*

It was both deeply weird and strangely pleasing. Weird, because having a power you couldn't feel, never mind control, was rather scary; pleasing, because Darius looked pretty impressed and Riley had been shocked and probably jealous. Part of his brain kept running over and over what had happened in the bunker. The other part of his mind was trying to keep up with what was going on around him.

Beside him, Bjorn prattled on about ratios and oil pressure while swinging a grocery bag he'd taken from Alec only a moment before, seemingly unmindful that that particular carrier held several bottles of carbonated drinks. Alec only partly listened. He hoped that Bjorn's motorboat would be one of those massive yachts all around them, with tons of sumptuous accessories. The guys would be totally jealous when he got back home after all this was over.

Bjorn turned down a narrow gangway, leading past several boats, finally stopping near the end of the

12

jetty. He pointed to the right. "That's her. The *Inga*."

Alec swallowed his disappointment. She was a dull, yellowish houseboat, with peeling paint and rust-stained metal fittings. She seemed forlorn, dwarfed by her more glamorous neighbours.

"Come on aboard." Bjorn cheerily led the little party towards wooden planking. The side of the boat rubbed up against several tractor tires looped against the jetty. It was an easy step down onto the deck.

"Come on, Riley," Darius said firmly.

Alec turned and looked. Riley had a mutinous look on her face, and was standing arms crossed and legs locked against further movement. "I told you—" she started.

"*Riley.*" Darius' hand went to his jacket pocket.

"Don't make me." It came out like a whimper and Alec knew from the sudden grimace that she hadn't wanted to sound so weak. He turned his back and pretended not to hear.

"I can and I will." Darius' voice had a hard edge.

Bjorn ducked through the opening into the galley-cum-cabin of what was instantly obvious as his home and Alec followed. A wide futon sofa lined the starboard side of the cabin; cupboards, countertops and kitchen appliances lined the port. A heavy table was bolted to the middle of the floor. A captain's chair was positioned in front of a wide bank of instruments under a row of windows forward of the living quarters. Everywhere, the detritus of a single man's life littered the cabin: clothes dropped onto the floor, crumpled newspapers all over the futon, an unfinished meal on the table.

Bjorn grabbed the books off the table and dumped them into a locker built under the sofa. He gave an apologetic smile as he swept the dishes away. "I made all of the modifications myself."

"It's impressive," Darius said politely. "Perhaps you wouldn't mind showing me the controls?"

"Don't," shouted Riley, hovering in the doorway, one foot still outside on the deck.

Darius gave her a sharp look. "Sit down and be quiet."

Slowly, she entered the cabin and crossed to the sofa. She sat on the edge and gritted her teeth.

"Please." Darius held out his hand, indicating the instrument panel. Bjorn nodded.

Alec stuffed another handful of chips into his mouth and chewed contentedly as he inspected the framed photos of sailing yachts along the wall.

"What the hell are you so happy about?" Riley muttered.

Alec glanced down. "Nothing."

"He's using you," she said, her eyes darting towards Darius, now deeply immersed in conversation. "You're just a pawn in some game he's playing."

Alec swallowed and took another handful, giving himself something to do until he'd thought of what to say. Cute girls always made his tongue tie up in knots.

"He's lying to you. Don't you get it? Telling you you're so special." Riley's voice was so low he almost couldn't hear her.

"It's not a game," Alec said slowly. "It can't be. You saw what I did."

"Huh. I have no proof you did anything. Only Darius said you did, and I don't trust him as far as I can throw him."

"How'd we get here then? Air Canada? How'd time go backwards?" Alec licked the seasoning off his fingers and dropped the half-eaten bag onto the table. He leaned back, looking directly at Riley. "Where'd my brother go? Who were those people who tried to kill me? If you've got another explanation, I'd love to hear it."

"I don't. Yet." Riley scowled. "But the minute I do, you'll be the first to know."

"If you don't like it with us, then go. I'm not gonna stop you."

The engine of the boat roared to life, then dropped to a thrumming that rose up through the floor and vibrated into their feet. Riley got paler.

"Look, please, you've got to help me," she whispered. "I don't want to be a part of this. I want to go home."

"Yeah, I doubt the going home part," Alec said. The memories of her suddenly rose up inside him. He'd *been* her, just for a second. In a dream. Or was it real? He couldn't remember.

Riley stood up, her small hands gripped his upper arms, and a look of frank pleading and vulnerability spread over her face. She gave him a little shake. "Help me get off this boat."

Alec shook himself away from her. She smelled too good this close. He glanced over at Darius, who was listening attentively as Bjorn pointed something out in the marina. Any minute they'd be casting off. An annoyed Darius was an unknown quantity, but on the other hand, it was pretty hard to look into Riley's navy blue eyes and refuse her. Maybe, if he helped her, she'd like him better. And if she liked him …

"Come on," he said quietly. He walked over to the doorway and leaned out. The *Inga* was straining away from the dock, seawater and refuse roiling with the thrust of the propellers. No one was walking on the jetty. In fact, the place seemed surprisingly deserted for such a beautiful, summer day. "You jump off and run. I'll slow him down."

She was shaking, Alec noticed. He gave her a little shove. "Go on."

Riley took a deep breath. Screwing her face up as if she were about to climb Mount Everest, she propelled herself forward. Two quick steps and she was over the side of the *Inga* and sprinting down the jetty. For someone so tiny, she was admirably fast.

"Hey!" Darius shouted.

Alec blocked the doorway but Darius brushed him easily aside and knocked him over. He leapt over the gunwale and disappeared down the gangway before Alec landed in a heap.

73

Alec rubbed a hand across his forehead, surprised at the force of Darius' reaction. Behind him, Bjorn stood silently beside the captain's chair, a blank look on his face.

"Don't worry, I'm fine," Alec muttered as he pulled himself to his feet. He glanced up at the sound of a strangled squawk. A moment later, Darius appeared with Riley unceremoniously slung over his shoulder. He crossed the several metres to the boat with impatient strides, brushed past Alec without a word and dumped Riley onto the sofa.

"Sit," he ground out.

Riley opened her mouth to speak, but Darius shouted "Silence!" before she could utter a sound. She grabbed at her throat and retched. Bjorn seemed to come back to life. Both he and Darius left the cabin and walked around to the bow of the boat. A moment later, they were heading aft.

The rope holding the *Inga* to the wharf arced through the sky to land in a heap on the jetty. Darius dashed back inside the cabin and deftly took the wheel. Bjorn held the rope in his hand and leapt off the *Inga*, landing easily on the wharf. Slowly, the houseboat pulled away from the jetty.

Alec grabbed the edge of the table to steady himself as the little craft rocked uneasily. Darius switched gears and the engine roared.

Alec ran over to the doorway and leaned out. The sharp salt spray blurred his vision for a second and the breeze, growing as the boat's speed increased, whipped his hair into his face, but even so, Bjorn didn't appear even aware that they were leaving him behind.

The *Inga* entered the open harbour and swung starboard. Darius opened up the engine and the boat strained forward.
For several minutes, no one said anything. Riley was rocking back and forth on the futon looking stricken. Darius was absorbed in navigating the small craft out of the harbour towards the open ocean. Alec was frozen in disbelief.

Riley had been right all along.

Alec sat down on the sofa beside Riley, unsure of what to do while Darius ignored them both and steered the houseboat beyond the safety of the harbour. Riley leaned back and closed her eyes, every line of her body screaming to be left alone.

There wasn't anything Alec could do. Jumping overboard didn't seem like a reasonable option. Within minutes they were far out in choppy water, filled with huge seagoing vessels that would easily mow down a tiny body bobbing in their path. There wasn't a phone to call the police and no sign of the Coast Guard. And besides, every time he tried to stand up and head outside to the deck an incredible sense of "not wanting to" washed over him, making him shiver. Only keeping still abated the sensation. Was Darius using some kind of weird mind control on him?

Alec rooted through the crumpled newspapers on the futon for something to do. It was the morning edition, he noted, the same day he'd been grabbed in Toronto. That meant that he had yet to go missing at home. Or did it? Could he be in both places at the same time, or was he not at home right now? And if he weren't at home now, how would he be kidnapped in order to end up here? Unable to figure out the rapidly confusing mess of time travel, he perused the sports section. It wasn't until he finished that and the entertainment news that he bothered with the headlines: *Riots in Toronto, Unprecedented Violence.*

13

The story went on to list several shootings, a looting of a mall overnight and multiple attacks on the subway system. The chief of police threatened a curfew. Some grey-bearded professor at the University of Toronto spouted on about economic unrest fueling the public's anger and Alec found himself grinning grimly at the photo. It wasn't economics. It was Rhozan. Whoever he was.

Darius slowed the engine down and hooked a small rope to the steering wheel, effectively locking the steering in place. He stalked over to the table, not quite so easy to do with the boat rocking back and forth, and began opening the bags of food. "We all need to eat something."

"I'm not hungry," Riley said, pouting.

"Tough. You're going to eat this even if I have to jam it down your throat." Darius didn't sound like he meant it. The anger seemed to have melted away as quickly as it had surfaced. He pulled out the two bottles of cola with a definite gleam in his eye, and set them down beside the fruit, bread, paté and cheese. "Alec, get a few plates and glasses."

No, thought Alec, as hard as he could.

"No need to yell," Darius replied conversationally. He squinted at the tiny writing on a small bottle. "This is made in France," he said to himself. "No wonder it's expensive."

"You read my mind," Alec accused him. There was no denying it now. "Didn't you?"

"Of course." Darius shrugged.

"Can all you aliens read our minds?"

"Hmm, no. And, I told you, I'm not an alien." Darius unscrewed the lid of the jar and stuck a finger into the drab yellow contents. He pulled it out and sucked off the mustard. "Yuck, this is awful. Riley, eat something."

Riley wiped the tear from her face, smearing the black track into an unbecoming smudge. "I'm not hungry."

"You are. There are other methods of proving your general dissatisfaction than self-starvation. You are not your sister."

"Leave me alone." But a loud grumbling of her stomach compromised the strength of her argument. Alec smothered his grin and began rooting in the untidy cupboards for glasses.

Humming to himself, Darius began dividing up the crusty bread and the cheese.

"Can you teach me to read minds?" Alec asked. This could be a useful skill, if he could learn it before escaping.

"Sorry, no." Darius placed several slices of cheese on a plate already laden with several thick slabs of bread and a large bunch of grapes and handed it to Alec.

"Why not?"

Darius shrugged and popped a grape into his mouth. He spoke while chewing. "You don't have the gift. It's not something you can learn. You either have it or you don't. Like Riley." He handed her a plate of food, then picked up a bottle of soda and began to unscrew the top.

"Stop!" yelled Alec, but it was too late. The excessive swinging had stirred up the carbonated liquid magnificently. Cola spewed in all directions.

Darius yelped, dropped the bottle and jumped back like a scalded cat.

Riley got to it first. With a quick twist of her wrist she closed the cap and carried the bottle at arm's length. She stepped onto the deck and carefully held the bottle over the side while she removed the lid. Excess soda foamed over the neck. Once finished she returned inside.

Darius was mopping his face and shirt with a rag that wasn't much cleaner. He raised his eyebrows. "I suppose you enjoyed that?"

Riley shrugged a thin shoulder but didn't smile. She handed him the bottle and sat back down on the couch, pulling her plate onto her lap. She picked up a grape. "Where exactly are we going?"

"Newfoundland." Darius didn't seem to notice Riley's wide-eyed stare or hear Alec's gasp of surprise. He was carefully pouring himself a tall glass of cola. He took a tentative sip and sighed with profound appreciation.

"Newfoundland? You've got to be joking." Riley jammed a hunk of cheese into her mouth, seemingly oblivious to what she was doing. "What on earth is in Newfoundland that you want?'

"Home Base," Darius replied. "We needed somewhere near the two main locations of Potentials: Ireland and Canada. Also somewhere off the beaten track but close enough to civilization so we can come and go without raising attention. Newfoundland has lots of little uninhabited islands. It's perfect." He took another swallow, then another. He drained the glass and poured one more. "This stuff is really good. I never got to have this before I left Earth."

"Newfoundland is about a thousand kilometres from here, across a famously treacherous sea. And we're in a *houseboat*, you idiot," Riley gasped.

"I don't have the time or the energy to regen enough to transport both of you," Darius explained. "In case you've forgotten, we were attacked recently and Anna and I had to fight off the Others, which happens to take a lot of energy. Add to that trying to control the teleport of a completely untrained and nearly unmanageable Potential," he gave a pointed look at Alec, "*and* enough mind control to hold your former boss in check, give us this boat and stop him from calling the police. Alec doesn't have any ID for an airplane trip and I don't have access to funds right at the moment."

"We could be killed out here." Riley shot to her feet.

78

"We *would have been* killed if we'd stayed in Halifax. They're following us, in case you haven't noticed. Every time we use an orb, Rhozan knows it."

"How do you know that?" Riley demanded.

"The Others fear orbs. They can't control the power of one. But they certainly seem to know when we use them." Darius grabbed onto the edge of the table as the little boat lurched sickeningly to port for a moment. Riley did likewise. Alec wasn't quick enough and he fell over in a heap, dropping his last slice of cheese to the floor. It was only as he pulled himself upright that he noted that far off on the distant horizon, dark clouds were nastily piling up.

"Uh, Darius," Alec said.

"Just a sec." Darius had his attention on Riley. "So keep your hands off your orb. Just touching it can send a signal."

Alec yanked his hand off his own orb with a pang of guilt. He'd gotten into the habit of mindlessly fiddling with it because it seemed to soothe him.

"You have no idea how to pilot this boat, do you?" Riley's cheeks were blotched with fire and her eyes snapped dangerously. "It's not like taking a cab across town, Darius. The ocean is a dangerous and unpredictable place."

As if to emphasize her words, the houseboat lurched again.

"Darius, the weather," Alec said, this time more loudly.

All three of them looked up and out over the bow of the ship. Far ahead, the sky was darkening ominously. Whitecaps dotted the undulating surface. A cold spray of seawater splashed over the bow and speckled the front window.

Darius frowned. He strode over to the steering wheel and unhooked the rope, taking control of the vessel himself. "Better look for lifejackets. We may need them."

Alec's stomach dropped to his ankles. Riley looked just as worried as she dropped to her knees and began rooting through the cupboards under the sofa. Alec headed to the back of the cabin and yanked open the door to the small storage room. The search took seconds. Nothing. Disgruntled, he slammed the door shut and leaned against it. "Any luck?" Alec asked.

"Does it look like it?" Riley banged her head on the handle of a pot as she rose to her feet. "I don't think he's cleaned the place. Ever."

Darius was holding the wheel with both hands now. The wind was rising quickly and the sky darkening rapidly.

"Look under the control panels here," Darius advised without taking his eyes off the ocean.

Alec complied. But the few cupboards were surprisingly empty of everything but wires and dust. He sat back on his heels. "What kind of idiot has a boat without lifejackets? We'll have to go back, right?" Everyone knew how danger-ous it was to be out in the ocean without a lifejacket. Even a landlubber like him. "I mean, what's so important that we have to go to Newfoundland right now? We can try again tomorrow."

"No can do." Darius fought for a moment with the wheel and the boat righted itself. "We're running out of time."

Alec tensed as a large wave smashed against the bow and drenched the windows. "Running out of time? How?"

Darius sighed. "You can't feel it, you're not trained to, but the rips are widening in Toronto and I'm sensing the same here. No one knows how to close them and you can't stop Rhozan, and whoever or whatever he has in there, from coming out."

A heavy silence fell over the cabin. Alec watched as the light faded and the sea took on a darker, more ominous shade of navy. The temperature seemed to drop as well. The swells got higher and rougher and the houseboat, not engineered for this type of weather, listed alarmingly from one side to the other.

If the boat went down, they'd all drown. They were too far from shore to even consider swimming for it.

"We're not drowning," Darius said quietly. "Worry less about what I'm doing and more about your companion."

Alec glanced backwards. Riley was huddled in a tiny ball, the picture of distress.

"She can't swim," Darius whispered. "Keep her company."

Rain began to lash at the little boat as Alec dropped to the seat beside Riley, and within a moment it was falling so thickly that visibility was reduced to almost nothing. The drumming on the roof increased in volume to a roar as the heavens opened. Without warning, Riley's hand shot out and grasped his wrist. He was surprised at her strength. For such a small person she was almost cutting off the circulation to his hand. Not that he was going to pry away her fingers.

"How close are we?" Alec had to shout above the rain.

"Nowhere close enough," Darius shouted back. "If this gets much worse, I'll have to call them."

There was no point asking "Call who?" because the wind began roaring and the thudding rain got much louder. Alec huddled next to Riley and shivered in the increasingly cool cabin, hoping that the rain and the storm would play itself out in the next few minutes. He didn't want to admit it, but he was getting scared, too.

14

Riley had never been so frightened in all her life. Even when that bizarre woman drew a knife on her at the outdoor festival, she had kept calm and acted in response to the threat. It had worked, too. But now, things were exponentially worse.

All her life, she'd been afraid of water. Sure, she could manage in a public pool, as long as her feet could touch the ground. Today, when they'd set off, she'd been too angry to really think about the miles of unending darkness below her. But nothing was diverting those thoughts now.

She glanced at the clock over the kitchen sink. They'd been out on the water for hours. Darius was still silently manning the wheel and so far had done an admirable job of keeping the houseboat the right way up. Whether or not they were even going in the right direction was another thing.

The boat hit a wave head-on and the bow lifted straight up for a second before dropping down and hitting the water with an almighty smack that knocked Riley and Alec to the floor. The door flung open and seawater rushed inside, swirling around the decking like a miniature tsunami.

"Alec, the door," Darius shouted. He was climbing up onto his feet, holding onto the wheel with one hand, his orb in the other.

Alec pulled away, but Riley convulsively grabbed onto him tighter. "Don't," she moaned before she could stop herself.

"I'll be right back. Promise." Alec's grin was jauntier than it should have been, considering that they were all going to die. He scrambled to his feet, slipping in the seawater, and managed to reach the door, only falling twice. He slammed it shut and slid home the dead bolt.

The boat keeled to the left and Alec toppled, sliding down the wet flooring to land in a heap at Darius' feet. "Any time you want to call for help."

Darius held the orb aloft for a moment, silently indicating the call was already in progress. Alec grunted and started to slop back towards the sofa where Riley was holding onto the table leg for dear life. He stopped dead.

Sparkles. In the air.

Alec screamed. "Riley, *move*."

Riley was frozen; her wide eyes focused on the rip and nothing else. Inside her head, the words *you fall into them and just disappear* were repeating over and over.

"Riley, get out of the way," Alec yelled.

Darius added, "You'll be pulled in if it touches you."

Alec dashed around the table, falling against it as the boat listed to one side. He groaned and grabbed at his hip, but didn't stop until he was directly beside her.

The sparkles grew brighter. She couldn't tear her eyes away. The rip was between her and Alec.

"Slide out," Alec urged.

The sparkles began to move. Closer.

"*Riley.*"

She forced her body to comply and slid to the floor, her head just missing the edge of the rip by millimetres. Alec, scrambling beside her, grabbed her arm and pulled her away.

"Door," she gasped as she tried to stand upright on the pitching deck.

Alec seemed to have the same idea, whether or not he heard her. He was already pulling her towards it. He

83

collapsed against the cabin wall and reached up towards the deadbolt.

"Alec, *no!*"

Alec froze, his arm outstretched. Darius' control was so strong Riley could barely move herself.

Sparkles. Hovering over the lock.

"Back up. Move out of its way," Darius shouted. The boat listed violently again and the steering wheel was pulled out of his hands. The walls of the boat groaned with the strain as another wave hit them broadside. With nothing to hold onto, Riley slid towards the table. Alec tumbled past her. She heard the crack of his skull against the wooden tabletop even above the howling wind and rain.

Alec groaned. His free hand grasped his forehead. A small trickle of blood seeped beneath his fingers.

"Okay?" Riley struggled for breath.

"No," Alec snapped. He cursed with proficient fluency.

"Alec, it's on the move again," Darius warned.

"I know, I know."

Riley grabbed Alec's hand. He tugged her back, away from the second lot of sparkles, which were slowly but steadily advancing towards them. The first cluster, under the table, was unmoving but getting larger in diameter. It was as if the two groups were planning on meeting each other: one moving closer and the other growing. They were sandwiched directly in between.

The houseboat bucked and thrashed. Darius scrambled wildly to reach the steering wheel, but another wave, this time larger and stronger than any previous, crashed through the windows over the sofa. Gallons of bitterly cold seawater poured in in a massive torrent.

Riley could do nothing but take a huge breath and steel herself for the inevitable. Alec's arms tightened around her as they were engulfed. She couldn't breathe. She couldn't see. She couldn't even fight.

Alec's arms pulled Riley upwards. Their heads broke

above water. Riley gave a strangled gasp. In the few moments she'd been submerged, several other windows had broken, including those over the bow of the boat and the cabin was halfway flooded. Sparks flew from the electrical panel. There was no sign of Darius. The sparkles were hovering just above the rising water and were still advancing.

"Dariu–" Riley tried to gasp his name, but another wave hit her directly in the face and she choked. Alec was still on his feet. How, she wasn't sure. One arm was like an iron band around her ribs. He was yelling something. She could feel the anger in him building and surging wildly.

Another wave, another mouthful of water.

Where was Darius Finn?

"That's enough," Alec shouted in her ear. "Stop it. *Now*."

Electricity, enough to light a city, exploded from behind her, through her and outwards. Alec's anger, in Tyon power.

A brilliant flash from the orb he held blinded her for a moment. Then, without warning, the boat blew apart.

Someone was holding him up by the scruff of his neck. His tee shirt was pulled taut and bit under his chin, enough to make it hard to breathe and impossible to swallow.

"Can you swim?" Darius panted behind him, letting go of his neck the moment Alec moved under his own control.

"Yeah." Instinctually Alec began to tread water. There was no sign of the houseboat anywhere. Only whitecaps and angry sky.

Darius was deathly pale and a deep cut over his left eye was bleeding sluggishly. He was holding Riley's head up under the chin. Her eyes were closed, her head rested on his shoulder and her arms and legs were spread like a starfish. Darius had his hand cupped around her mouth to prevent her breathing in the seawater.

"What happened?" Alec strained to be heard above the keening wind and the sloshing water.

"Save your strength," Darius yelled back. "Won't be long."

The last thought Alec clearly remembered was the sparkles getting closer and water sucking at his arms and legs and attempting to drag him down. He recalled feeling furious. He vaguely recollected grabbing at his orb while he struggled to stay above water, but then what?

He felt as if he'd run a marathon or stayed on the field for an entire double championship game. Alec desperately tried to keep Darius and Riley in sight. The fierce swells and the might of the wind seemed to conspire to pull them apart.

The water temperature, even for July, was bitterly cold. His arms were aching and his legs seemed leaden. Alec's mind became numb and the easiest thing seemed to be to drift off to sleep. He forced himself to think. About his mother, his father and friends in Toronto. What drowning would feel like. The orb in his pocket. Darius Finn, and Riley. Guess she'd never kiss him now.

A wave slapped him across the face and he choked.

The minutes stretched out and then ceased to matter. The waves continued to heave around him, tossing him up and dropping him down with sickening regularity. The wind blew rain and seawater without end.

It was getting harder to keep close to Darius and Riley. Harder to move his arms. Harder to keep his head above water. He desperately wanted to sleep.

There was a crack of distant thunder.

Call for help. He weakly pushed his thoughts towards Darius. *Call and save us.*

Riley dreamed she was swimming. It was a pleasant dream, too, which was very odd. She was vaguely aware of the water's chill and Darius' presence, but they didn't seem to matter. She distantly heard him shout something, but the sloshing water deafened the sound and she didn't much care. She felt his arm grab her around the waist and drag her body under the water. She rather wished he wouldn't.

Something huge moved directly beneath them.

Suddenly the dream state was gone. Riley's senses returned to her in a massive rush.

She was in the ocean.

She wasn't wearing a lifejacket.

And she couldn't swim. "Ahh …"

16

Darius loudly grunted as she thrashed about in panic. "Stay still for God's sake."

What had happened? Where was Alec? Or Bjorn's houseboat? She had just opened her mouth to scream again when something hard hit under her feet and propelled her upwards like a rocket off a launch pad. She and Darius were pushed right out of the water.

Seawater poured off the dark, curved surface of the craft as it rose upwards to float on top of the waves. Darius, still holding her so tightly she could hardly breathe, fell to his knees on the shiny surface. Riley fell under him. There were no protrusions to grab and the surface was slippery as ice. They were starting to slide off. Riley squirmed as hard as she could to free her arm. She slammed her palm onto the surface of the ship and tried to halt their inexorable slide.

It wasn't working.

The metal began to vibrate as if a thousand furious bees were just underneath the surface. Suddenly the hull of the ship pulled apart beneath her and she and Darius fell into darkness through the open hatchway.

Riley landed face-down in something soft and spongy that almost immediately curled around her and held her tight. Rain poured in until the hatchway closed. She thrashed about, trying to free herself but the material didn't allow any movement. She could see, even with the dim light, that she was inside a small craft and that Darius had fallen beside her. Hands reached out to roll him over on his back.

"Get the boy," Darius croaked.

"Zeroing in on target," said an unfamiliar male voice.

The lights inside the cabin rose smartly to an almost too-bright level. Riley squinted as two hands clasped her shoulders and pulled her upright. A hulking blond man with a crew cut and pale blue eyes picked her up effortlessly and carried her to a narrow bunk against the wall. She sat up and looked around.

They were inside some sort of ultra-modern submersible ship. There seemed to be only the one small, low-ceilinged cabin. A bank of what might be controls lined the far wall with two chairs mounted to the floor directly in front. There were no windows or view screens. Whoever had designed the ship had watched way too much *Star Trek*, Riley concluded derisively. The smooth lines, limited furniture and ultra-modern appearance were right out of a movie. Except this was real.

Both the strangers wore one-piece, grey jumpsuits, similar to fighter pilots, and serious expressions. The only familiar person on the ship was the woman cradling Darius and soothing his forehead with her palm. The unflappable Ice Queen from the bunker.

Darius' eyes didn't open to Anna's gentle ministrations, nor did he respond in any way when Anna pulled out her orb and held it over his chest.

The hatch in the roof opened without warning. Rain and Alec fell in.

The hatch slid closed again. The foam circle lowered quickly until it was flush with the metal flooring. Alec lay unmoving in the middle of the foam, which retracted from around his body as the man who'd carried Riley moved to Alec's side and rolled him over onto his back. Riley had a glimpse of Alec's pale face before the man pulled an orb from the back pocket of his overalls and held it closely over Alec's chest.

The man frowned. Riley's breath caught in her throat. The man placed his hand on Alec's forehead. He closed his eyes and concentrated.

Riley shivered violently. The interior of the little submarine was warm, but her clothes were soaked and her body deeply chilled. Hypothermia, she muzzily realized.

"Is … is he okay?" she asked, her teeth chattering.

"He will be," the man hovering over Alec answered. He had the same non-descript, clipped accent as Anna. He straightened up and removed his hand from Alec's forehead.

"You must be Riley," he said. "I am Dean. Our pilot is Tyrell. And you know Anna."

Anna glanced up and gave Riley a quick nod, before turning to Darius again. Tyrell didn't turn at the mention of his name. Whatever he was doing seemed to take all his attention.

Dean lifted Alec easily and carried him over to the bunk beside Riley. He pulled straps out from under the thin mattress and snapped the belts across Alec's waist. Dean nodded towards Riley's bunk. "Secure yourself. We're about to dive."

Riley's fingers struggled to fasten the unfamiliar clasps

together and, without comment, Dean finished for her. Despite the warning, the little ship moved so quickly her stomach dropped to her knees. She grabbed onto the edge of the bunk, fearful of falling off despite the restraints. The pilot, Tyrell, waved his hands over the controls, not quite touching any of them. Riley caught sight of an orb in his right hand.

Dean didn't seem affected by the wild movements of the ship that was now straightening and propelling rapidly forward. He crossed to Anna and reached over her shoulder. He waved his hand and a small drawer appeared in the wall. Dean reached inside and pulled out a metallic beaker. He carried it across to Riley. Hesitantly, she took it.

"Drink it," Dean advised. "It will help with the cold."

"What is it?" she asked. They wouldn't go through all the trouble of saving her just to poison her now, would they?

"A heated restorative," Dean informed her. He turned and sat in the chair next to the pilot.

Steam rose from the milky beverage and bathed her face. Actually, it didn't smell too bad. She took a tentative sip. The liquid, although unrecognizable, was quite palatable and gloriously warm. She took another mouthful, savouring the heat as it spread through her body.

"We're heading to Home Base," Anna said.

Riley looked up in surprise. Anna sounded almost pleasant. She continued to stroke Darius' forehead, her free hand pressed over the neck of her jumpsuit, almost as if unaware she was doing it.

"Darius said it was in Newfoundland," Riley replied.

"Under a small island off the south coast, yes."

Riley considered this for a moment. Then she voiced her concerns. "Is he all right?"

"Alec or Darius?"

Riley glanced over at Alec's pale face on the bunk beside her. "Both."

"They will both recover. Both Darius and Alec have more intense effects from the cold, as Darius was able to protect you somewhat from the elements. In addition, they are suffering from psychic and physical exhaustion. Both have extended significant Tyon power in the last several days."

Riley frowned. What power did Alec use?

Anna answered her unspoken question. "Alec destroyed the boat you were on. We felt it as far away as the Base. It is a wonder he didn't kill the three of you."

Riley bit her lip. She remembered the surge of electricity just before she lost consciousness. Was that *Alec*? He had no more training with these crystal balls than she did. It was totally unfair.

"Alec's ability is certainly remarkable. But highly dangerous. What was happening at the time?"

Riley took another mouthful. "There was a storm. Darius was trying his best, but Bjorn's houseboat wasn't meant to handle that kind of weather. Then these, I don't know, sparkles appeared. Darius called it a rip. He got totally freaked. So did Alec." She paused to drink again. "They were after us. Darius said we'd die if they touched us."

Anna was frowning. "There were more than one?"

"I saw two. Don't know if there were any more." Riley wrapped her hands around the now-empty mug as she remembered. "The windows blew out. The boat took on water. Darius couldn't control it anymore. We started to sink."

"And then?"

Riley shrugged. "I dunno. That's the last I remember."

Anna's fingers ran distractedly through Darius' hair. She seemed to be deep in thought.

"How long until he's okay?" Riley frowned. It was annoying the way Anna was touching him, as if she had a right to.

"Unspecified. He's seriously overextended himself, saving you two. I hope you appreciate it." Anna gave Darius a severe look, then eased herself out from under his inert form and stood up. She walked over to the controls and leaned over Dean's shoulder, busying herself with reading the various screens.

Riley clamped her lips shut and glared at Anna's back while the ship continued its silent journey. It was impossible to tell how deep they were or in what direction they were travelling because of the lack of windows. She felt the ship slowing before anyone said anything. Dean rose from his seat and came over to kneel by her bunk. "We are docking in a minute. Remain secured until I have indicated otherwise." He leaned over Alec, checking that the strap was still fastened.

The boat slowed rather abruptly. There was a slight rubbing sensation, as if the outer hull was nestling against something solid, then the craft was still. A humming sensation that Riley hadn't even been aware of until it stopped, ceased. A doorway materialized in the wall right beside Darius. The doors slid open.

A tall, wide-shouldered man, older than any of the others Riley had seen before, marched onto the ship. He wore his grey uniform like armour. His blue eyes glittered with ice. The man glanced down at Darius. Riley noted the flicker of contempt before it was hidden.

"Is the boy, Alec, on board?" The man's imperious tone cut through the silence. Riley's spine stiffened. He glanced over at her dismissively.

Anna walked over to the newcomer. "He's unconscious, Logan."

"Finn?"

"Seriously weakened, but alive."

Logan's lip gave a slight curl as he ordered, "Bring him to Med Ops. Anna, come with me."

He turned and left the ship, his shoulders nearly

brushing the sides of the doorway as he passed. Anna fell in behind him without another look in Riley's direction. They were out of sight in a second.

Two more blond men, both wearing coveralls identical to Dean and Tyrell's, entered without comment. One pulled a baton from his pocket, and with a flick of his wrist, the object unravelled to form a simple stretcher. Within seconds, they loaded Darius onto the contraption and bore him away.

Dean undid the buckle and tossed the restraining straps off of Alec's hips. He lifted the boy up into his arms. "Follow me, Riley," he instructed.

She undid the buckle and got slowly to her feet. Where else could she go? What else could she do?

R iley stepped out into a cool, dank tunnel of dark chiselled rock. The curved ceiling was so low she could almost touch it with her fingertips. The walls were practically oozing water, and here and there dark puddles had formed small mirrors in the depressions of the floor. Intermittent sconces held yellow, softly glowing lights, providing enough illumination to prevent tripping.

Dean carried Alec in his arms in front of her, blocking most of her view. Tyrell was right on her heels.

The tunnel sloped slowly downwards and the air cooled. After they had walked for several minutes, the tunnel curved and levelled. The walls widened out to form a crude room with several other tunnels joining at odd angles. There wasn't a door anywhere nor any indication what the room was for. Which tunnel led the way out wasn't indicated either. Perhaps none of them did?

17

Riley shivered. She wished they'd hurry up and get wherever they were going so she could change into dry clothes.

Two more Operatives, a man and a woman both wearing grey jumpsuits and both holding orbs, walked out through the widest tunnel. Neither looked particularly friendly.

"Scanned and affirmed," the woman said to her companion. Both lowered their orbs. Tyrell nodded to them and walked past, entering the tunnel without a backwards glance.

The newer man came forward and scooped Alec from Dean's arms. "His readings are off the curve."

Dean smiled. "Just so."

"What does Logan say?"

"You know Orions. Never a word when silence will suffice." Dean grinned. "Come along, Riley." Too cold to argue, Riley fell in behind him.

Within steps, the tunnel stopped at a metallic double door, which was wide open. Several different-coloured lights grouped in unusual patterns on the wall blinked as she passed. Riley stepped into the room and stopped in awe.

The chamber was enormous. She craned her neck upwards, following the curved lines of the smoothly cut rock until it arched high overhead in darkness. Here and there, wide, flat panels of glowing lights hung over the floor space, illuminating the people below with a soft and pleasant yellow glow. Oddly, there were no cords or wires suspending the lights, nor were they held up from the ground. She squinted. What on earth was keeping them in place?

Someone gave her shoulder a gentle push and she automatically followed, but her feet trod without attention. She was too busy gawking.

The cave was nearly the size of a football stadium and partitioned with divider walls, most of which came up to her shoulders, no higher. By pivoting around on tiptoe she could see the entire room, but walking from one side to another might be complicated. The configurations of the dividers looked like a maze.

They passed what seemed to be a kitchen of sorts and some kind of recreation area, but Riley, trying to keep up with Dean's long strides, didn't have much time for a close look. The most interesting feature, apart from the free-floating lighting fixtures, was the movie screens. There were eighteen of them, she counted, all playing movies, but all silent. They lined three of the four walls and were nearly the size of those found in the local Cineplex. How odd.

Dean turned abruptly down a side corridor and entered what Riley immediately determined to be the medical facility. Several raised beds circled a large central console, like spokes of a wheel. Two women in white jump suits were in attendance: one at the console, peering at a screen with absorbed interest, and an older woman standing over Darius Finn. Darius, Riley noted, lay naked and pale under a grey sheet. Alec slept on the bed next to him.

The older attendant left Darius' side to inspect her second patient. She raised her orb, ran it about six inches above Alec's body in a waving motion, and frowned. Riley stood at the end of his bed and shivered.

"This child has expelled a formidable amount of Tyon energy," the woman said, with a sharp rise of her grey eyebrows. "How?"

Dean nodded towards Darius' unconscious body. "He permitted him an orb, Martje. The boy is untrained."

"Well, of course he's untrained," snapped Martje. "He's a child. And a Terran. They have only potential, not skill or knowledge. And certainly not enough power to do this sort of damage. Who did it to him?"

"Apparently, he did it himself." Dean shrugged one shoulder. It didn't have any effect on the older woman, whose aura of authority permeated the very air. Riley recognized it easily. She sat around a dinner table with it regularly.

"Nonsense." Martje pulled a face. "It isn't possible. Finn must have channelled it or boosted it somehow."

"He didn't," Riley piped up. "Darius was underwater, drowning or something."

The woman turned her eagle eyes in Riley's direction and held her immobile. "Terran?" she asked abruptly.

Riley nodded. "Yeah, what of it?"

Martje gave a sniff and turned away. She waved her orb again over Alec, pausing for a longer reading over his head.

The second attendant walked over and raised one of

Alec's eyelids with a finger. "All the readings are correct. He did expend an extraordinary amount of power." She gave Darius a pointed glance. "Two, in such a short period of time."

"Must be the electromagnetic force of this planet," Martje muttered in a low voice. "We must study this more closely."

Two what? What made Darius and Alec so interesting to these people? And why weren't they as interested in *her*? Riley shivered again and this time her teeth chattered. She was about to demand something dry to wear when Logan and Anna entered the medical area and the temperature dropped even lower.

"Report," Logan barked.

"The Terran Operative is suffering from exhaustion. He requires significant regen, but will recover. The boy is experiencing the same condition."

Martje didn't seem particularly cowed by Logan's presence, but the other one didn't meet his eyes and shuffled her feet a bit too much. Logan directed his words to the older medic.

"Ensure both receive rapid regen, Martje. Conditions are deteriorating."

Martje nodded. "He'll be ready by change over."

"Perhaps that is too quick to be safe?" Anna ventured with no change in her placid expression.

"Scars are secondary." Logan's tone brooked no argument.

Riley swallowed. What were they going to do to Darius that would scar him?

"The boy?" Logan asked.

Martje glanced with interest at Alec for a moment, and then resumed her implacable stance. "He is weaker and not trained to accept regen. I will have to proceed much more slowly."

The lines around Logan's mouth tightened, but Martje

didn't blink. Anna stared at Darius with a veiled look that Riley couldn't decipher and wasn't sure she wanted to.

The younger medical attendant spoke to Riley. "Come here and I will scan you."

It wasn't a suggestion. Riley felt the invisible tug and immediately stiffened her spine. "You can cut that 'forcing me with your orb thingy.'" The effect of her tone was undone by her chattering teeth. "Ask nicely."

The younger attendant cocked her head, as if she were inspecting an interesting new species.

"Go on, Nara," Martje said, fixing Riley with a pointed look.

Nara wasn't pleased, but did extend her arm to indicate that Riley could seat herself on a bed. With an impatient sigh, Riley hopped up and dangled her legs over the side. Nara pulled out her orb and waved it over Riley's body. There was no sensation.

"Mild hypothermia, physical fatigue, minor contusions, nothing else." Nara addressed her comments to Martje.

Riley's interest burgeoned. This could be a cool tool in medical school if it both diagnosed and treated people. Maybe she *should* learn how to use one.

"Give her a uniform and a restorative compound," Martje instructed Anna. "Have her rest. Use your orb if she resists."

Riley scowled. *Use your orb*, indeed. Heaviness was settling in all her limbs and she found it hard to keep her eyes open. She wasn't able to stifle the yawn.

"Dean can do it." Anna didn't bother even glancing in Riley's direction. Her eyes never left Darius. "They are my responsibility. I will wait until they are recovered."

Martje pursed her lips but said nothing. She nodded at Dean.

The overhead lights took on a slightly reddish hue. Riley looked up in surprise and felt her heart flip. Not again.

99

The pilot from the submarine ran into the Med Ops and came to a sharp halt at Logan's elbow. He spoke tersely in an unfamiliar tongue.

Logan had already pulled his orb from his pocket and was staring intently into its yellow depths. Riley didn't need to speak the language to understand the profanity. He whirled around, his long strides taking him out of the Med Ops and down the corridor in the blink of an eye.

"What's going on?" Riley asked.

"Sensors indicate the presence of the Others," Anna said as she turned and followed Logan.

Riley hopped down and took off behind Dean, ignoring Martje's shout. There was a sharp mental tug as someone tried to use their orb, but Riley instinctively grabbed her own and squeezed tight. She hurried after Dean, desperate not to lose him in the maze of corridors. Something important was happening and she sure as heck was going to be a part of it. The mental tugging stopped.

Dean turned right, then left, and left again. For a second she lost sight of him around a higher wall, but as she rounded the corner, she nearly ran into him.

Several Tyon Operatives clustered around a huge circular console, which rose up twice the height of Logan. Anna, Tyrell, Dean and several other serious-faced men and women peered at a variety of translucent, free-hanging screens, their fingers flying over the moving symbols. None of the

18

symbols were familiar, but the glowing red image could only indicate trouble.

Logan pointed at his screen and Tyrell nodded, his fingers rapidly enlarging an image. Several Operatives gathered over his shoulder to watch, but his frown a moment later indicated the lack of success.

Logan barked several incomprehensible commands and the majority of the small crowd immediately dispersed. Only Anna stayed at his side, peering silently at the screen Tyrell had vacated. Dean hovered behind them, uncertainty on his face. Riley slipped behind him and gripped her orb as she willed herself to remain unobserved. She wished they would speak English, as they had at the medical station. It would make it much easier to learn what was going on.

Logan spoke sharply to Anna. Other than a tell-tale blush, Anna did not reply. Her eyes remained fastened on the glowing symbols. Logan growled something else and pointed towards the medical station. Anna shook her head.

Dean tugged on Riley's arm and silently pulled her away from the argument. With one last look, Riley allowed herself to be escorted back down the corridor.

"What's going on?" she asked.

"Logan thinks there is a traitor among us."

Riley shivered at his words. "He thinks it's Darius, doesn't he?"

Dean pursed his lips as his strides lengthened. Riley almost had to run to keep up. "Finn is a Terran. Logan has always mistrusted off-worlders."

"But?" she prodded. She could almost feel Dean's worry and some other conflicting emotion through her fingers on his arm, but of course, that was impossible.

"No one would willingly assist the Others. We're sworn to stop them." Dean looked distressed. "When the Celestial Council created the Collective, it was the primary mandate. We've all taken an oath."

"Not everyone takes promises seriously." Riley was

thinking out loud. Darius Finn was hardly the soul of sombre reason.

"Anna has access to his mind at all times. It was the agreement for permitting this posting. She would know if he was influenced or working for the other side."

Riley bit her lip. Would Anna tell anyone if Darius had turned rogue? She'd seen the way the woman looked at him.

Above them the light returned to pale yellow.

"Is the threat over?" She glanced up at the hovering lights.

Dean nodded. "Initial readings suggested that the Others were somewhere inside the perimeter, but it must have been an anomaly. This compound is impervious to their invasion."

Riley rolled her eyes but said nothing. She owed no allegiance to these people. In fact, she was a prisoner. An attack, like at the Toronto bunker, would only work to her advantage. She was more likely to be able to escape in a moment of mass confusion.

Her thoughts turned to the scene she'd just witnessed. The commander of this group thought Darius was some kind of mole working for the other side, and only Anna knew if he was or wasn't. The Others breached the bunker in Toronto and, now, here, despite Dean's assurances. But had Darius orchestrated it, or had he just been in the wrong place at the wrong time? Would you know if the Others had taken you over? Could Anna be under their influence as well?

Who could she trust?

"This is the most unflattering piece of clothing I have ever seen. Where are all the cool futuristic clothes TV aliens always wear?" Riley complained as Dean handed her a grey jumpsuit. "And how come you all wear the same thing?"

"The Collective requires uniformity in purpose and practice," Dean said as he led the way into the huge co-ed bathroom next to the sleeping area. "As we are a collection of various cultures and peoples, similar language, dress and function is mandated to develop similarity of purpose." He stopped in front of several stalls that, even with their unusual design, were clearly showers. "I want you to bathe quickly and don this uniform. As soon as you are ready, we will obtain nourishment and enter Rest."

19

There wasn't much choice. She was frozen to the bone and her wet clothes were sticking to her in most unpleasant ways. Shooing him away with a shaking hand, Riley complied. It took a few head-scratching minutes to figure out the controls, but soon she was feeling much better and the shivering had stopped. She dressed quickly and left the bathroom.

She followed Dean through the confusing corridors until they arrived at the kitchen area. Dean indicated that Riley was to seat herself, and a moment later brought her a large mug of steaming liquid.

Without delay she wrapped her hands around the metallic beaker and drank deeply. She was starving. "How many Operatives work here?" she asked as the rise in her blood sugar nudged her curiosity.

"Twenty," said Dean as he got up to refill the beaker.

"And how many bunkers do you have on my planet? Like the one in Toronto."

"Twenty-two. Several have been abandoned as there were no Potentials in that vicinity. Operating a station without Potentials is a waste of resources."

Riley licked her lips and thought for a moment. "So there aren't people like me everywhere? Just in a few places?"

"Correct. There hasn't been enough time for the resistor to spread adequately throughout the population. The main concentrations are in Ireland and here in Canada. Specifically, Southern Ontario, Newfoundland and Nova Scotia. A few in Australia, Scotland, Norway and the Philippines. We've concentrated our operations there."

Riley pursed her lips at the reminder of her genetic manipulation but decided to lodge her protest on that subject at a later time. There were too many things she needed to know now. "And how many of us do you have so far?"

Dean shrugged. "Several dozen. For the time being. We've lost more in the last few days than we'd hoped."

"Why?" Riley placed the beaker on the metal table.

"Rhozan is targeting Potentials faster than we can pick them up. Somehow, he's learned to spot them faster than we can. It's frustrating."

"Yeah, I'll bet."

Dean didn't seem to hear the sarcasm. Several lines had formed between his eyes. "It is very unusual. We have encountered the Others before. Seen what they can do to decimate a civilization. But this is different. Several Operatives are working on it."

"Yeah, Anna mentioned that they had guns and that was really odd."

"Yes, choosing armed Emissaries is new. How or why Rhozan has changed his tactics, we don't understand." Dean pulled the empty beaker from her fingers and stood up. "You should rest now."

"I'd like to check on Darius and Alec," Riley said. "Just to make sure they're all right."

"I assure you that our medical personnel are more than competent—" Dean began, but Riley smiled with her most endearing expression and he stopped.

"Darius saved my life," she wheedled, batting her eyes in what she hoped was an appealing manner. "Please."

Dean pursed his lips and appeared to think the request over. "If you will be quick, I'll permit it. There is something I must see to. I'll show you where Med Ops is and collect you shortly."

Riley got up and contained her smile of satisfaction.

Med Ops was fortunately close to the kitchen. Dean skirted around two high dividers and stopped. He pointed to the opening at the end of the short hall.

"I'll be right back," he said. "Don't leave without me." Dean disappeared down a side corridor without a backwards glance. Riley paused. What could she say to Darius with those medics watching that would get him to agree to get her out of here? What if he was still unconscious? Considering the options, Riley shuffled down the hall.

She heard Logan before she saw him.

The Tyon leader was almost shouting. Riley slipped up to the opening of the Med Ops area and ducked to the side of the entry, hiding herself. She peeped around the corner and crossed her fingers they were speaking English.

Logan and Anna stood at the side of Darius' bed, which had been raised into a sitting position. Darius was leaning back in the bed, his eyes half open, his head lolling weakly to the side. Martje was holding her orb over his chest and frowning, alternatively at Darius, then at Logan. Nara hovered in the background, looking nervous.

Darius' eyes fluttered and he licked his lips. His reply sounded horribly weak, Riley thought with a start. How badly was he hurt?

Logan spat something else at Darius, and Riley watched both him and Anna wince. Darius shook his head. Anna interjected, but her argument was lost on Logan. He held out his hand. Riley heard Anna gasp. Darius didn't speak.

Martje seemed to be in disagreement, but her words meant nothing to Logan. A moment later, a dark frown creasing her forehead, she rooted through Darius' jeans pockets. She handed over his orb and Logan pocketed it without comment.

Anna placed her hand on Logan's arm. Her voice was low and carefully modulated, but whatever she was saying seemed to make no difference. Logan shouldered past her and stormed out of the medical facility so quickly, Riley barely had time to flatten herself against the wall and out of his way. She took a deep and steadying breath as she watched his back disappear around a corner. Why had he taken Darius' orb? What was going on?

Riley again leaned as carefully around the wall as she could.

Anna was still standing ramrod straight, her face carefully purged of emotion. Other than the twin blotches of fire on her cheeks, there was no indication of what had just transpired.

Martje said something in a low voice.

Anna lifted a shoulder then dropped it. As if she had heard something, Anna suddenly turned and caught sight of Riley. Riley straightened her shoulders and entered.

"I wanted to check on them," she said demurely, trying as hard as she could to stop thinking about what she'd just witnessed.

Anna nodded.

"I was worried."

Anna said nothing.

"Your boss looked pretty riled. What's his problem?"

Anna's lips tightened, but she still refused to answer.

Riley swallowed the sigh and headed for a more neutral subject. "Is Alec going to be okay?"

Anna turned her back and stared at Darius, whose eyes had closed again. The medic nodded. "He's young, healthy and surprisingly resilient. He should be up and around in two periods."

"How long's a period?" Riley frowned.

"Twelve of your hours," Martje replied. "Our schedule is similar to this planet. Twelve hours of work alternating with twelve of rest." She glanced down the short hallway and frowned. "Where is your Guardian, Dean? You should be resting."

Riley forced the smile. "He had an errand, but he'll be right back."

Martje turned her back and peered at a transparent screen. Anna turned away and left Med Ops without a word.

Riley's hands curled into fists. There wasn't anything else she could learn here now. Darius was unconscious, Alec was asleep and Anna certainly wasn't about to unburden her hard little soul with an outpouring of girly heart-to-heart.

If she wanted to get out of here, she was on her own.

Alec awoke with a start. One moment he'd been in deep darkness, the next he was sitting bolt upright, his heart pounding out of his ribs, the area behind his left ear aching badly, and a feeling of inescapable doom smothering him. Immediately someone was at his side. Alec swung his arm in defense, but it was immobilized by a strong grip before he could hit anything. He twisted around to see his captor.

"Steady on, Alec," the grey-haired woman with the tired eyes said softly. "You've nothing to be afraid of here."

"Where am I?" His mouth was dry and his tongue almost stuck to the roof of his mouth.

"You are currently lying in bed in Med Ops of Home Base." The woman released his wrist and gave a cool smile. "I am Martje, the chief Medic for the Tyon Operation here on Terra. You were injured and required medical attention, hence, your stay in my facility."

The wild pounding of his heart started to slow as memories tumbled into place. This made sense. Darius had said someone was coming to get them. Obviously someone had.

"Is Darius okay?"

"Recovering as expected." Martje stood to the side and Darius' thatch of spiky hair was visible in the bed next to his. He was curled on his side, fast asleep, and looked only a few years older than Alec.

Alec lay back down and thought for a moment. He was wearing the same grey jumpsuit that Darius was and his own clothes were not in sight. He had no idea how much time had passed and that was disconcerting. "What about Riley?" he asked. The last thing he could remember was the houseboat taking on water, Riley flailing about and the rips getting closer. He'd been so mad.

"She is well and assimilating into our unit with assistance from her assigned Guardian. You too will be assigned for training, once you are medically fit."

Alec flexed his fingers and wiggled his toes experimentally. "I feel fine."

"I will scan you to confirm. Then I will call Logan." Martje turned her back for a moment and disappeared past the head of Alec's bed.

"Who's Logan?" asked Alec as he twisted around on one elbow to watch her.

"Commander Logan is in charge. All Tyon Operatives on this planet report and take their orders from him."

"What's he like?"

Martje pulled her orb out of her pocket and gave him a slight shove to make him lie down again. She waved the orb above his body.

"Just what can you see with that thing?" Alec asked. Darius said that orbs could concentrate power, but Alec couldn't fathom what other properties they might have.

"It can determine injuries and provide treatment. If you are destined for healing, you will learn the skill."

"So, I can't learn it if I'm not destined?"

"Every person with Tyon power is different. None have identical skills or aptitudes. For example, you will not read minds or influence another's behaviour, but your female companion might. That is, if she trains hard enough." Martje pocketed the orb. "You appear well. I will have Logan debrief you before you are sent for assignment."

Alec sat back up. Debriefing sounded like a good idea

but assignment didn't. What were they expecting to do with him here, anyway? Before he had a chance to ask Martje, a tall, severe looking man entered Med Ops at a brisk march. Anna followed at his heel. Neither looked happy.

"You are Alec," said the man in a deep voice that had no warmth and even less friendliness.

"Yeah." Alec shrugged.

"You will respond with 'yes, sir,' or 'no, sir.'"

Alec didn't answer. His fingers slowly curled into fists.

"I am Commander Logan. I am in charge of this operation on Terra. From this moment forth, you will follow my orders implicitly. There will be no questions, no disobedience. Do I make myself clear?"

Alec didn't stop the frown. Logan narrowed his eyes, and the muscles around his jaw tightened perceptibly. Alec thought he heard Martje clearing her throat, but he wasn't going to toady up to some know-it-all. Principals, schoolyard bullies, Tyon Commanders – it didn't matter. *No one* ordered him to jump and told him how high.

"I don't like to repeat myself, Alec. Did you hear me?" Logan's pale eyes were now freezing.

"Sure. Whatever."

He felt rather than heard Anna's sharp intake of breath. Logan took the one step that separated them and grabbed Alec's jumpsuit at the neck so quickly the thought of retreat didn't enter his head. The material bunched under his fist as he pulled Alec right off the bed.

"Listen to me, *Terran*," Logan said coldly. "Your uncontrolled power is a danger. You cannot be permitted further freedom. Nothing that endangers the safety of my crew is permitted. You *will* follow my orders."

"You don't … scare … me," Alec gasped. His hands scrabbled to release the pressure, but Logan's grip was like steel.

Logan barely smiled, just enough for Alec to see the glimmer of pleasure. His orb seemed tiny in his massive fist.

He let go of Alec without warning. Alec fell to the ground on his hands and knees, gasping for breath. He was just about to scramble backwards as an overwhelming sense of unease and danger flooded his veins, but it was too late. The Commander was faster. The hand holding the orb clamped onto Alec's right temple while his other hand grasped his left. His head was jerked upwards until he was on his knees and staring straight at Logan's face. The Commander held him immobile.

A searing pain where the orb touched his skin drilled right through his brain. But it was the invasion of his consciousness that was truly horrifying. There was nothing he could protect from Logan's probing invasion. Everything he was, everything he thought, every memory he'd ever stored was laid bare.

It only lasted a moment, yet felt like forever. Logan released him and he fell backwards against the bed. His heart thudded wildly between his ears. He was soaked in sweat and trembling so hard he couldn't have stood even if he'd wanted to.

My God, what had Logan done to him?

Logan straightened and dropped his orb back into his pocket. Behind him, Anna stared straight ahead.

With that, he turned and left.

Alec stayed in a heap on the floor, his eyes open but not seeing, his mind in turmoil. How had Logan done that and, more importantly, how could he stop him if he wanted to do it again? Why hadn't anyone come to his defense?

It took several minutes to get his breath back and his body under control. He ducked his head and surreptitiously wiped his cheeks with the back of his hand before pulling himself unsteadily to his feet. The profanities raced along his tongue, but he managed, with great effort, not to say them aloud. The last thing he needed was Anna summoning Logan back, and he wouldn't put it past her to jump at the opportunity.

111

"I will show you to your quarters," Anna said without emotion. "You will receive nourishment and begin your training." She turned and walked out.

Alec considered refusing to follow her, but reconsidered. A sudden vision of Logan reaching out to probe him again flashed across his conscious mind. He shuddered. Not again.

Swallowing his pride and his temper, he obeyed.

ogan's attack had emptied Alec's mind of all emotion but fear. He noted the vast chamber and its busy occupants without awe. He wove his way through the various sections of the bunker without stopping to gawk. He didn't bother looking for Riley.

He did notice vaguely that everyone watched him pass. He felt their eyes burn into his skin. He rubbed the tender skin behind his left ear absently as he trudged behind Anna. Only when she arrived at the farthest corner did she stop and turn to face him. Two bunks, a table and two chairs were enclosed behind a partition.

"We will stay in this section of the Base," Anna said. "You will not pass the perimeter without permission. Bathing and toilet facilities are installed for your personal use. Food and drink will be brought here."

They hadn't given him much space to live in. Six paces in one direction, maybe, and less than that in the other. It was a cage. Anger started to seep through the fog in his head.

A silent Operative entered, bearing a tray in her arms. She gave Alec a long, rather intrusive look but said nothing as she laid the tray on the table and left.

"Eat," Anna instructed.

Logan had stolen his appetite. He crossed his arms and said nothing.

Anna pointed to the chair. "Sit, then. And listen."

Alec counted to ten. Just as she opened her mouth to speak, he took a step towards the table. As slowly as he could, he crossed the short distance, pulled out the metallic chair and seated himself.

"I recognize that your life has changed dramatically in the space of a few days. I understand your fear and concerns. However, it is vital that you begin your training immediately."

"Yeah, sure you do." Alec didn't curb his insolent tone. If she was going to hit him, let her. He might not like it, but he'd hit her back. He wasn't as muscled as a grown man, but he was still strong enough that the blow would hurt. He'd wrestled his dad to the ground last month, hadn't he?

Anna cocked her head to one side. "You fought your father?" she asked, puzzled.

Alec stared at a section of divider to the left of her shoulder. He didn't answer.

"He hurt you, didn't he?" she continued.

Alec felt the angry flush burning his cheeks. If he hadn't told the social workers at the hospital, he sure as hell wasn't going to tell these jerks. Time to change the subject. "Why am I a danger?"

"Your power is too strong and too uncontrolled. You destroyed the houseboat and could easily have killed Riley. Only Darius' intervention prevented that, and your own death."

"Logan was hinting at something else," Alec pushed.

Anna frowned. "Your lack of control has serious implications for this world. We must prevent any further damage."

114

"Look, I know you guys think these orb things are the greatest thing next to sliced bread, and you use them for all sorts of stuff. But I can't. I don't know how. So cut with the 'you-made-it-happen' crap. I didn't." Alec stood up so quickly he knocked the chair over. Ignoring it, he began to pace. "I don't remember doing anything with the orb. I mean, I was holding it. But I wasn't trying anything."

"What were you thinking?" Anna reached down, pulled the chair upright and placed it at the table.

"I dunno."

"Think, Alec. You were scared. The rips were advancing. Darius couldn't help you. Riley was in trouble."

"How do you know?" Alec paused mid-step.

"I obtained the information from Darius," Anna said, folding her hands in her lap and directing an untroubled look at Alec. "I did not intrude on your privacy."

Alec snorted. "Did you ask Darius' permission?" These aliens were so high-handed, she'd probably rummaged around in Darius' brain without a second thought.

"Darius and I have an understanding, to which you are not privy," Anna said. "I will ask permission before I enter your mind. Unless it is a matter of life and death."

"Yeah. And I can totally trust *you*."

"For the time being, Alec, there is no one else you can trust. I will be your Guardian and your only contact within this facility."

"Maybe I don't want you." Alec glared at her. Logan was the last person he wanted training him for anything, but Anna was a close second. He hadn't liked her in Toronto, and now, surrounded by her cronies, he liked her even less. Standing by while Logan hurt him was unforgiveable.

"Neither of us have a choice. I am the most experienced officer to train Terran Potentials. Hence, my assignment."

"You don't want this any more than I do, is that what you're saying?" The anger was building inside him.

"Stop shouting," Anna ordered.

"I'll shout if I want to! Try and stop me."

"I will, if force is required." Anna stood.

"You put one finger on me, and you'll be sorry." Alec backed away. She'd better not come any closer.

"Stop moving, Alec. You're about to touch the perimeter."

Alec inched farther away. Anna was holding her orb in her left hand. He hadn't noticed it before, but now he couldn't take his eyes off it. He'd hit her first, he vowed as she took a step towards him.

"Alec, stop moving. *Now.*"

He didn't.

The surge of electricity struck him squarely between the shoulder blades. For one horrible second he was held immobile, zapped by something stronger than the current in the electrical socket he'd stuck his finger into when he was a child. It suddenly stopped and he fell to the ground.

Anna crossed over and crouched down. He saw two of her for a moment as she stroked her cool fingers across his brow. "I did warn you."

She sounded amused and that only fueled the white-hot fury. Alec knocked her hand away. He scrambled to his feet. He grabbed at the table, picked it up and threw it as hard as he could towards the space between the dividers that opened to the rest of the Base. Anna ducked in time. The table sailed out and landed with a dull clang. The chair followed.

"You'll need an orb to move the beds," Anna advised.

Alec was past listening. Furiously, he yanked and pulled with all his might, but Anna was correct; the beds didn't budge. He slammed his open fist against the brackets that held them together. Once, twice, three times. His palm began to bleed. "I want out," he yelled.

Two Operatives arrived at the opening but did not enter. Anna shook her head. "I am not in danger."

"Leave me alone," screamed Alec.

"Lower the dampening fields and withdraw," Anna instructed. Both left silently. "Alec, if you cannot control your anger, then I shall have to do it for you. You put us all in danger when you do this."

Alec swore violently and began to kick the toilet cubicle in the corner.

"This is your last warning. I must subdue you if you do not stop."

Alec was past stopping. He was enraged with a kind of anger he couldn't control. There was a red haze floating across his mind, blocking out all reasonable thought. He'd only felt this once before.

"Enough." The word penetrated his mind like a hot knife cutting through butter. Its force scattered his fury. For several moments there was nothing but the word, echoing over and over in his mind. His heart slowed down. The wild power in his muscles slipped away. Anna's voice seemed far away. She was saying something, but he couldn't quite hear her. Not that it mattered. Nothing did.

"Look, get your hands off me," Riley snapped. Jacob had been hovering at her elbow for the last hour and she'd had enough. Actually, she'd had enough two hours ago, but Dean had insisted that she work with the weasely little Potential from Chicago.

Jacob sat back in the metal chair and dropped his hands to the tabletop. He was nearly a year younger, three times as wide, and probably half as intelligent. His eyes had lit up with the fire of a zealot the instant he'd seen her and nothing she'd done so far had discouraged him.

"Dean told you to practice with me." Jacob's nasal whine was only slightly more annoying than his constant sniffing. "They'll put you in confinement if you don't."

"They have already. It's no big deal." Riley got up from the table and stretched. There were several other Potentials, mostly from Canada and a few from Ireland and Europe, all in pairs and all working on orb exercises. The four Guardians supervising the lesson stood side-by-side, staring impassively at the group and waiting to deal with an outburst of frayed nerves. Dean, as always, watched her. He raised his eyebrows in question.

"I need to stretch my legs," Riley replied to his unspoken query. "Twenty minutes, okay?"

Dean gave a curt nod and came over to take her seat. Jacob wiped his nose on his sleeve and scowled. "How come she gets a break?" he muttered.

"Riley understands the consequences for disobedience and has agreed to refrain from further disruptive behaviour," Dean said as he pulled his own orb from his pocket and held it up in front of his face. "Focus on your assigned task, Jacob."

Riley headed out of the study area and past Food Dispersal at a brisk pace, eager to have a reprieve from the constant lessons and prying eyes. It was so rare to have a moment to herself.

She marched around the outermost part of the station, letting the rhythm of her steps cool her irritation. In the week she'd been held prisoner, most of her energy had gone into reacting negatively. It had taken her several days to control her temper enough to avoid punishment. Pretending to acclimatize to her situation increased her chance of successful escape, she reasoned. It was really just like high school. The more you acted like you hated it, the worse everyone treated you.

The Tyon Base functioned like a highly protected military unit, with each individual having a specific function. This could be a weakness, she mused. The Tyons were mostly from two planets and, despite looking similar, each group had traits that the other disliked. This too could be an advantage, if she could only come up with a way to exploit it. The technology they had was more advanced than anything she'd ever even dreamed of and she still had little understanding of how to use it, despite asking a lot of questions. Using her orb for anything other than picking up a vague notion of someone else's emotions was a bust. That was definitely a problem. Unless she magically learned how to use it in the next couple of days, she was going to have to either convince some Tyon to help her or get Darius to do it.

Darius was a bigger problem. She hadn't spoken a word to him since she arrived, and from what she gleaned from overheard conversations and the dark looks Dean gave her when she brought the topic up, Darius was persona non grata within the entire Tyon fold. He was being watched more closely than she was. How would she get close enough to convince him to abandon his Tyon training, throw in his lot with her *and* get them both out, despite constant surveillance?

Alec was the biggest problem. He was still being held in seclusion and as far as she knew, no one but Anna was allowed to have any contact with him. The rumours about him were rampant: Alec had killed two guards; Anna was using such strong control Alec couldn't even feed himself any longer; Alec had enough power to destroy the world. Riley had heard them all.

Whatever she was going to do, it had to be soon. The Tyons' daily reports of increasing violence coupled with the real-time transmissions of events unfolding the world over, playing constantly on the surrounding screens, were deeply disturbing.

As if her subconscious had led her there, Riley realized she was right in front of Alec's private section. The lights were low in his partitioned area but she could still make out his dark hair on the pillow of the upper bunk. He was facing the wall and had pulled the blanket up to his ears.

Anna sat at the table reading a glowing handheld screen and holding in her fist something attached to the ever-present chain around her neck. She glanced up.

"Is he all right?" Riley asked.

Anna let go of a long, glowing rectangular crystal and dropped it and its chain underneath her collar. She didn't reply.

"When's he allowed out with the rest of us?" Riley forged ahead. "I mean, you can't keep him locked up forever."

"Can't I?" Anna's expression didn't change.

"He'll go crazy. That's what solitary does to you. I studied that in psych." Riley bit her tongue. Swearing at

Anna would get her back in confinement and that was the last thing she needed.

"Then I hope that Alec will learn to obey us soon. Time is running out."

"If you keep trying to force the guy, he'll only fight you harder. Don't you know anything about human behaviour?"

"He is challenging."

"More challenging than Darius was?" Riley smiled coolly. "Dean told me you trained him, too."

"Darius was much younger when he began his training, and despite his penchant for humour and an irreverent attitude towards work, he did comply eventually."

"Alec's a different kettle of fish," Riley advised. "You need a carrot, not a whip, with him."

"I already provide nourishment."

Riley snorted. "I wasn't being literal."

Anna sat back in her chair. Then she nodded. "Kindness."

"Just a thought." Riley shoved her hands into the jumpsuit pocket and fingered her orb. "Depends on how badly you want success."

Anna picked up the screen and began reading. Obviously the conversation was over.

Only supreme effort prevented Riley from giving Anna the finger. Muttering under her breath, she marched back down the hall eager to put as much distance between herself and the insufferable Tyon as possible. Hopefully she had prodded Anna in a different direction. The faster the restrictions around Alec lifted, the faster she could escape with him. She rounded a corner so quickly she nearly walked right into Dean.

"Feel better?" he asked, falling in beside her as she charged through the rec area.

"No," Riley grumbled. "I want to go home."

"I've told you, this is your home. I realize that you miss the life you had before and your family of origin, but it is best if you forget them."

Riley stopped and gripped her hips. "You want me to forget my entire life before I met you guys? That I have parents? A sister? Well, I suppose I can forget Deborah, she's a bit of a tool, but not my dad. Or mom. Did you?"

"Tholans are raised communally. We have little ties to blood relatives. I suppose that makes things easier if we are selected for Tyon training," Dean conceded.

"Yeah. Just a tad." Riley couldn't help fuming. These Tyons were so high-handed. "I love my parents. I'm worried sick about what might happen to them. My dad's probably having an aneurysm right now, with me missing."

Dean started walking again and Riley found herself keeping pace with him. He looked thoughtful.

"What?" she asked.

"You know that we're going to have to leave this planet, don't you, Riley? That the issues we've spoken of are greater than the concerns of just one person?"

Riley crossed her arms and stared straight ahead. "With the Others?" she answered reluctantly.

"Yes. You're aware we're constantly monitoring the situation. Should the threat be considered insurmountable, we'll evacuate earlier."

"What's insurmountable?"

"Global war. Nuclear weapons."

"Cripes," Riley breathed.

"They manipulate the population through the rips. Like puppeteers. They seem to feed off the negative energy created by manipulation. They've started wars on the three planets we know they invaded and likely many more we're not certain of yet. We know so very little about them."

"But that doesn't make sense. What life forms have their food source destroy themselves?"

"Bacteria?" Dean said. "Or us? Humans are notorious for killing their own planets and destroying their sources of food and water. It's even happening on this planet."

"Did you guys destroy your planet?" she asked.

"Tholos is not destroyed. Nor is the Orion homeworld."

"So, if Logan and Anna's world is fine, why do they give a toss about mine?"

"Terra is important. Its inhabitants are important." Dean replied.

"But you guys didn't want Darius, did you?" Riley jibed.

Dean didn't bother to deny it. "Finn was picked up during our initial scouting stage. He was a spontaneous mutation. And remarkably strong. Our leader felt he could be useful as an Operative with local knowledge, if the time ever came to infiltrate. Turns out it was a wise decision. The Others arrived just as Finn was completing his training."

So Darius hadn't had a choice either. The Tyon Collective had made another one of their high-handed decisions and used him.

"You must return to your lessons," Dean said. The companionable tone of voice was gone. "There is much to learn and time is running out."

Riley quietly followed as he led the way back to the study area. Her brain was buzzing. If the Others got the upper hand, she and the rest of the Potentials would be waving goodbye out the stern-side window of a spaceship. Dean was right. Time *was* running out. She had to escape, and soon.

Alec paced. Six long strides one way, six back. Anna sat at the table, as usual. She'd said nothing to him as she handed him his breakfast, nor did she speak as she cleaned up the mess when he threw the bowl across the room. Other than a distinct tightening of her jaw, there was no expression.

Alec told himself he didn't care. He focused on staying angry. It wasn't too difficult. He was miserable here, separated from the only people he knew and forced to try and study something he didn't want to, day after day after day. The confinement was driving him crazy. He hadn't been able to go for a run in *ages*. On top of that, his mom would be frantic and his dad would be ballistic by now. He'd missed all his exams and that would mean repeating a grade. His summer on the provincial team was over before it had even started, and that was the only thing he'd been looking forward to in ages. Someone was going to pay for this.

23

He was concentrating so intently on his internal fury that he didn't hear Logan's footsteps. He nearly paced right into him. He scrambled away as fast as he could.

"Alec, remember June thirteenth." The Commander gave no greeting.

"Huh?" Alec's heart lodged in his throat. "Why?"

"Obey me," Logan demanded. He stepped closer.

The edge of the table hit the back of Alec's thighs. He glanced for help at Anna, but she was staring rigidly straight ahead. "I don't remember," he croaked.

"You do." Logan stopped an arm's length away. He pulled out his own orb and held it out, palm upward. The light within was slightly yellow and pulsing. "Don't move," he instructed.

Anna took a breath, as if she were about to disagree, but didn't actually speak. Alec tensed. He wasn't going to just stand here and let that …

Logan reached out with his free hand. Alec faked left, then turned right, ducking under the Commander's hand. He wasn't fast enough. Logan lashed out and grabbed Alec's wrist, twisting it cruelly up behind his back. Alec couldn't stop the cry that tore from his lips as his shoulder was nearly dislocated. He dropped to his knees.

"Disobey me and you are punished, Alec. Learn this well."

Tears welled up in his eyes. It was only the barest of touches, but Logan's fingers burned. Alec started to jerk his head away. Anna slipped behind him quickly and her hands gripped his shoulders. She was tremendously strong. He couldn't move.

The power probed and scorched as it moved through Alec's temple and into his mind. If he was screaming, he couldn't hear it. As quickly as the invasion started, it was over. Logan removed his hand. Alec would have collapsed if Anna hadn't been holding him.

"Instinctive. Spontaneous," Logan said to Anna. He seemed interested as well as angry, but Alec was still reeling and heard the words without comprehension.

"Is it certain?" Anna asked.

"Appears that way. Triggered by extreme anger. It's all there. Beyond extraordinary." Logan stepped towards the doorway. "He did it without an orb, Anna. There may be power we cannot detect. He's too dangerous to keep."

"Inside he's shielded. He will not cause any further damage."

"We cannot be sure of this. It is prudent to negate danger once identified. You grow sentimental for this race."

"I only wish to explore his potential. Should he be able to harness this, the possibilities are endless," Anna replied in an even tone.

"Your argument was similar about Finn."

"And Darius has completed all levels of his training. His evaluations were exemplary. Despite your personal feelings, Logan, he surpassed any expectations we had of a Terran. Alec may do the same."

Logan said nothing. He turned and left, his footfalls almost silent. Anna let go of Alec's shoulders and took her place at the table. When the nausea had passed and he was finally able to look up, he saw she held her head in her hands.

"Are you ready to begin your lesson?" she asked quietly.

Alec gave her the finger. A woozy, shaky retort, but all he was capable of.

"We will continue with the concentration exercises and emotional control. It is vital."

Alec climbed to his feet and staggered across to his bed. He collapsed onto the lower bunk and stared with unseeing eyes at the underside of his bunk.

"I do not wish to use physical force, Alec."

He didn't respond, other than to clench his fists. Sure she didn't. Who held him down – Santa Claus?

"Your anger controls you, Alec. It dictates your actions. You realize this as well as I. Once you let go of it and immerse yourself in the training, you will be much more at peace. When you attain a certain level of control, I will lift the restrictions you live under. You will be able to socialize with your peers."

Alec refused to look at her. He wasn't *that* naïve.

"I wish you didn't make this so difficult," she said, so

quietly he almost couldn't hear her. "Why are Terran males so implacable? My experience is limited to two, but both of you are a study in frustration. There must be something in the water here that limits your ability to surrender to imposed instruction."

Alec still didn't say anything.

"It took less time to convince him, but he still dug his heels in at every new concept," Anna murmured. "It was a wonder he ever finished the training. But now, he's one of the best we have. You could be like that." She paused for a moment. "Do you understand what Logan was saying?"

Alec turned his head to the wall.

"Alec, you're anything but stupid, but what you fail to understand is that time is running out. The violence is worsening hourly. We've done our calculations. The genetic resistance is far too low to protect your planet. Unless we intervene, your society will destroy itself. Once North America dissolves into chaos, the rest of the world will follow.

"Logan is convinced that your uncontrolled power constitutes too great a risk. If you don't comply and learn to harness your emotions, he will have no choice."

The silence stretched on for several uncomfortable minutes. Then Anna surprised him. She got up out of her chair and skirted the edge of the table. She looked over her shoulder as she sat gingerly on the edge of the bed. She leaned over and whispered. "Alec, he'll have your mind erased. For the sake of your own life, please, stop fighting me."

Alec sat bolt upright. Without question, he knew she wasn't lying. He took a deep breath to calm the wild beating of his heart and stared at the opening of this tiny cell. Could you live with a blank mind?

"No," Anna said, leaning over and speaking closely to his ear.

A cold sweat drenched his body.

"Start your training in earnest. He'll leave you alone if you seem to be no danger."

Alec didn't want to give in, but being brain-dead wasn't much of an option. Could he trust Anna? Could he trust *any* of them? Was he a coward or being sensible? "What's he looking for, in my head?" Alec croaked.

Anna looked away. "Alec, I—"

"I have to know. It's my mind he's messing around with."

Anna stood up abruptly. She walked over to the opening in the dividers and stared out at the Bunker. The lights were low in the main section. It was rest period and most of the occupants were sleeping. Finally, she turned around. "Logan is convinced that the Tyon power you unleashed last June caused the initial rip in the fabric of time and space. It was that rip which allowed the Others to gain access to your world. He fears your power may open the rips even further."

If Alec hadn't already been sitting, he might have fallen over. How in the world had he done something so, *so unbelievable?*

"I d-didn't," he stuttered.

"You did. The confrontation with your father was the catalyst. Can you remember it?"

Alec turned his face away. Sure, he could remember. It was damn hard to forget. But force an opening between this dimension and another? No way. Wouldn't he have noticed?

"You were angry, Alec. Remember?"

Alec's fingers clawed into the blanket around him. "I had good reason."

"Tell me."

Alec's jaw clamped shut. It was still so raw, so painful, that even thoughts of that evening, when everything had fallen apart, caused him to break out in a sweat.

"Alec, I need to know what triggered that sort of hatred. If I don't, I can't protect you or teach you how to avoid it again. Logan will consider you unreachable. He won't hesitate to remove any threat."

Alec flung himself off the bed and started to pace.

"What did your father do to provoke such anger? What did he say to you?"

"He didn't *say* anything," Alec ground out.

"But you engaged in a physical altercation. I saw it in your thoughts. You tried to kill him."

The words triggered the memory, as bitter and heart-breaking as it had been the night it happened.

"Stop making excuses for him," Alec's father yelled. Red-faced, he swung around to face them. Alec's mother stood framed in the doorway of the kitchen, still clutching the principal's letter, and Alec cowered in the dim light from the bathroom halfway down the hall.

If only his dad hadn't lost another job the same week Alec got suspended for fighting. He should have let those guys make their empty threats and walked away. Let his bookworm brother fight his own battles.

His father took an unsteady step forward and the reek of the afternoon's binge assailed his nostrils. Alec couldn't help the grimace.

"Wipe that grin of your face, you worthless little shit," his father growled.

"That's enough." His mom stepped in between them. "I've dealt with the school and with Alec. I'll handle it. I handle everything else nowadays."

He knew it was the wrong thing to say the instant he heard it. Alec almost didn't see the blow. One minute his father's lip was curled in disgust; the second, his arm was swinging through the air. His mother's face jerked towards him, so brutally that the flecks of blood from her mouth and nose flung outwards and splattered the far wall. Her eyes were wide with shock and fear.

Time stopped.

Nothing Alec had ever seen or heard or felt compared to this. The anger exploded inside him. He literally saw red. He stopped thinking.

His own arm swung wildly and connected with his father's stubbled chin. His father grunted and toppled to the right. He slumped momentarily against the wall. Lost in the conflagration of wild rage that consumed him, he barely noticed his father's returned blow.

He fell slowly, almost in slow motion, and landed on the thin carpet in front of his open bedroom door. He was only dimly aware: the desk light shining weakly inside his room; the bitter taste of copper filling his mouth; denim-clad legs walking towards him. Then, the legs halted and the bedroom door closed.

He heard shouting in the distance. A slow, insidious darkness crept in around the edges of his vision. Straight ahead, in the corner of the hall, a tiny speck of sparkling lights danced and shimmered. He tried blinking but it didn't help. They were still there.

I'm going blind: the thought drifted across his mind, just before the darkness claimed him.

"Damn him to hell," Alec spoke out loud. He glanced up in time to see the noticeable distaste on Anna's face. "Did you get that?"

Anna turned away. For a moment, her long hair obscured her face. Then, she turned back. Her emotions were once again masked. Without a word, she crossed over to the storage cupboard and pulled out another bowl of food. She carried it over and placed it on the table.

"Protection of those weaker is always commendable," she said.

Alec stopped his pacing. For a moment, their eyes locked. "And cowardice?"

"Peter has to live with his actions, the same as you do. He had his reasons for not standing up for either you or your mother."

She pulled out the chair and signalled he was to sit. Alec didn't move. Now that they'd been unleashed, the memories were playing in a continuous loop. He bit his lip. There was something there, hovering on the edge of his consciousness, something he should pay attention to. What was it?

"What did you see before you lost consciousness, Alec?" Anna prompted.

His eyes locked with hers as he remembered.

Logan was right. In the hall of their apartment.

Sparkles.

Riley lay on her bunk in the dim twilight of rest period, working her way through a multitude of options for escape. It was the only time she could be reasonably sure no one was listening to her thoughts. She stifled a yawn. So far, every idea was overflowing with flaws. There was only one door and it was guarded around the clock. She couldn't teleport past the perimeter, even if she knew how. Dean rarely left her alone and her orb was linked to his somehow, meaning he'd know if she used it to force her way outside. And besides, they were hundreds of metres below the surface and she had no idea how to get on top of the island or how to get off it once she did.

A slight rustling caught her attention. Someone was creeping along the divider wall that separated the sleeping quarters from the main chamber. Riley sat up and squinted. There was something familiar about that silhouette.

The shadow slid up to her bunk and a hand whipped out of the darkness to clamp across her mouth. "Shh," Darius hissed. "Stay quiet."

Riley peeled his hand away. "Just what the–"

Darius gave her shoulder a shove and dropped down onto her bunk beside her. He lay back, tugging her arm so that she would lie beside him. "Don't attract attention," he whispered.

"Get out of my bed," Riley ordered as she shoved him.

"Just a sec. We have to talk."

"We can talk at meal times," Riley began, her voice starting to rise with annoyance.

"And everyone will see us," Darius said quietly. "Haven't you noticed they're keeping us apart?"

Riley's jaw clenched. She'd been planning to casually sit next to him at a meal or "accidentally" wander into his work station, but this was way too obvious. If Dean woke up ...

"Do you have your orb?" Darius asked.

"Sure. Always," Riley nodded. No one had told her to do it, she'd just felt odd, leaving it on the pillow or in her locker. Like taking off her arm and leaving it somewhere else.

"Good. Never let it out of your sight. You're the only one of the three of us who has one now."

"Doesn't Alec?"

"No. They're preventing him access. I have a good idea why, though."

"So?" Riley shoved his arm with her elbow. "Spill."

"No one has told me directly. Anna's not talking." He sounded bitter about it. "But I've looked in Logan's files and overheard a few things."

"Does Logan know you're rooting through his stuff and eavesdropping?" Riley interrupted.

"Don't be an idiot."

"Oh for heaven's sake, Dare," Riley said. "He'll have your nuts in a sling if he catches you."

"He's gotta catch me first."

She could almost hear the grin in his voice. He rolled over onto his side. His breath was warm on her cheek. "Look, Riley, here's the point. Logan's convinced that Rhozan has somehow tapped into the kid's mind and is using his knowledge of this world against us."

Riley sat up with surprise. "What the–"

"I know, it's crazy." Darius grabbed her shoulder and pulled her back down until her head lay on the pillow beside his. He was silent for a moment. When he did speak his voice was low and urgent. "Logan's only given another two work periods for Anna to break through and get Alec under control. Or else."

"You've got to be kidding."

"I'm not."

"Then you're mistaken. Logan's the Mr. Spock of this little party. He's hardly going around yelling 'off with their heads.' I've watched this guy for a week. He hardly has any emotions."

"I don't know who this Spock fellow is, but I know Logan. He's seriously worried. And when Logan gets worried, he gets rid of whatever worries him. I've worked for the guy for years, remember?"

Her heart did a nasty twist inside her chest. Logan had seemed pretty pissed the day she arrived, even if he hadn't shown a flicker of it since. "What are we going to do?"

"That's my girl. I've got a plan."

Of course he did. Darius' eternal optimism that he could work things out was one of the most attractive things about him. Next to his lips, his smile, and of course, his killer eyes. She hastily amended her thoughts, in case he tapped into them. Which wasn't easy because he smelled really nice and his lips were so close he could just ... She forced *those* thoughts out of her mind completely. "How are we going to stop Logan from–" she couldn't make herself say "kill"; it sounded so melodramatic "–doing Alec in? Can we get him out of here?"

"Anna's watching him around the clock. She's pretty tough to outwit."

"But you have, right?"

She heard his smile. "I have the access codes to get in and out of the Base. And I know the way to the surface. But without an orb I can't use the codes, get past the guards and transport us off this island."

"What about a ship? How close are we to the mainland?" Riley's mind was racing. They'd need transportation,

ID and probably money. Did she still have her wallet somewhere? What had Dean done with her clothes?

Darius shook his head. "You can barely see the main island from here, and only in good weather. A few fishing vessels pass by, but you can't count on one being there when you need it. And besides, the bloody rock above us is completely surrounded by cliffs. We couldn't get down to the water's edge, even if we saw a boat." He rolled on his back and clasped his hands behind his head. "Getting off this island is going to be a huge problem."

"Can't Alec transport us? He did before."

"Pure instinct is one thing, trying to do it under pressure is another. Even with me guiding him, just the off-chance thought, and we could end up in Outer Mongolia. Look what happened last time."

"That's better than Alec dying here," Riley summarized succinctly.

Darius gave a deep sigh. "Yeah, you're right."

Without warning he partially sat up and leaned over. The kiss was warm and quick and threw her heart into overdrive. "I hate to leave a lady curious," Darius chuckled as he slipped off the bed. Within a second, he'd rejoined the shadows and disappeared to his own bunk at the other end of the row.

Wow. The man really knew how to kiss. It took ages to fall asleep.

Riley sat across the table from Dean. She lifted another spoonful of the highly nutritional meal replacement she'd named Goop to her mouth with a distinct lack of enthusiasm. Dean was typically tucking into his meal as if he hadn't eaten anything for days. The stuff didn't actually taste bad, but the appearance and the consistency made her stomach turn. Not to mention they ate it five times a day.

"We have another hour after we eat," Dean informed her between mouthfuls, "so we can continue with your exercises, if you feel up to it."

They'd worked hard that morning and Riley had a slight headache. Hours of lying awake after Darius' news hadn't helped either. She was shaking her head when Darius and Tyrell approached their table. Darius swung his leg over the back of the chair opposite Riley and sat down with a wide grin. He was quite flushed, as if he'd run a marathon, and his eyes were sparkling. Tyrell sat down more demurely on the other side of Dean. He nodded at Riley and began to eat without saying a word. As usual.

"I just bested Ty," he said to Dean. "Two out of three. Anytime you want to try?" Darius smiled at Dean.

Dean raised an eyebrow and glanced at Tyrell. "He's not as physically strong but he's fast and fights dirty." Riley listened with surprise. Tyrell never spoke in her language. She hadn't been sure he could. "He's up for the challenge."

Dean dropped his spoon onto his empty plate

with a clatter. He leaned back in his chair. "If you think you can take me on, Terran, then mark the segment and we'll meet."

Riley looked from one man to the other. Darius' colouring was more emphasized: his cheeks pink with health, the glow of his skin more pronounced. Both Dean and Tyrell had longer, leaner limbs and fingers and their features were more delicate. Side-by-side like this, it was obvious who was the alien. Pass them on the street and you wouldn't notice a thing.

Darius grinned. "I'm in."

"I thought everyone was panicking over the destruction of my civilization?" Riley remarked. "Not running off and engaging in testosterone-fueled exhibitions of virility."

Tyrell didn't crack a smile. "We were sparring. Physical exercise is mandatory to maintain conditioning. Guardians must be prepared to engage in combat at all times."

"Anytime you want to learn a few moves, just ask." Darius winked at her.

Riley felt Dean's intake of breath and waited for the rebuke but it didn't materialize. She watched as Darius' facial expression changed abruptly, and a façade of disinterest slipped over his features. He dropped his eyes and focused on his food. Riley didn't need to turn around. She knew exactly who had walked into the eating area and was now standing directly behind her.

Tyrell scooped the last of his meal into his mouth and stood, picking up his plate and spoon. He gave a brief nod and then left.

"I thought you had alternated your schedule with ours?" Dean said.

"I did." Anna walked around the table and stood behind the chair that Tyrell had vacated. She didn't sit. She didn't look at Darius and he was studiously not looking at her. "Why have you lifted the restrictions?"

Dean gave Riley a quick look. "She is progressing well.

Interaction with the Collective is not a risk now."

"What–" Riley began, but stopped when someone kicked her ankle. She caught Darius' eye only for a second before he focused on his meal.

"Why are you sitting with this Terran? Logan ordered no contact," Anna asked Darius.

Darius lifted a spoonful of goop to his mouth. He shrugged. "It was lifted this morning."

Riley changed the subject before Anna could put the restrictions back in place. "How much longer is Alec in seclusion? I'd like to talk to him."

"He has nothing to say to you," Anna said dismissively.

"Yeah, well, I'll be the judge of the that," Riley snapped.

"Alec is working and cannot be disturbed," Anna said. "Dean, I require your assistance."

"I can help you," Darius volunteered, his voice a study of ultra-casualness.

"I prefer Dean. Riley, return to the study area immediately," Anna said as she turned away.

Riley watched Darius gaze at Anna as she left. It was highly surprising that he'd never learned to always conceal his emotions, despite spending years with these people.

"I shouldn't be too long," Dean said to her as he got to his feet. He dropped his empty plate on the counter and followed Anna out.

Darius took another couple of mouthfuls before he spoke. "Guess my little nighttime visit was unnecessary. They've left us together."

"Don't waste the opportunity." Riley leaned forward. "What's the plan?"

138

"Don't be so obvious," Darius advised.

"Well, isn't that the pot calling the kettle black," she retorted.

Darius frowned. He cleared his throat and spoke a little louder. "If you're finished eating, we'll go to the Study section. Practice your concentration." He dropped his voice to a whisper. "Always conduct your secrets out in the open."

Darius led the way to the tables already occupied by several Guardians and their students. There were two new Potentials, Riley noticed, and both looked pale and frightened.

She and Darius sat side-by-side at a table in the middle of the section. Riley pulled out her orb and held it in the palm of her hand. Already the repeated exercise felt completely normal, the orb almost a part of her.

"Focus on deep relaxation," Darius said loudly. Then he whispered, "Both the guards Anna uses when she leaves Alec are pretty junior. I shouldn't have any trouble with either of them. We'll have to take Alec during our Rest period. There are too many up and around during Work."

Riley nodded.

"The main problems are Logan and Anna. Dean will be resting and unless the alarm goes off, he sleeps like the dead."

Riley shuddered at the analogy.

"If we can distract Logan long enough, it will give me time to get through the defences. There are so many Operatives coming and going right now, it'll camouflage us."

"How on earth will we distract Logan?" Riley muttered.

"Haven't got that far yet." Darius was chewing his lip. "But I'll think of something."

"And what about Anna? She's going to be onto you in a minute."

She felt rather than heard Darius' sigh. She definitely heard the expletive. "Leave her to me."

"Look, you haven't thought this through. There are a million holes in your plan. I think we should wait a bit. Logan's not going to off Alec in the next couple of hours. He has to give the guy some time."

Darius reached over, ostensibly to readjust her grip on her orb. She felt his breath on her ear. "He's not going to wait."

"She doesn't need your assistance." Dean stood directly behind them. His arm snaked through the space between Darius' face and Riley's ear. Darius was forced backward.

Darius got to his feet and stretched languidly. "Sure, no problem. She's making good progress." Without a backwards glance, he sauntered out of the area. Several of the female Potentials watched.

Dean sat down. His smile was somewhat forced. "I'd prefer if you had nothing to do with Finn, even with the restrictions lifted."

Riley feigned surprise. "Why? He's a Terran, like me. What's he done?"

Dean pulled out his own orb, preparing to start the lesson. "Let's just say, he's an unpredictable entity."

"You're afraid I won't see through the animal magnetism." Riley smiled. "You think I'll fall for him."

"You wouldn't be the first," Dean remarked dryly. "Now, show me what you've remembered from the previous lessons."

Concentrating on her lessons was nearly impossible for the rest of the Work period. She knew Dean was disappointed in her lack of focus, but there were too many things colliding inside her brain. What if their only chance blew up in their faces because they'd missed something? Both she and Darius would end up in solitary, just like Alec, and Logan would be free to do what he liked with all of them. The man already hated Darius. She couldn't imagine his reaction if he caught them trying to sneak Alec out.

No. They had to rethink the plan and fill in all the details before they could take the chance.

Riley headed for the recreation area. Dean had suggested that a good workout might improve her fidgets and she'd quickly taken him up on the offer. She turned a corner and immediately wheeled around in the opposite direction. She wasn't fast enough.

"Hey there," Jacob called, running to catch up with her.

"Hey, yourself." Riley inwardly groaned. Why did every loser attach themselves to her like a leech?

Jacob wiped his nose on the sleeve of his jumpsuit. He smiled hopefully. "Wanna watch the wall?"

"No thanks." Riley kept walking. "Gotta study."

"Aw c'mon. It'll be great. I know how to find porn."

What kind of idiot thought that a girl would want to watch pornography with him on a jumbo screen in full view of an entire complement of Tyon officers? He was so stunned, it hurt.

"Tempting? No." Riley turned to walk away, but Jacob grabbed hold of her sleeve. She was about to tell him what he could do with his mucus-covered fingers in no uncertain terms when he interrupted her train of thought.

"Logan thinks Alec caused the first rip."

Riley startled. "What did you say?"

"Alec's the strongest Potential. Ever. I heard Logan talking with Anna. He thinks Alec started this whole thing off."

"Back up and start again," Riley ordered. "And if you're pulling my chain …"

Jacob sniffed a couple of times. He looked around covertly. "Honest. I overheard them." He held up his orb. "I was sitting on the floor, next to Alec's quarters. They didn't see me."

Riley could easily picture the snotty little weasel hiding under a table, listening for any crumb of information. "Go on."

"Anna said she thought the kid needed a break or he'd crack up."

"What'd Logan say?"

141

"He was pissed. Thought she was too soft. She was angry but didn't answer him back. I don't blame her. He scares the bejesus out of me."

Cornflakes would scare you, Riley thought unkindly. She waved her hand to indicate he should continue.

"She said she was going to give the kid a break. Logan reminded her that Alec's temper probably caused the first crack in the time/space continuum. He told her the kid was dangerous and if she couldn't teach him control, he'd have to terminate him next Work period. Isn't he your boyfriend?"

Darius hadn't been exaggerating. Logan *was* planning to kill Alec if he didn't cooperate. Riley chewed her lower lip for a moment. They had to have more time.

"Thanks," she mumbled. She turned and walked away, only vaguely aware that Jacob was following. She glanced around the bunker. Eighteen screens flickered with violence. Murder, fighting, rape, riots. It was all there. Everywhere you looked. *And all because of Alec.* The knowledge would destroy anyone, and Alec was just a kid.

She whirled around. Jacob jumped backwards. "You can't say a word of this, not to anyone." Riley leaned over him, piercing him with the force of her stare. "Promise."

Jacob sniffed. He looked around him for back-up but no one was nearby. "But–"

"I mean it. I'll twist your balls right off and feed them to you."

Jacob backed up until his back literally hit a divider wall. He blanched.

"Swear it," Riley demanded, leaning over him like an avenging angel.

"I s-swear," Jacob stuttered.

"Remember, I can read minds," Riley boasted. "I'll know if you blab. And I'll know where this info came from if anyone else knows."

Jacob scuttled sideways, inching his way out from under her. He gave her another terrified look, and then bolted.

Riley leaned against the wall and waited for her pounding heart to slow down. Darius was right. There was no more time.

142

Riley set off at once in search of Darius. She'd made an entire tour of the busy Base, including a rather embarrassing moment with Tyrell in the communal bathroom, before she finally found him.

Both Dean and Darius were stripped to the waist and facing each other across the outline of a five-sided figure on the raised, cushioned flooring of the rec area. At some unseen signal both men dropped to a crouch. Dean lunged, Darius feinted and contact was made. A bone-crunching smack reverberated as they hit each other. The display was a vicious combination of martial arts and street fighting.

26

Darius struck out with what looked to be a highly illegal move, knocking Dean to the mat with a dull *smack*. There was a collective intake of breath as Darius leapt on him faster than she could blink, wrestling Dean onto his stomach and twisting his arm up, behind his back.

Dean yelled and Darius immediately let go. He jumped to his feet and rubbed his chin ruefully. Dean got to his feet as the crowd quietly dispersed. Darius stuck out his hand, and after a brief pause, Dean awkwardly shook it. They both seemed to notice Riley at the same time.

"Well?" Darius was panting.

"Dean was amazing," she deadpanned.

"Their reflexes are faster than mine, and their muscles, stronger. But I've learned a few tricks,"

Darius said with a sideways look at Dean. Dean's frown was revealing.

"Riley, return to your studies," Dean ordered. He reached down, grabbed a cloth that was lying on the corner of the mat and used it to wipe his face. "I'll join you immediately." He didn't give Darius a glance before heading to the communal washroom.

Darius was still panting, and from the way he was favouring his right leg, probably more injured than he might want to advertize. He wiped the sweat from his brow and looked around. Two female Operatives and one male were lounging at the far end of the mat, sending occasional sideways glances his way.

"Look, Darius, I've got some news," Riley said.

"Sure, I can teach those moves," Darius said, somewhat louder than necessary.

"For Pete's sake, will you pay attention?"

"Any time you like," Darius replied cheerily. Without warning, he pulled her close and twisted her so that her back was pulled tight against his chest, in a simulation of a move Dean had used on him only a few minutes before. "Can you stop being quite so obvious," he whispered directly into her ear. He shoved her away with a dramatic flourish, parodying another wrestling move. "See, just like that. It's easy."

"Again. I missed it," Riley said, cottoning on.

Darius went through the moves, slower this time, his head bent close to hers.

"Logan *is* convinced that Alec caused the rips in the first place, and he's going to do him in next Work period.
You were right. What're we going to do?" she whispered, pretending an obvious interest in where Darius' hands went and how he pivoted her around.

"What makes you so sure?"

"Jacob the weasel overheard him."

Darius swore quietly. His facial expression was

completely opposite to his anger. Maybe he had learned to conceal what he was feeling after all.

"So?"

"I'm thinking."

"Dare, we have to get him out of here."

"Riley, your lessons." Dean had approached them unheard. He had showered and changed back to the grey uniform incredibly quickly. His tone of voice brooked no refusal.

Darius let Riley go and stood back. His lopsided smile was no different from usual, but the sparkle in his eyes was missing. "Sure. Any time you want to learn–"

"Any survival or combat skills, she'll learn from me, Finn." Dean gave Darius a stony look.

Darius shrugged. "Sure. No problem." With one last wink at Riley, he turned and sauntered towards the lingering Operatives.

Riley followed Dean back to the Study section, her mind in overdrive as she considered and rejected various plans. She nearly walked into Dean when he stopped abruptly. She looked up. Gino and Mary Beth, the only survivors of the Toronto bunker, were deep in conversation with Jacob in the Study section, and three Potentials from Norway were standing next to Dean and their Guardian, a young woman with an even more severe expression than Anna.

"What is going on?" Dean asked.

"You missed Logan," Jacob volunteered. "He's got bad news."

Missing Logan was definitely a good thing, in Riley's opinion. "What'd the great chief have to say?" she asked.

"More trouble in your city."

"Halifax?"

"No, no. Toronto." Jacob pointed over the dividers to the far wall where the farthest screen showed a riot taking place. Police officers, several on horseback and all in riot gear, were doing their best, but it didn't look promising. "Rhozan's started a huge fight."

Riley frowned. For a moment she glimpsed the CN Tower in the background. Then the camera, or whatever equipment was transmitting the image, panned lower, to the people again.

Rioting wasn't an insurmountable problem. Toronto had lots of police. "Why was Logan so worried?"

"He said the Operatives wouldn't be able to get in any longer. Too many dangers. He said there were still Potentials there, but they couldn't get close to them."

That meant kids like her, with the same gift in their genes, were in danger. And no one was trying to save them. "Oh come on. With all their power?" Riley turned to Dean. "A few idiots running wild in the streets shouldn't frighten big, strong aliens like you."

"There are rips everywhere," Dean said patiently. "We can't get close. Anyone with an orb is spotted faster than we can zero in on the Potential, grab them and go. It isn't as easy as it sounds, Riley."

"Yeah, but come on. Kids are dying, right? You're going to do something, aren't you?"

There was silence. Riley looked from one Tyon to the next. None seemed too concerned. All the other Potentials were looking anywhere but at her. Even Jacob found the floor more interesting.

"So you're going to stand around and watch." Riley's hands went to her hips. "You're a bunch of cowards."

"You are ignorant."

The voice came from behind her. Riley whirled around.
146 Tyrell wasn't smiling. Riley was relieved to notice he was wearing clothes now.

"Enlighten me," she challenged.

"Come." It was an order, not a suggestion. Tyrell strode past her and continued out of the teaching area.

Riley gave Dean a withering look before marching after

Tyrell as quickly as she could. The pilot had much longer legs and he made no effort to ensure she was following. She glanced back. All the Potentials and the other Guardians were trooping behind her, Dean leading the pack. Mary Beth squeezed past him and joined Riley at her elbow.

"You're pissing everyone off," Mary Beth whispered, her eyes darting from Tyrell's back to Dean's stern countenance. "Do you want us all punished?"

"Get a grip." Riley didn't bother even looking at her.

"They will, you know. They've put Alec in solitary and they'll do it to us, if you aren't careful."

"I'd like to see them try," Riley muttered.

"Don't you understand anything? They hate us. They're just looking for an excuse to wipe us all out."

Riley grabbed Mary Beth's arm. "What makes you believe that? Got any proof?"

"I'm not an idiot." Mary Beth lowered her voice as Dean passed. "I keep my mouth shut and my eyes open and I hear a lot of things I'm probably not supposed to. You should try it." She jerked her arm away from Riley and joined the rest of the group that was now huddling around Tyrell.

"Riley," Tyrell shouted.

Riley took a calming breath and blanketed her mental worries before someone plucked them out of her skull. Tyrell took out his orb. He waved it at the screen. Riley couldn't help but marvel at the technology. She could practically smell the heated asphalt.

"Sound, five," said Tyrell. The sound rose from silence to barely audible.

147

It was a view of Yonge Street, looking north. Most of the shop windows were broken and several signs torn down. The mob surged and retreated like an undulating mass of serpents. They were all shouting but their words were unclear.

Here and there, the police came into view and were beaten back. Riot sticks whaled in the air. Canisters were tossed onto the ground and rolled under the feet of the closest rioters. Almost instantly, everyone nearby began clawing at their eyes. Thick, bluish smoke belched into a noxious cloud, but even those affected didn't stop their destructive and dangerous behaviour.

"Sound to zero," Tyrell said, and the sound of the riot instantly disappeared. "There are two Potentials in this crowd. Our sensors have just discovered them in the last few minutes. Can you spot them, Riley?"

Well, of course she couldn't. How did you spot a Potential anyway? "No," she said. "Can you?"

"No." Tyrell pointed at the screen where the crowd had now turned on itself instead of the police. A young woman with a haircut similar to Riley's was simultaneously bashed on both sides of her head. Her eyes rolled back and she fell to the smoke-obscured ground. The crowd trampled her, ignoring the body beneath their feet. Riley's stomach heaved, but she couldn't wrench her eyes away.

"Without an orb, none of us could distinguish a Potential in this crowd." Dean's voice startled her. "Normally, the signal is weak when we first find it. It grows stronger as the genetic trait activates. That's why it generally takes so long to find you. Searching in this crowd with the amount of energy present and the influence of the Others so strongly dispersed would be nearly impossible. Can you spot the Emissaries here?"

Riley shook her head. They all looked the same to her: wild, out of control and highly dangerous. The cold, unemotional danger she'd spotted before was nowhere to be seen.

"Protecting myself would be almost impossible, particularly from this." Tyrell waved his orb and the picture froze. He pointed at the lower-right corner, between two women who were halted in mid-slap. Sparkles. Hovering just above the thickest smoke and impossible to see until you stepped into them. Riley gulped.

"We're skilled but not magicians. I would ask you to tell us how we ought to manage this situation." Tyrell waved his hand again and the screen went mercifully blank. He stared at Riley over the heads of the other Potentials. She shuffled her feet.

"Well?"

"Okay, so I don't know. I'm the trainee, not the teacher, remember?" Riley pulled a face at Mary Beth's scandalized expression.

"I would suggest that all of you heed Logan's words." Tyrell was now speaking to the group. "This world is in serious trouble. We have begun transportation of all training centre personal and Potentials to this facility. Over the next Work period, decisions will be made concerning the future of this planet. All Potentials should increase their effort towards orb mastery.

"Work has ended. Please obtain your meal and retire for Rest. Dismissed." Tyrell turned and left. The three Norwegians and their Guardian followed him, muttering amongst themselves. Riley stood as if rooted to the ground.

These smug, high-handed aliens were doing nothing to save the innocent kids in the middle of a small-scale war. What if Rhozan turned his attention to the Base? How far would the Collective go to protect her and the others?

Alec lay on his top bunk and listened as the melodious gong reverberated throughout the bunker, indicating the last hour of Work and the beginning of Rest. Of course, his schedule was opposite and right now he should be just waking. But he'd been awake for hours. Thinking.

He'd had a dream, the same kind he'd had before in the last couple of weeks and he'd woken in a cold sweat. Nothing actually happened in the dream, but it bothered him anyway. He was in a dark place, unable to see or hear, but he knew that someone was coming. A sense of impending doom enveloped him and then he'd wake.

He'd first had that dream in the hospital, the night his father gave him a concussion. Even though the nurse woke him nearly every hour to check his pupils and vital signs.

27

Below him, Anna got up from her bunk and padded barefoot to the table. Her hair was loose for a change and flowed down her back in a smooth, pale cascade. She waved her orb and the computer screen winked into being.

He didn't hate her anymore. The dislike and impotent anger had faded, leaving a residue of disagreeable, distant memories. She wasn't engaging like Darius, or funny like Riley, but she wasn't wholly unpleasant now. They had worked for hours in the last Work period. While Anna wasn't effusive with her praise, she was surprisingly encouraging, and Alec found himself wanting to please her, despite himself. Rarely had Alec ever found himself on the positive side of a teacher's opinion, except on the sports field. Part of him suspected that Anna's encouraging feedback was manipulative, but he couldn't help himself responding. It felt so *good* to be good at something. He wished Riley could witness his growing proficiency.

"I know you're awake. Are you hungry?"

"Yeah, I guess." He sat up, swung his legs over the side and dropped easily to the floor. He headed to the toileting/shower cubicle. He closed the door behind him and stared into the small shiny area that doubled as a mirror. Did he look any different from yesterday? He felt changed.

He shaved with satisfaction the fuzz that had collected over his upper lip, showered and dressed in a clean overall. He finger-combed his hair, spending more time trying to attain a casual windblown look that he knew Anna would like and smiled to himself. He might not be as handsome as Darius, but he would soon be taller. There were girls out there in the main bunker, including Riley, and Anna had promised she'd let him mingle as soon as his emotions were under control. Other than the creepy dream, his emotions were fine. Maybe she'd let him out today?

Anna had placed their breakfast on the table by the time he came out of the bathroom. He slyly observed her expression. Other than an overlong glance at his hair, nothing.

"Did you sleep well?" she asked.

He shrugged as he resignedly tucked into the bowl of what reminded him of tapioca pudding. Right now he'd cut off a leg for a batch of his mom's blueberry pancakes. Thinking about home produced a hard lump that was difficult to swallow around. He focused on his meal. "Uh-huh."

"Do you feel well?"

"Yeah."

"Did you have any bad dreams?"

Alec paused with the spoon halfway to his mouth. He stared at the bowl. "What's with the inquisition?"

"Scanners sensed something in the bunker during the last twelve hours," Anna said.

"Sensed what?" Alec scraped the bottom of his bowl and looked around. Anna usually had extra for him.

"We're not sure exactly. The signal was similar to an Emissary's. Of course, no Emissary could be created inside the Base. The reading was too faint to identify perfectly." Anna got up and procured a second bowl from the cupboard. She watched him closely as he started in. "I wonder if you might have felt anything unusual during the time it was recorded."

"Why?"

"Because you are particularly sensitive to the Others. If Rhozan was trying to gain entry to the Base, you might be a portal."

Alec dropped his spoon to the table. "Are you saying that Rhozan might try and get to you guys through me? Are you out of your mind? I don't even know the guy."

"I'm not implying that you would willingly help our enemies, Alec."

"I bet Logan thinks I would," he muttered angrily. He pushed the half-eaten bowl away. Great. He'd started the day okay, and there she was, annoying him before the first meal was even over. He might not like these Tyon Operatives, might think the whole orb training was beyond boring, but he wasn't going to open the doors to the enemy and yell "Come on in."

"Logan doesn't trust any off-worlders. He never has. He even gives the Tholan Operatives, like Dean, a hard time," Anna explained.

"Yeah, well, he hates me."

"I agree that many of Logan's tactics are harsh," Anna said quietly. "I dislike how he treats you but—"

"But nothing," Alec burst out. "Anna, it was a complete

violation. You know it. You didn't even try to stop him."

Anna pushed her own bowl away and crossed her arms. She stared at the opening to the rest of the bunker. "No. I did not." She was quiet for a long moment. "I apologize."

This was the last thing he expected her to say. "So, why didn't you?" he asked after a long pause.

"Logan has been my commander for many of your years. I began my first assignment with him." She gazed intently out towards the bunker, but Alec had the impression she wasn't seeing anything. "When an Operative finishes their training and is assigned their duties, they take an oath to obey their commander in all things. It is one of the worst crimes to refute that oath."

"So, he locks you up for a while or something. Big deal." Alec grimaced. "You should have said no. My Guardian's supposed to protect me. Not hold me down while someone rapes me."

A heavy silence surrounded Alec's harsh words. Finally, Anna licked her lips and spoke. "How could you tell Logan crucial information, when you are unaware of it yourself? Were you aware of the results of your anger the night you attacked your father?"

Alec abruptly got up from the table. He was sure he didn't want to hear this.

"There is no other way to recover what has been deeply hidden inside you, Alec. Few from my home planet are skilled enough to try, and none who can do it gently are here with us on this planet. Your world is being destroyed, even as we speak, and you are angry because the Commander chose their lives over your discomfort."

"Yeah, but—" he began.

"Is a momentary unpleasantness more important

153

than trying to save the life of your mother? Because, like it or not, that is exactly what Logan is trying to do. Protecting the people of Earth, your parents included, from Rhozan. And he was convinced the key to doing that was somewhere inside your mind."

This was not what Alec had expected to hear and with every word he felt himself burning with shame. He'd do anything to protect his mom. He already had. Alec scowled and kicked the table leg.

Suddenly, the overhead lighting changed to a reddish hue. Anna jumped up from her seat. "Stay here," she ordered, before she ran out through the dividers and disappeared into the bunker.

The instant she was gone, Alec swung himself onto his upper bed and stood up on the mattress. The entire Base lay spread out in front of him with a sea of pale, yellow heads bobbing and scuttling around the divider walls. Anna could be any one of them and could have gone anywhere. There was a large cluster of Operatives near the tall cylindrical tower in the Command Centre. Anna would probably go there. No one had said anything to confirm it, but he was sure that Anna was pretty high up on the chain of command.

He scanned the rest of the Base. Most of the movement seemed to be around the perimeter or the Command Centre. He shifted his attention to the walls where at least one or two people stood watching the action before each screen.

He peered closely. There was something uncomfortably familiar about the scene unfolding on the screen just to his left. The picture widened to show a vacant street lined with pale grey, concrete high-rises, rusting metal balustrades sagging over each narrow balcony. The dusty, packed earth in front of each building might, at one time, have been covered with grass, but now endless feet had trampled even the most hardy of weeds into oblivion. The occasional

154

spindly sapling, pegged with nylon ties to hold it upright, lined the cracked cement walkways. On the corner, a convenience store with the "Super Fast Mart" sign, broken in two places, looked deserted.

Wait a minute, this was his neighbourhood. He'd spent hours fooling around in the store's stock room, hanging out with Chin while he did his chores, or swiping licorice under the nose of Chin's elderly grandmother. A cold trickle of dread ran down his spine.

Several cars appeared at the farthest end of the street. They skidded to a stop in front of the store. The car doors opened and several dishevelled people clambered out.

Alec was too far away to hear the sounds of their shouts, or perhaps the sound was low on the screen. Armed with clubs and other weapons, they barrelled inside, pulling the door off the hinges as they passed. One man with a blank expression and too many tattooes swung a golf club at the plate-glass window, shattering it all over the sidewalk. Alec cringed. That window had been broken twice in the last year and cost a fortune to fix. Alec's hands clasped into fists.

He didn't realize he was holding his breath until the gang spilled out of the store, jumped into the cars and peeled out of sight. His relief was short-lived. The explosion might be thousands of kilometres away, but he felt it all the same. The remaining glass blew outwards and grey, billowing smoke roiled from the open door and window.

"Get out," Alec breathed. "Hurry up."

As if they could hear his whispered plea, several small figures stumbled from the open doorway. A tiny woman pulled someone by the legs. She collapsed, her body racking with coughs, over the limp body of a tee-shirt clad figure. She shook the body several times, but the dark-haired boy didn't respond. A teenage girl, her long, black hair obscuring her face, crawled out of the entrance and collapsed.

Alec swallowed the lump in his throat. This couldn't be happening. That was Chin's mom and sister. He couldn't see Chin's face but the cold sensation in his stomach swelled with fear. Where was old Mrs. Lee and Chin's dad?

"Get up," he pleaded. Chin didn't move.

A sudden ball of flame leapt through the open door. Mrs. Lee and Mei Ling flattened themselves to the ground, Chin's mother protecting her son with her body against the scorching inferno. Alec's heart leapt into his throat. The fire broke through the roof, engulfing the entire building, but neither Mei Ling nor her mother stirred.

"Move," Alec yelled, only half aware they couldn't hear him. He desperately scanned the nearby corridors for an Operative. If the transmission could come into the Base, couldn't he get a message out?

Too late. He watched with horror as the brick building seemed to actually *bulge* with the second and more powerful explosion. Bricks, mortar, glass, all blew outwards so fast he almost didn't see it, levelling the building into nothing. Alec's legs gave out from under him and he dropped to the bed with shock.

Sudden knowledge seared Alec's mind. Rhozan's puppets had done this. It didn't take a genius to understand the plan. Rhozan was after *him*. The Other's attempt at infiltrating the Base had a purpose. Rhozan *knew* Alec was safe inside the protective boundaries of the Base. Like any good tactician in the video games Alec loved, he was going after those Alec knew, planning to take them out, one by one, until the real target showed up to demand retribution.

156   Alec's stomach dropped to his knees. If Rhozan was going after his friends, it wasn't going to be long before he turned his attention to his family.

He had to get out of here. *Now.*

Riley dropped her spoon into her bowl with a loud clang as the light around her changed from yellow to red. Across the table, Jacob wiped his mouth on the back of his sleeve and looked around for a second helping.

"Attention Potentials," Dean said as he stood up. "This is a warning signal. All Potentials are to gather outside of Med Ops and wait for further instruction. Proceed there immediately." With that, he headed out of Meal Dispersal.

The Norwegians stood up as one and headed towards Med Ops silently. Mary Beth gave Riley a sharp glance before scuttling off behind them, Gino in tow. All the others followed but Jacob.

"Come on," Riley said, standing up. Her heart was dancing a funny little jig inside her chest. Silly to be scared when the Base was filled to the brim with fully trained Operatives and Logan was commanding. Whoever Rhozan was, she couldn't imagine him wanting to take on the Tyon Commander.

28

Jacob reached for someone's half-empty bowl. "Why? What's happening?"

"Don't you pay attention to anything?" Riley snapped. If the perpetuation of the human species was dependent on Jacob, she rather hoped the lot of them died out.

"I'm hungry," he whined, lifting an overladen spoon to his mouth. "They hardly feed us anything here. If we're under attack, I'd rather die with a full stomach."

"Why am I not surprised," Riley muttered to herself as she headed towards the Med Ops Console behind what seemed to be the entire Tyon company. Wait a minute. *Alec.* Wouldn't he be left alone right now? Riley stopped mid-step. This could be the perfect opportunity. If the Base was truly in trouble, this might be their only chance to escape.

She turned around and headed back the way she'd come, glancing at the screens as she passed. On every one, scenes of violence, worse than she'd ever seen before, flickered and changed. An entire city block was ablaze. Which city wasn't immediately apparent, but it didn't look like somewhere in Canada. Another two screens displayed the smoldering ashes of what looked to be a factory, and another screen showed a refinery engulfed in flames, while several fire trucks impotently waited a safe distance away.

Tyrell was right. Rhozan, whoever he was, certainly seemed to be upping the level of violence.

She ran around another corner and slipped into the back corridor. It was deserted. She stopped at the perimeter. Dean had warned her that it was armed. With what exactly, he hadn't said.

"Come to say hello, or just admiring the scenery?" Alec asked. He was pacing back and forth, his shoulders bunched by his ears and his hands jammed into his pockets. He didn't break his stride.

"Neither," Riley snapped. "I've come to get you out."

"Yeah, right. The border's armed."

"Well, duh." Riley frowned. This required some serious thought. "Guess you have no idea how to disarm it?"

158   "Well, duh," Alec mimicked before he stopped and faced her. They were only a few strides apart, but it seemed like miles. Riley had forgotten how tall he was. "So you couldn't be bothered to come and see me all this time, but now that something interesting is going on, you come rushing in to the rescue."

"Gimme a break. I've come by lots of times to check on you, and you've always been asleep."

Alec's annoyance seemed to drain away like water. His eyebrows rose into his thick thatch of dark curls. "Really?"

"Well, yeah." Riley leaned on one hip. "It's not like I completely desert my friends."

A grin split Alec's face, just for an instant, rendering him remarkably handsome. "So, we're friends."

Riley snorted. "Don't get your hopes up." She looked around intently. "How's the alarm work?"

"I dunno." Alec walked over to the edge of the floor space that was still inside the divider. He peered closely at the floor and walls. "When I try to cross this area, I get a pretty wicked shock. I can't make myself go past it. I don't see any wires or anything."

How can you disrupt an alarm you can't even see? The lighting turned a darker red. "Maybe you can just run at it?" Riley suggested.

"Tried that."

"What does Anna do to go in and out? Have you watched her?"

"Course I have. And she doesn't do anything. She isn't even holding her orb when she walks through. No one does. The alarm just doesn't zap *them*."

"It's primed just for you then," Riley considered. "Thought it might be."

"So?"

"So, I'm thinking." Riley's brow furrowed. Most of the orb lessons focused upon learning to concentrate deeply on what it was you wanted to happen and *willing* it. Would that work with a highly sophisticated alarm system? 159

"Hurry up," Alec urged. "I've got to get out of here."

"Hold your horses." Riley chewed on her bottom lip. There was only one way to find out if her idea was workable. "Okay, here's what we're going to do. I'm going to come in. Then we're going to both hold my orb and concentrate on walking past this alarm system without triggering it. Then, we're going to find Darius and get the hell out of this place."

"Since when do you know how to use an orb?" Alec looked skeptical.

"Since I've been training how to use one of these thingies, and you haven't," she scoffed without meeting his eyes.

"It's not my fault Anna won't let me keep one," Alec muttered.

"Stand back." Riley squared her shoulders and gripped her orb. She kept her hand inside the overall pocket. No need for Alec to see how white her knuckles were.

The alarm didn't trip as she stepped over the threshold. For a second she just stood there, surprised at herself, then quickly rearranged her features into an expression of utmost seriousness and superiority. "'Kay, hold onto my orb at the same time as me and keep your mind entirely blank," she ordered. "Don't think about anything. Don't break your concentration for a second. No matter what. Let me do all the thinking."

"Are you sure about this?" Alec was frowning. "I mean, it's all right for you. You won't get your skin fried off. I will."

"Look." She turned, hands on her hips, cocking her head to stare up at him with the most intimidating look she could muster. "Do you want to leave this joint or not?"

Alec glanced bleakly towards the movie screens. He gritted his teeth. "Yeah, I do."

"Well then stop being such a wuss about a bit of electricity. I'll pull you out if I have to."

160 Alec grabbed her hand, engulfing her small fist in his larger one. She twisted her fingers for a second to allow him contact with the orb. His hand was warm and a little tingle of static electricity zipped through her fingers. She shoved him into position in front of the perimeter. Only one stride to freedom.

"Ready?" she said, unable to look at him. *If this didn't work …*

"Do it."

"On three," said Riley as she tried to focus on her single thought rather than the warm fingers gripping her own. "One, two, *go*."

Before she could rethink the plan, Riley took a deep breath and stepped across the barrier, focusing her attention fully on blocking any negative effect from the alarm system. She was concentrating so hard she walked straight into the divider wall opposite. She opened her eyes, blinked, rubbed her nose and tried to look nonchalant.

Nothing had happened. It was rather anticlimactic. Riley pulled the orb out of Alec's grasp and dropped it into her overall pocket.

"Now we find Darius and get the hell out of here," Riley said. It was too late to have second thoughts now. "We've got to keep you out of sight, though. The second anyone notices you, they'll be onto Logan before you can blink. And, Alec, the guy doesn't like you."

"Yeah, tell me about it."

They ran down the narrow corridor, Alec hunching over so that the top of his head wasn't visible over the upper edge of the divider walls. Riley went ahead by several paces, stopping at each junction and scouting the area first before waving him on behind her.

They twisted and turned multiple times. If Alec was confused as to his whereabouts, he said nothing, and Riley was too concerned with getting him to the bathroom without anyone noticing to direct him.

She turned another corner and slammed on the brakes. Alec almost knocked her over. She shoved him backwards with urgent hands. The Norwegian Potential's Guardian and one of her charges stood together in front of the bathroom doorway. Whatever they were talking about, it was an intense subject, with the Potential waving her arms around and yelling. Riley cursed under her breath.

"What?" Alec looked behind him for a second, then leaned over her shoulder to watch the two others argue.

"They're right in front of the bathroom."

"So?"

"Where did you think I'm hiding you, you dork?" Riley grimaced as she shoved him back.

As if they responded to her unspoken plea, both the Guardian and her sullen charge suddenly turned and walked away, heading towards Med Ops. Riley watched until they were out of sight.

She ran across the floor to place her palm against the smooth metal of the wall. The doorway rapidly materialized and opened. Riley stepped inside and Alec followed her a moment later. The door closed behind them with a slight *whoosh*.

"Whoa," Alec breathed. His eyes were wide as he took in the bank of open shower stalls. "Are you sure I'm allowed in here? Isn't this the girls' bathroom?"

"It's co-ed," Riley said, watching his face for the first hint of a tell-tale blush.

Alec didn't disappoint her. "No way." He cleared his throat. "Have you ever wondered about these guys' obsession with metal?"

"It's some sort of creepy living metal," Riley said as she pushed open a stall door and indicated with a flourish of her hand that Alec should enter. "Dean told me the whole place is made up of this stuff. They just tell it what they want and it grows to make it."

"Really? Cool." He suddenly looked serious. "How long are you going to leave me here?"

"Just as long as it takes to find Darius and organize our escape." Riley was already pulling the stall door closed but Alec grabbed it.

"Don't be long. Some city named Trondheim has burned

to the ground. The military's been called in. It's really bad."

Riley stared up at him with a combination of amazement and concern. "You could understand that conversation?"

Puzzled, he looked down at her. "Well, yeah."

"I didn't know you spoke Norwegian."

"Look, what's with this Norwegian stuff? All I speak is English. I even failed French this year."

"Both those people were speaking another language, Alec." Riley chewed on her lower lip. "I couldn't understand a thing. How did you do that?'

Alec scowled. "Riley, you're wasting time. Get Darius. Get me out of here. If a city in Norway is falling apart, then sure as hell Toronto is. The rips started there. Rhozan's at his strongest there. And *my* family lives in Scarborough."

He was right. They'd sort through Alec's new linguistic abilities later, when they were out of the Base. "Don't move," she ordered. "Stay quiet and don't leave here for anything."

Alec wished for the twentieth time that he had a watch. How long had Riley been gone? What would happen if she didn't come back? Was he supposed to wait in the bathroom forever? No one had come in since she'd left and the red lighting had deepened slightly, so that the walls and floor seemed like they were burning. It was pretty creepy.

The door of the bathroom opened with its almost silent *whoosh*. Alec gulped. He eyed the locking mechanism on the stall door, reassuring himself that it was fastened securely, and hopped up on the rim of the seat as quietly as he could, settling down to wait. Several long seconds passed. Then several more. He listened intently but heard nothing. Did someone know he was there and was just waiting for his nerve to break? The urge to peek under the stall door grew stronger. What on earth was going on?

"You really need to learn to blanket your mind."

Darius' voice startled Alec so badly he fell. Slamming the wall with the palm of his hand to halt his fall, he glanced upwards. Darius was watching over the top of the stall next to him.

"Jeez, give me a heart attack, why don't ya." Alec straightened up.

"Get out and follow me."

Alec undid the lock with shaking hands and stepped out into the bathroom, only wondering a second later if Darius was alone or if he'd walked into an ambush. Relief flooded him as he glanced around.

"Good time to think about a trap, after you've come out of hiding," Darius said with mild rebuke.

"Gimme a break," Alec muttered.

"You're hunted now." Darius wasn't smiling. His stony countenance indicated a harder and less sympathetic man than Alec had seen before. "Time to start thinking like prey and smarten up. This is not a game."

The words sparked a chill down the back of Alec's neck. "Then what are we standing around talking for? Shouldn't we be going?"

"Absolutely. Stay close."

Darius crossed to where the door had been. He leaned against the wall, almost as if trying to listen through the metal. Apparently satisfied, he pressed his hand against the wall and the door materialized and opened. Darius leaned out and looked around.

"We're heading to the entrance. Several transports are due in dock in a couple of minutes. With all the new Potentials arriving, there should be enough distraction for us to leave. The barrier will be down only for a moment, so we have to be ready to leave the instant I tell you," Darius instructed quietly. "Follow me and stay right behind. Say nothing to no one. Don't look anyone in the eye. Pretend that you know what you're doing and that you belong here."

"Won't everyone know who I am?" Alec whispered nervously as they stepped out of the bathroom and into the wide corridor next to a long series of bunk beds. "I'm supposed to be locked up. Won't they try to stop me?"

"The Collective is a bit distracted at the moment, Alec. Keep your mind blank and no one will pick up on your worry about being caught. My thoughts will indicate this behaviour is required. Now, quiet."

Darius' reassurance made no sense to Alec, but he was not in a position to argue. Darius had already headed out of the sleeping area and was striding down a long, wide corridor. Alec sped up to catch up to him. All he needed was to get separated.

"What about Riley?" Alec muttered after they had crossed the computer terminal area and turned yet another corner. They were now heading towards the far wall of the cavern. He looked around nervously. If she didn't meet up with them in time …

"She has her instructions," Darius said. "Concentrate."

Alec bit his tongue and took a deep breath. He couldn't imagine what she was doing that was so important. Heart in his mouth he strode along, head down, as if lost in thought. It was a lot harder to manage Anna's exercises now than it had been at the little table in his quarters.

His heart almost stopped the first time a Tyon Operative turned a corner ahead of them and passed by so closely he could have reached out and touched him. It only started beating again once the man passed without a comment.

Darius turned right and headed through a more populated section of the Base. Operatives, all waving their hands furiously over computer consoles, paid no attention as they passed. The very air was humming with frantic activity. Once through that section, Darius turned right and stopped. The outer wall of the chamber was directly ahead, with a set of closed double doors only metres away. There was no obvious lock nor was anyone on guard. Could they just walk out?

"The guards are outside these doors." Darius didn't bother with the semblance of politely ignoring Alec's telepathic broadcast. He backed up a couple of steps to return to the partial protection of a divider wall and gave Alec a slight push to keep him from stepping too far out, into sight.

Several Operatives marched into Alec's line of sight and halted in front of the doors. Eerily, no one spoke as they waited. A sudden pang of worry coursed through him. Darius' coveralls were not as loose as Riley's had been, but if Darius had an orb on him, Alec couldn't see it. Darius wasn't planning to get out and make a run for it unarmed, was he?

Darius turned his head and mouthed the words, "Stop worrying," before turning back to watch the crowd. Alec took a deep breath and tried again to purge his mind of every thought.

Several Operatives ran through the milling crowd and skidded to a stop in front of the doors. Both pulled out orbs, held them in the palms of their hands and directed a brief flash of white-blue light towards the doors. There was a grating sound, like rock rubbing against rock. Then the doors swung open.

Alec tensed to run, but Darius reached out and held his upper arm. The two Operatives walked through the doorway and disappeared into the dark corridor beyond. None of the others moved. Like Darius, they waited for some sign. Alec felt rather than heard it. A weight he hadn't actually been aware of lifted off his shoulders. Around him, the Operatives surged forward. Darius did likewise. Alec followed.

The corridor was low, domed and cold. It was dark, too, and Alec would have tripped had the stone floor been uneven. Darius walked at his side, his shoulder occasionally bumping into Alec's as the crowd jostled them.

Almost as quickly as they had entered the tunnel, they exited into a large chamber with a low roof and several dark tunnels leading out of it. The room was filled with people. Alec had the impression of scores of teenagers, many crying, and at least twenty Tyon Operatives, grim-faced and wearing the ubiquitous grey coveralls. Several of them were holding blood-soaked clothes to their faces and their uniforms were dirty and torn. Whatever had happened to them, it wasn't pleasant.

Darius tugged him to the side and out of the way. The Tyons from the Base surged past them, dividing the group into many smaller clusters with the minimum of instruction, and set about sending them all into the main chamber with military precision.

"Follow me," Darius whispered. He turned and walked around the perimeter of the crowd with every appearance of having something important to do. He nodded to several of the newly arrived Tyon Operatives but spoke to no one. Alec followed. He kept his eyes on his feet and off the frightened faces of the other kids. It took nearly a minute to circumnavigate the crowd.

Darius turned suddenly and stopped. Alec halted mid-stride, turned his back to the crowd and leaned in to hear Darius' whisper. "The tunnel right behind you leads to the outside. Riley will join us there. Don't look like you are making your escape. Be casual. I'll follow. Go."

Alec nodded once. Glancing surreptitiously around him, he walked around Darius and headed towards the dark opening just off to his right. Heart pounding, he passed the tunnel opening and then paused, pretending to bend down and adjust his shoe. Once certain no one was paying attention to him, he stood up and ducked down the tunnel. The second he was sure he was out of sight, he broke into a run.

The tunnel was darker than the chamber, and the lights posted on the wall few and far between. Alec ran with his hand out, trailing it along the surprisingly smooth stone to keep himself oriented. There was a turn to the right and another to the left. The floor sloped gently upwards.

He stopped to listen. Other than the *drip, drip* of water pooling into the small puddles that dotted the floor and a faint whistling of the air as it blew past him, the tunnel was silent. Alec leaned against the cold wall. He had no idea if he'd run far enough or not.

The minutes inched past. No one approached and nothing broke the silence. Alec ground his teeth and started to pace. Where the hell was Darius? Had something happened? What if Anna stopped him? Sweat trickled under his arms, making him shiver in the cooler air. A soft scraping caught his attention. He whirled around.

Someone walked into the faint pool of light. The young man was tall and blond, with wide shoulders and angry, pale eyes. He came to a stop only a couple of strides from Alec.

Alec swallowed the profanity. There was no point in running. Whoever he was appeared to be in peak physical condition, and no doubt he had an orb. The best Alec could hope for was preventing Darius and Riley from walking into the trap. "Who are you?" he challenged loudly.

"I am Riley's Guardian, Dean." The man cocked his head on one side. "Where is she?"

Alec shrugged. "No idea. What's it to you?"

"Riley's safety and training are my responsibility," Dean said in his clipped and accent-less voice. "I must prevent her foolish actions."

"What foolish actions?" It was pretty lame, but for the life of him Alec couldn't think of anything else to say.

"She plans to liberate an orb from another Operative and meet Finn here, in this tunnel. I cannot permit it."

"Because she doesn't want to stay or because Darius is telling her to?" Alec hadn't missed the inflection Dean gave Darius' name.

"Both."

"You don't like him, do you?"

"Finn is unable to maintain the impersonal distance required in the Collective. He's *attractive*."

This was not what Alec had expected to hear. "So you guys don't like him, because you *like* him? That's totally weird. Not to mention stupid."

"Attraction and personal feelings have no place in the function of the Collective. The only goal is to serve and protect against the Others. Emotional attachments are permitted once an Operative's duty has been discharged. Not before." Dean seemed to tire of the conversation or he had realized Alec's purpose in keeping him talking. "Turn around, Alec, and start walking," he ordered.

So Dean knew exactly who he was, which meant he'd also know to tell Logan. Fighting the sudden urge to lash out, Alec turned and took a step back down the tunnel towards captivity, his mind working furiously. If he could somehow overpower Dean, he might still make a run for it. He just had to catch him unawares.

He almost walked into Darius, who had been standing in the shadows.

"He's leaving with me, Dean." Darius' voice was quiet but the menace unmistakable.

"Sometimes I wonder about you, Finn," Dean said. His voice seemed to echo in the half-dark. "It's as if you just don't understand how sub-standard you really are to all of us. You have no orb. You're physically my inferior. And yet, you oppose me? There is little hope for this planet if you're a representative sample."

"I know this is particularly difficult for you, after all the training we've done together. But I'm leaving now. And Alec is coming with me. *You* are not going to stop me." Darius reached out and grabbed Alec's arm, shoving him roughly against the wall and out of his way before Alec could react. He took a threatening step towards Dean. "Let's just settle this, once and for all, why don't we?"

"This isn't Rec training, Finn. I won't hold back. You'll die."

"Then kill me."

Alec held his breath. There was no way you could duck an orb blast. What the hell was Darius *doing*?

Darius grinned and didn't move. The light was so poor it was hard to tell for certain, but Alec couldn't see an orb in his hand. Was he just going to stand there and let Dean murder him?

"If you have a God, you should pray to him now," whispered Dean.

"And *you* should hope that no one finds out that you plan to murder a fellow Operative in cold blood, without a weapon of his own. Logan will be severely annoyed to see one of his own defy the Code. But then, maybe your feelings for me drove you to it. A crime of passion, hmm?"

The swear word Dean used was completely new to Alec, but the hatred and hurt behind it were not.

Someone clutched at Alec's arm. Startled, he turned away from the two men for a split second. Riley was hidden by shadows and had approached so quietly he doubted the others even knew she was there. Dean couldn't see her, Alec realized. She could still get away.

He shook his head mutely, willing her to run. She didn't. Alec tried to yank his arm away from hers, but her grip was so strong that all he did was unbalance her. Riley stumbled against Alec, grabbing on to his other arm to break her fall. He felt an orb drop into his pocket. With a sudden flash of insight, he pushed her away again, hoping she'd understand and melt back into the darkness, now that he was armed. But she either didn't get his silent message or had an agenda of her own.

"Don't hurt him," Riley gasped. Her voice echoed eerily in the tunnel. "You don't want to. I know you don't."

"He's defying orders." Dean managed to get the words out, despite his clenched jaw. "I must stop him."

"You'll have to go through me first," Riley challenged. She made as if to fling herself in front of Darius, but Alec grabbed her arms to stop her. He pinned her against the cold stone, shielding her from Dean.

"You're making a grave mistake. We're helping the Terrans. We're not the enemy, Rhozan is," Dean said, his eyes never leaving Darius.

"Yeah, really?" Riley's voice was scathing as she squirmed impotently against Alec. "So why's Logan planning to kill Alec, eh? Explain that."

Alec's breath caught in his throat. *What*? He barely saw Dean's eyes flicker from Riley to himself and back again. "There has been no order given to terminate Alec. You are mistaken."

"There has and it is you who is mistaken."

Dean whirled around.

Anna stepped out of the inky darkness. In her hand was her orb, its wintry blue glow strengthening with every step. Her expression was cold and unemotional. She might have been made from ice.

Alec's heartbeat racked up a notch. *What on earth had she said?*

"You knew all along what Logan was planning and you went along with it." Darius sounded bitter. "You kept that from me."

"I made my promise to Logan, long before I made mine to you."

"Then it was all lies? Everything?" Alec couldn't see Darius' face but his back was rigid.

"No. Not everything," Anna said slowly.

"Has Logan ordered a death mark for this boy?" Dean kept his eye on Darius but spoke to his supervisor. He sounded confused, or at least wary. "For what reason?"

"Alec is the strongest Potential ever created. Stronger than Finn," Anna said without taking her eyes off Darius. "But unlike Darius, he's been tainted by contact with Rhozan. The link has been confirmed. That magnitude of power cannot be permitted to be corrupted."

Alec recoiled. This couldn't be true. He'd know if someone that powerful came knocking at his mind. Wouldn't he?

"He's not in league with the Others, Anna," Darius said, his voice persuasive. "You know it, as well as I. Any link that has been forged was done by them, not him. You've worked with him for days now. You've seen inside his mind. He's only a child. He can still be trained. Any link can be broken."

Alec could hear that Darius was pleading for his life, and yet at the same time he couldn't help but bristle at Darius' description. The last thing he felt like was a child.

"You *agree* with Logan?" Riley shouted over Alec's shoulder. "You *bitch*."

Alec tightened his hold on her as she squirmed wildly. "Let me go, you dork," she grunted, kicking at Alec's shin with surprising accuracy.

Anna looked away from Darius and pierced Alec with a look he couldn't quite understand. Then she transferred her gaze to Riley. "Orders and obedience. Two concepts that continue to be unfamiliar to you, Riley. You cannot proceed with your training until you understand both of these. *Do as you've been instructed.*"

Riley stiffened. Then, before Alec could react, she reached into his pocket, grabbed at the orb. Alec tried to stop her. His hand succeeded in grasping around hers as she pulled it out, the warm smoothness of the orb only touching a fingertip. But it was enough. Darius' hand snaked out of the darkness and clasped over his.

"Now!" Riley shouted in the same instant Darius' message slammed into his mind. Alec had no choice. The power awoke inside him, straining to join in. He added his response to theirs. The light from Riley's orb flashed brilliantly in the confined space, for a moment searing an image of Dean, his hands upturned in defence, his own orb brilliant with power, and Anna, standing still, her hands by her side, into Alec's brain.

In the same instant, someone else was there, hovering at the back of Alec's mind, touching it tentatively, like a caress, but colder and impersonal. Alec shuddered. The sensation began to slip away.

The light faded to nothing, leaving the tunnel even darker than before.

For several seconds Alec could do nothing but blink furiously as tears streamed down his cheeks. On all fours now, he felt cold and disoriented. Wetness was seeping through the material on his knees. He was wrist-deep in a puddle. He couldn't concentrate.

"Get her orb," Darius was saying in the distance.

"What about Dean's?" Riley called back to him. Both of them seemed awfully far away. Alec shook his head to clear it, but the cold, *touching* feeling was growing again. It was getting harder to think.

"Alec, get up." Darius' hand grabbed under his arm and a forceful yank pulled him upward. He swayed. "Here, hold onto this." Someone dropped an orb into his hand. It was all he could do to concentrate on closing his fingers around it.

"Dare, I think they're—" Riley wailed.

"Don't think about it," Darius responded. His voice, too, was muffled.

"We can't just *leave* them."

Darius said something indistinct. Riley gave a sob. Alec

swayed again. His feet were miles away. He couldn't see. What had happened? Why didn't he care?

"Riley, we've got to leave. Now. Otherwise her sacrifice will be for nothing." Darius was urging Riley and tugging at Alec's arm at the same time.

What sacrifice? Alec reached up to rub his eyes and knocked the orb inadvertently against his forehead. Whose orb was this? Irritated and muddled, Alec slipped the orb into his pocket and stopped resisting Darius' tugging. He took a tentative step into the darkness, didn't fall, and took another.

He was pulled up the slope one laborious step after another. Lights came and went, creating faint pools of brightness, then fading to inky darkness once more. He felt as if he were somewhere else, then back again inside his own skin without any indication that he'd moved. He felt anger and triumph, then dizzy and confused. Pictures flashed through his mind. Battles, monsters, mayhem. What was real and what were fantasies? He couldn't concentrate.

The slope became steeper and the air around him warmer. The tunnel outlines took on clarity as the sunlight from the world outside filtered downwards. Alec was mostly oblivious.

By the time they stepped out into the sunshine, he didn't even notice.

Riley leaned against the tunnel entrance and held on for dear life. The stitch in her side was fading now, but she was still gasping. Not that the run up the long tunnel had been overly strenuous.

Killing two people had been.

She couldn't believe it. Darius had ordered her to knock out anyone who opposed them and that he'd guide her. Those were his implicit instructions. He hadn't said anything about *murdering* them.

Nothing had gone right since finding Alec. It had taken ages to find Darius and agree to a plan. She hadn't been able to find the orb he'd hidden, despite his instructions, and she'd had to swipe two from distracted Potentials. Then getting out of the Base separately had nearly failed. It was only a complete lack of attention on the part of the two guards that allowed her to slip past unnoticed. She'd nearly missed the correct tunnel, too. Only after she'd travelled halfway down one and met a party of teenage Potentials, crying and frightened out of their minds, had she realized she was in the wrong place.

Now, despite her best intentions to merely incapacitate her Guardian and Anna, she had bumped off the both of them. It defied belief.

And, as if that wasn't bad enough, Darius was mute with what could only be grief, and, any minute now, the entire Base of Tyon Operatives would realize that a) they'd escaped, b) they had Alec with them, and c) they'd assassinated two colleagues.

31

Could things get any worse?

Riley let go of the rocky outcrop and stepped into the welcome sunlight. The tall grass rippled in a sea of dark green as a brisk ocean breeze whipped across the hilly meadow. On all sides lay the brilliant navy of the ocean. Above, the wide sky was dotted with heavy clouds and wheeling seabirds.

Riley took in a deep, shaky breath of sea air. She hadn't realized how much she'd missed the sun on her skin and the tang of salty air on her tongue. She gave herself a mental shake. There were far more pressing issues at hand. They had to get off this island and hide somewhere. Fast.

But where?

Riley headed out onto the grassy knoll and lumbered up over a cluster of grey, sun-warmed stones. Perched on top, she had an excellent view of the entire island. She twisted around. Other than Darius, kneeling in the grass several metres to her right, and Alec, slumped against the entrance to the dark maw of the tunnel, they were completely alone.

If she squinted, the faintest outline of far-off, haze-shrouded cliffs came into view, across a wide expanse of water.

Riley kicked at the closest rock in frustration. He'd gotten them out of the Base, but so what? He'd warned her that teleporting after fending off an attack would be nearly impossible. Unless there was a ship hidden somewhere along the bottom of what appeared to be cliffs *and* he knew of a safe way down to it, they were stuck there, waiting until the Tyons realized what had happened and came marching up the tunnel to take them into custody. There wasn't even something to block the tunnel entrance.

Some escape. She slammed her hands into her pockets.

Wait a minute. Could *she* move them? She pelted back to Darius and dropped to her knees beside him.

He was almost doubled up, his face pressed into the sweet-smelling grass, his knuckles white as he gripped clumps in a stranglehold. Riley hesitated. What on earth could she possibly say? Tentatively, she reached out, touching his shoulder with only the faintest of pressure. Waves of distress rolled off him like a storm surge.

"Darius," she implored, as gently as possible. "We've got to get off this island."

He jerked his shoulders from her touch and turned his face away.

"Please," she tried again. "They'll be after us any minute."

"I …" Darius couldn't seem to finish. His voice was bleak, as if the light had gone out of his world. Perhaps, considering Anna, it had.

Riley glanced up at the tunnel entrance. Alec was still slumped against the rocky opening, his face pale and drawn. His eyes were oddly blank. He didn't seem to be aware of his surroundings. Heaven only knew what had happened to him, but he was obviously not going to be any help to anyone in his present state. It was up to her.

"Logan will kill all three of us. Is that what you want?" Riley shoved Darius' shoulder. "Get up and get yourself together. You're the only one who can get us off this miserable rock. So do it. Now."

Darius raised his head. His eyes glittered with anger, his skin was white and bloodless. His breath came in rapid, shallow pants. Riley took a step back. He'd never frightened her before, but this man was clearly on the edge.

She took a deep breath and held out her orb. "You have one now. So does Alec. I'll move us. You just need to show me how."

178   Darius glanced once at the orb in her outstretched palm. Without a word, he turned and looked at Alec, then back at her face. Almost snarling, he lunged. He grabbed Riley's arm painfully and pulled her along beside him. Her feet barely touched the ground. He stopped at Alec's inert form. With his free hand he reached down, grabbed

hold of Alec's upper arm and yanked him upright. Alec swayed.

"Get your orbs out," he rasped.

Riley couldn't suppress the shiver as she held her orb in her outstretched palm. Discretion stopped her voice. She had no idea what Darius might do in this state. Warily she watched him plunder Alec's pocket for the orb that Alec seemed too disoriented to find.

"Here," he said, thrusting the small globe into Alec's slack hand. "Hold it. Pay attention."

"What's the matter with him?" Riley asked. Alec's eyes looked like they were crossed. And was he *drooling*?

"Rhozan," Darius barked. "Focus on me, Alec. Nothing else. Nothing but me is real."

What was Rhozan doing to Alec? Would he turn into an Emissary and try to kill them?

"Rhozan can't control us like normal people, that's why he doesn't like us very much," Darius said, answering her unspoken question. "Hold your hand out so our orbs are touching. Like this." He grabbed at Riley when she didn't obey quickly enough.

"Hey," she yelped. His grip was bruising. "I'm doing it."

Darius ignored her. He positioned each hand and orb so that they were touching. The glass clinked together. He pulled Alec's hand close so all three orbs touched each other. "I'm wiped from the fight with Dean, so you'll have to boost this. I'll direct you."

"Where are we going?" Riley asked, but Darius ignored her.

"Alec, pay attention."

Alec squinted and bit his lower lip. The war between 179 what he wanted to do and what was preventing him from complying waged across his face. Riley reached out with her free hand and clasped his shoulder.

"Don't distract him," Darius ordered. "Focus on what you have to do, Riley. Now."

Riley swallowed the angry retort and tried to comply. It wasn't easy. Despite the lessons she'd taken, every time she tried to empty the thoughts from her mind, create the blank slate as she'd been taught, thoughts of Dean intruded. Dean's patience with her endless questions, his exclusive focus on his job, his exasperation with Darius' popularity. A huge lump formed in her throat. Stop it, she berated herself. Don't think of anything.

She felt the first tentative touch of Darius' thoughts the same instant she heard the pounding of feet in the tunnel.

Ohmygawdtheyrecoming.

"Focus," Darius barked. His mental slap was painful, pulling her attention and fear from the approaching Operatives onto him. As required.

Desperately she tried. Purged the fear, purged the thoughts. Blank.

A picture formed inside her mind. A city landscape. Towering office blocks. Glass and steel and impersonal beauty.

Shouts, far away and getting closer. Darius' anger surged.

Ignore it. Focus on the task.

Escape.

Alec's thoughts touched her mind. He was scattered, flitting from one thought to another. A fairground, a tent, a pretty Asian girl, soccer cleats. Riley gasped in amazement at his strength.

Darius fought for control.

Riley squeezed her eyes shut. Leaned into it and followed Darius' lead.

She could feel the power building like a huge electrical charge under her skin. She tried to breathe through it. Add her own strength to his.

"*Finn!*"

Their pursuer's cry was the signal. The dam of energy broke its boundaries.

Then nothing.

A huge farmer's field stretched as far as the eye could see. Row after row of waist-high, yellowed corn stalks rustled in the breeze. On either side, the dense darkness of the forest stood resolutely impenetrable until out of sight. Overhead, the broiling midday sun had the sky to itself. Even the birds were hiding.

Alec wiped the sweat from his brow and anticipated another hour of walking with intense dislike. Who the hell had teleported them into the middle of nowhere? This was some escape. "Keep going?" he asked Darius.

"'Fraid so," Darius replied.

They stepped out into the wide path bordering the field. Tractor treads criss-crossed the earth like gigantic tic-tac-toe games. A tall wooden fence separated the three of them from the field beyond. Darius climbed over and dropped to the other side and carried on walking. Riley followed suit and Alec took up the rear, nearly tearing his hand on a protruding nail. Riley tugged on Darius' sleeve to slow him down.

32

"Do you actually have a destination or are we just going to walk until we collapse?" she asked.

Darius pointed to his right. Off in the distance, the sun-bleached, red tiles of a barn roof were just visible behind a huge grove of trees. There was an old-fashioned windmill not far from it, creaking as it turned slowly in the humid air.

Alec perked up. With a farm came farmers and

food and a method of transportation. Darius would have to use his Tyon power to convince the people who lived there to feed them, hand over the car keys, and maybe, Alec tugged at the collar of his jumpsuit, loan them some decent clothes. He sprinted to catch up with Darius and Riley.

"So, listen," Riley said as she wiped her bangs off her wet forehead with an exasperated sigh, "I've been thinking about a few things and I've got some questions about this organization of yours."

"It's not my organization now." Darius stared straight ahead.

Riley ignored that statement. "We walked right out of the Base. No one even gave us a second glance. What's up with that?"

Good question, Alec thought. He could remember everything clearly until he touched the orb in the tunnel and woke up in the middle of a cornfield an hour ago. The lack of interest the Tyons displayed had been unnerving, if not downright weird.

"Orions and Tholans are the most logical and unimaginative group of beings you'll ever meet." Darius stopped abruptly and reached down. Grasping a handful of leafy shoots, he yanked. A bunch of carrots, thick with dirt, appeared. Darius smiled coldly. "And that's the key to staying one step ahead of them. No imagination. They couldn't begin to believe that we'd try to escape by walking out right in front of everyone. So, when we did, the assumption was that we were supposed to be there, had some purpose. As long as our thoughts didn't betray us, we were fine."

182   "But if Anna or Logan had seen us …" Riley yanked a few carrots out herself before Darius started walking again.

"Sure, they'd have known what we were up to."

Riley paused, frowning. She glanced at Alec for a second as if wondering how to phrase the next question. It was probably the same one on his mind. Why had Dean sent a killing bolt of power at them?

"He didn't want to kill you," Darius sighed. "He was after me."

"I wish you'd stop reading my thoughts," Riley snapped.

"It's faster. There's no reason to pretend now. And besides, your thoughts are so interesting."

"Get out of my head, you creep." Riley smiled, smacking his backside with her carrots. Darius gave a brief laugh.

"So, if Dean were only after you, why'd Anna get blasted?" Alec wondered aloud.

"She didn't repel it. Didn't try. I don't know why." Darius' voice was hard and his jaw set. He started to walk faster towards the farm, as if trying to put some distance between the uncomfortable topic of conversation and his own feelings. For several minutes they walked in silence.

The farm slowly came into view, appearing fully as they climbed over the hedge and dropped down into an untidy yard of overgrown grass and haphazardly planted fruit trees. The clapboard house was a dilapidated affair with three small additions tacked onto the main one-storey building, all in different styles and all in need of repair. The two barns were in much better condition, freshly painted and the grass cut short around them. The larger of the two's main doors were partly open where the raised gravel path met them.

The place was silent except for the buzzing of wasps around the cherry trees, whose bountiful branches were weighed down with bright red fruit. Alec plucked a handful as he passed and popped them into his mouth, savouring the sweetness with satisfaction. Riley caught him wiping cherry juice from his chin and grinned. He tossed her a couple of cherries before grabbing a few more for himself.

There wasn't a car or pickup truck anywhere, nor were there any signs of people. No radio, no music, no voices, no laundry hanging on the clothesline.

183

"Alec, take a look in the house," Darius instructed. "See if anyone's around. Riley, you come with me. There's probably a truck or something in that barn we can borrow."

Alec grimaced but said nothing as he headed towards the back of the house. The back door was unlocked. Alec knocked, waited for a moment, then took a deep breath and swung it open, half expecting someone inside to shout. A cat streaked past his ankles and he nearly jumped out of his skin. When his heart had slowed, he stepped inside.

The flowered curtains had all been pulled closed and the main room was dim and suffused with a sickly greenish hue from the material. It was like submerging himself in a murky pond. The musty air was still. It took a moment before his eyes adjusted to the darkness.

The room was as dilapidated inside as out. A grimy woodstove dominated the corner like a squat spider, and battered furniture, cracked linoleum, and cheap oil paintings indicated that the owners cared little for their surroundings.

They'd left in a hurry, whoever they were. The cupboard doors were still open, and several plastic shopping bags were half-full of canned goods and bags of flour. The small table in the corner still had the remains of their last meal, three places set and three cups of half-drunk tea, scraps of food on three plates.

Alec's foot hit a bowl on the floor and he jumped at the sound. *Muffin*'s dish rattled along the tiles, coming to a stop under the table. Likely that was Muffin making his escape only moments before. Alec was pleased to see, when he opened the fridge, that the electricity was still on but was disappointed to find that the kitchen telephone didn't work.

184

Suddenly, a horrible sensation swamped him. He felt violently sick. Panic gripped his heart. *Riley*. She was badly hurt. Without pausing to consider how he knew it, he ran. The back door slammed on its hinges as he unerringly headed for the smaller barn, instinct guiding his feet.

An old tractor was lying on its side just inside the barn doors. Deathly pale, Riley was pinned underneath it.

"*Darius!*" Alec screamed. He grabbed at the metal frame of the machine and pushed with all his might. The tractor didn't budge.

There had to be a way of lifting the machine off her. His eyes raked the ceiling. No holder for a pulley, no external beam to throw a rope over. No ropes either, he realized with a pang of horror. There was nothing in this barn but the tractor, the raised boards it had been driven up onto and the pile of tools and oil cans the farmer had used to service it.

"Darius!" he yelled again.

He heard the rapid rush of footsteps the instant before he saw him.

"Rhozan attacked her," Alec panted.

Darius dropped to his knees, pulled out his orb and touched Riley's forehead. For an interminable moment he didn't speak. Then he shook his head. "Not Rhozan. An accident. She was trying to reach a kitten under here. I think it wasn't braced properly." He gave the tractor an ugly look.

"I can't lift it off her and there's nothing to make a pulley." Alec shoved against the dirt-splashed machine but it didn't shift a millimetre.

"Forget it, I'll do it." Darius shimmied closer. "The second I have it off her leg, pull her out. Don't waste time. I won't be able to hold it up for long."

"Give me an orb," Alec beseeched desperately. "I can help. You know I can."

"Absolutely not," Darius grunted, his eyes already closed and the power of the orb starting to build. "Don't interrupt me."

"But what if you can't—"

"Shh."

Impotent anger surged through Alec's veins, but he

managed to hold his tongue. He got down on his knees next to Darius and grabbed at Riley's shoulders, trying to slip his hands under her armpits to get a firm enough grip. Beside him, Darius was straining. Sweat beaded his brow. He began to pant. His orb pulsed with brilliant light. The tractor didn't move.

Alec gulped. If he couldn't raise it …

The seconds inched past so slowly they almost seemed to go backwards. The only sounds were Darius' panting and soft grunts of exertion and Alec's rapid breathing. He wiped the sweat from his brow onto his shoulder, poised for the second the tractor lifted and he could–

"Now," Darius grunted.

Pulling with all his might, Alec scrabbled against the gritty wooden floor and slid the unconscious Riley out. The second her feet were clear, the tractor crashed down the last few inches again with a resounding *crack*. Dust flew.

Darius collapsed on the dirt floor beside it, his face bloodless, his shoulders shivering with effort.

"Carry her into the house."

Alec had to strain to hear Darius' whispered instructions. He awkwardly pulled Riley into his arms and straightened up. She was lighter than he expected. Terrified that any movement might cause her more pain, Alec trod carefully over the uneven ground towards the back door of the farmhouse, shoving it open with his hip. Riley didn't stir.

Darius' trudging footfalls followed him. Alec headed straight for the biggest bedroom. The bed looked the most comfortable and was closest to a bathroom. He laid her down on top of the flowered duvet as gently as he could, getting a clear look at the swollen and bloody left ankle as he turned to straighten out her leg. Bile rose to the back of his throat.

"She needs a hospital," Alec said hoarsely as Darius entered the room and leaned for a moment against the doorjamb.

Darius mutely shook his head. His voice was barely audible. "Find some painkillers. Get her some water."

"She needs an operation." Alec pointed at Riley's foot. "Her ankle is probably in a million pieces. She's going to need it pinned."

Darius crawled onto the bed, every movement proclaiming the serious toll mentally lifting the tractor had taken. He curled up next to Riley's ankle, dragged a pillow down from the head of the bed and shoved it under his ear. Pulling his orb out of his pocket, he placed it directly on Riley's bloody ankle and covered it with his own trembling hand. A sickly glow seeped between his fingers.

"This is going to take hours," he panted, his eyes closed. "Make me something to eat, would you?"

Alec didn't bother to lower his voice as he swore. Was he Darius' new servant or what? He left the room, barely squeezing between the dresser and the bed, shoved the door out of his way and headed to the messy kitchen. He flung open the freezer and dumped the half-filled ice tray into a dishtowel, scattering ice all over the counter. More quietly, he eased back into the room and leaned over Riley. She was still not conscious. He took a deep and steadying breath before placing the pack gently around her rapidly swelling limb. Darius didn't open an eye.

A quick check of both medicine cupboards revealed nothing but antacids and bandages. It was only in a drawer in the living room desk, of all places, that he found a small bottle of prescription painkillers. Feeling slightly more accomplished, he filled a glass with water and returned to the sick room.

Riley hadn't moved an inch and Darius, pale and sweating, was still curled up at the foot of the bed working his healing magic.

"Give her one of these when she wakes up," Alec advised. His mom had plied her nursing trade on the family as well as on strangers for as long as he could remember. "One every six hours. These are pretty strong, but they won't do more than dull the pain."

Darius cracked open an eye. One golden brow arched upwards.

Alec shrugged. "Before I gave up kickboxing last year, I was always dislocating or breaking something. I've used these. They make you sick as a dog, but they work." He rattled the little bottle before placing it on the dresser beside the glass of water.

Darius nodded.

"How long's this gonna take?" Alec couldn't tear his eyes from Riley's pale face.

"Couple of days, max," Darius whispered. "Don't worry."

"I'll get you some soup or something," Alec grumbled. Riley looked so weak and helpless. He almost ached with wishing he could help. "I'm warning you, though, I'm a lousy cook."

"Thanks." Darius managed a weak smile before he closed his eyes again and settled against his pillow. The orb's glow strengthened, filling the room with a comforting light.

Alec closed the door behind him.

Darius was too optimistic. It took more than a week for Riley's ankle to heal well enough for her even to put weight on it, and several days after that for her to walk. Day after day, hour after hour, Darius lay weakly beside her, his orb pulsing softly in the curtained twilight, neither of them stirring. For the first two days, Alec was nearly out of his mind with worry. Darius was too weak to do more than sit up for a mouthful of food. Every ounce of energy he had went into healing Riley's ankle.

Other than brief moments to be carried to the bathroom and swallow a painkiller, Riley barely woke up until the third day. Her ankle swelled horribly and the bruising and discolouration went almost halfway to her knee before whatever Darius was doing started to work. Alec spent endless hours lying on the sofa across from the bedroom door or pacing the scuffed wooden floor, listening to her moans and feeling helpless and exposed. He couldn't rest. Every sound seemed excessively loud and a dozen times a night he was sure armed troops were driving up the lane. Several times helicopters *whumped* overhead, and the second afternoon the endless drone of heavy trucks had lasted until darkness. But his worst fears did not come to pass. Riley's ankle began to heal, Darius slowly re-gathered his strength and no one came banging on the door, guns drawn.

Once Darius was on his feet, the anger simmering beneath Alec's skin started to erupt with increasing frequency. Every worrisome issue he'd tried to keep out of his thoughts vied for space in his already crowded mind: his brother was missing; his parents were in danger; he had a dangerous power burning beneath his skin he had no idea how to control; Rhozan wanted him.

Why weren't they *doing* something?

He began having nightmares again, the same ones that had started the night of his concussion. He knew it was stupid not to tell someone, but the last thing he wanted was Riley thinking he was a child.

Once Riley was over the worst of her injury, Darius insisted that they both continue the lessons they'd begun at Home Base. Darius still refused Alec direct access to an orb, telling him that Rhozan would feel the connection and instantly know where they were. What was even more annoying was that, despite their hours of lessons together, Riley was just as indifferent to him as she had been when they first met. The second Darius indicated the lesson was over, she'd snatch her hand away and hop one-footed to the rocking chair, gingerly raising her swollen ankle to the footrest and sighing with profound relief. She seldom talked to him in anything but scathing tones and rarely caught his eye. What had he done to her to make her treat him like he had some kind of contagious disease, anyway?

He started spending more and more time outside, digging up vegetables, mowing the lawn, anything to be physically exhausted at the end of the day. He never saw anyone during his labours, only the occasional plane cutting its way through the clouds or the rumble of a distant truck that gave him any reassurance the world outside the farm was still there. He'd turned to the television for comfort but the stupid thing wouldn't work, and even after hours of fiddling with its innards, he couldn't make it produce a picture worth looking at. He'd started listening to the radio whenever indoors.

One morning, Darius sprawled on the cushions next to Alec and rested his feet on the armrest. He clasped his fingers together behind his head and stared at the plastered ceiling while the news program time signal chimed.

With the sound of the announcer's voice, Riley hobbled in from the kitchen. She dropped into the rocking chair by the wood stove and started to creak back and forth. Alec tried to ignore her.

"… And in devastating news from the East Coast where the violence, so pervasive in Ontario, has started to rise, reports indicate that weapons' fire from our own naval forces frigates hit the downtown early this morning. A spokesperson for the Canadian navy issued a brief statement this morning: 'Unauthorized use of weaponry by several military personnel resulted in torpedo fire from the HMCS *St. John's* at oh-five-twenty-eight this morning. Approximately six torpedoes were launched towards the downtown Halifax area, resulting in serious damage and multiple casualties. The perpetrators have been apprehended and a full military investigation is underway.' Few details are available. At the moment, we know that several buildings in the business area of Halifax are on fire and the premier has declared a state of emergency. Citizens are urged to—"

Darius shut off the radio with a sharp twist of his wrist. He glanced at Riley. She was pale and unmoving in the rocking chair, her eyes staring straight ahead. It was only when Darius crossed over the floral carpet and sank to his knees in front of Riley, pulling her hands into his, that Alec made the connection.

"Your house is out in the country. I'm sure your dad is fine," Darius said.

"The hospital is downtown." Her voice trembled. "He's often there all night."

"They would have said if the hospital had been hit," Darius said. "Don't grieve about something you don't know for certain."

Riley said nothing. She turned to Alec. For a second, her gaze seemed to connect with his, but the pain reflected in her dark blue eyes was too much. He dropped his gaze to his knees and when he'd gathered the resources to face her again, she was already on her feet.

"I think I'll go to bed," she said. "I'm tired."

"It's lunchtime," Alec blurted. "You just got up."

Riley didn't even look in his direction. Stiff-backed, she headed for her bedroom.

Darius gave Alec a pointed look. "She's pretty upset," he said.

"Yeah, no kidding," Alec muttered.

"She could use a bit of human kindness," Darius suggested.

"Couldn't we all," Alec said.

Darius gave an impatient sigh. "Alec, why don't you—"

Alec bounded off the sofa, leaving Darius' question hanging in the air. He carried his plate to the kitchen and dropped it in the sink. He was not going to follow Riley into her room and put his arm around her. Wild horses couldn't drag him in there and leave him open to one of her scathing comments.

Darius followed him and leaned against the doorway to

the kitchen. Alec could feel his eyes burning into his shoulders, but he made a pretence of getting ready to wash the dishes.

"You constantly wonder how to get women to find you attractive, and yet, a golden opportunity lands in your lap and you run in the opposite direction. For heaven's sake, Alec, how do you expect to gain any sort of sexual experience with women, outside of the Internet, if you're afraid to be in the same room?"

Alec viciously squirted the liquid soap into the sink.

"She's in there crying."

Alec turned on the water with a jerk of his wrist.

"She's desperately hoping you come in to check on her."

Alec swirled the water ferociously to create bubbles.

"She likes both of us. You could tip her affections in your favour with one easy move, Alec."

There was a long silence while Alec furiously scrubbed the plates and cups from lunch and breakfast. Finally, he heard Darius' footsteps back into the living room.

He heard the soft knock on Riley's door a moment later. A searing stab of jealousy burned his chest before he threw the dishcloth into the sink and stormed outside to do a thousand push-ups.

If they didn't leave the farmhouse soon, he was going to go right out of his mind. Every minute that passed was another minute closer to Rhozan finding his parents and killing them. Every minute close to Riley was torture trying to guard his tongue from spilling how he felt. Every minute practicing a skill he wasn't actually allowed to do, but somehow had to master, was driving him up the wall. If Darius didn't let them start off for Toronto by tomorrow morning, Alec decided, he was going to go himself.

And no one was going to stop him.

Riley switched off the radio and lay back on the bed, a sick feeling gurgling around in her stomach, like it was exam time and she'd completely forgotten to study. Except worse.

The entire radio broadcast was now taken over with constant updates of road closures, new rules of conduct, military crackdowns and edicts by the prime minister, all amounting to a picture of mass hysteria and confusion. Rhozan was doing a great job.

Riley rolled onto her side and stared blankly at the panelled wall opposite. It was so stupid, just staying here, practicing with the orbs, and monitoring the outside world as it went down the toilet. Alec was right. They should be *doing* something.

33

Alec. She was *not* going to think about him. He was a kid. She was not. End of story. Darius, on the other hand, was older, experienced and the most attractive man she'd ever met. As if he were reading her thoughts again, the bedroom door swung open and Darius poked his head through. "You want to do something? Then get up and grab something to wear out of the closet. We're leaving."

Alec was standing by the bay window, his arms crossed and a mutinous expression plastered across his face when she walked in. Darius was in the kitchen pulling cans down from the cupboard and dropping them into a canvas rucksack.

"Where exactly are we going?" she asked the room in general.

"Toronto," Darius replied. He pulled the drawstrings tight on the bag and placed it on the counter before rooting in the next cupboard.

"Walking?" Riley scoffed.

"Actually, we are." Darius pulled out a Tetra Pak of milk from the pantry and squinted at the best-before date.

"You've got to be kidding. You're back to normal, aren't you? Can't you just," she snapped her fingers, "take us there?"

"Have I significantly regenerated my power? Mostly. Am I going to risk setting off a huge signal to Rhozan that we're on our way? Not likely. We're sneaking up on him, not taking out an advertisement that we're coming."

This didn't make sense. They were at least a couple of hundred kilometres from their destination. It would take weeks to walk that far, never mind probably wrecking her ankle completely. Alec's parents were sure to be dead by then. Riley glanced over at Alec's stiff back. Obviously he'd come to the same conclusion.

"We're not walking the entire distance, at least I hope not," Darius said. "This farm isn't too far from a village. There's a map in the desk drawer over there. I figure there will be some mode of transportation we can avail ourselves of, and hasten the journey significantly."

Riley translated. "You want us to steal a car."

"Yup."

"Are you out of your mind? Haven't you heard a word on the radio? The military is everywhere. The penalty for theft is immediate incarceration. There are prison camps being set up all over the place to deal with looters and arsonists. And you want us to steal a car?"

"Yup."

"You've lost your marbles."

"We have no choice. I cannot use Tyon power to bring us closer to Alec's apartment. Rhozan will follow the energy signature and be waiting when we materialize. We can't stay here. Eventually, the minimal power we're using by touching the orbs will be noticed, if it hasn't been already, and Rhozan will show up. Haven't you heard the helicopters overhead? Any worries who might be inhabiting the pilot, hmm?"

Riley hadn't given a thought to the idea of Rhozan using soldiers as Emissaries, but now that she did, she shuddered. There were thousands of military personnel tramping across Southern Ontario and all of them armed. "But we have orbs and he's afraid of them, isn't he?"

Darius carried his knapsack and a plastic bag with the last of the supplies into the living room. "Orbs won't be much good if thirty soldiers show up at the door with automatic weapons, Riley. Sure, we think the Others fear the orbs and that's why they're so focused on destroying anyone who can use one, but we're not a hundred percent sure."

Alec said nothing. He merely brushed past her and stomped into the bedroom he shared with Darius, slamming the door behind him.

"What's with him?" Riley stared at the closed door. Alec had been grouching all week about getting a move on and heading out to rescue his family. Now that they were, he was in a huff. And they thought *girls* were hard to understand.

No one spoke as they tramped down the rutted driveway to the dirt road beyond. The sun was out and the air already warming uncomfortably. A breeze caressed the upmost branches, emitting a faint moaning sound, but didn't blow low enough to give any respite from the humidity. Riley wiped the sweat off her brow and tried to ignore her ankle. The unpaved road was more uneven than it looked and several times she'd slipped. Though she'd not fallen, it was enough to jar her newly knitted bones.

Before lunchtime, they found a pickup truck parked haphazardly in the front garden of an A-framed cottage with gingerbread trim. Darius crept forward to peer in through the ground floor window. He straightened up and walked back to them, a look of disgust on his face.

"What?" Riley asked.

"An example of why gun control is so vital to any country," Darius replied curtly. Alec gave a considering glance at the house, but Darius stopped him before he'd taken a step. "Don't go looking in the windows, Alec."

"Why not?"

"Because this is not one of your video games. There are real people in there who have really blown each other's heads off, and despite your belief that you're totally cool with death in a million forms, I'm assuring you that reality is much worse than pretend." Darius squinted at the standard gearshift with mild concern. "Can you drive this, Riley?"

"If it has wheels and an engine, I can drive it." Eyes carefully avoiding the house, she walked around to the driver's side and clambered up into the dirty cab. She reached up and pulled the keys down from the visor with a little smile. Honestly, what idiots left the keys in their truck?

"I can drive, too," Alec muttered. He was giving the house an intent stare, as if weighing the distance to the window and Darius' ability to stop him.

"Unfortunately, you're underage. Riley isn't. She's also a much better liar than you are and will probably be able to convince any military checkpoint we come across that this is indeed her truck and she has every right to drive it."

196 Riley startled. Twisting the truth so it would fit her needs was a lot more accurate.

"You just like her more." Alec turned on Darius. His cheeks were red and his eyes blazing. "That's the reason you butter her up all the time. You want to get in her–"

Smack.

Darius dropped his hand and stood entirely still. Alec raised his hand, almost unbelievingly, to his cheek.

"Don't *ever* suggest that I would take advantage of Riley," Darius said in a low and cutting voice. "I am now her Guardian and there are rules in place for any relationship between us that I could *never* break. If I praise her efforts, it is because, unlike you, she recognizes the utmost seriousness of our situation and has tried her best to learn what I'm teaching. You, on the other hand, still seem to think this is a game. It's not, Alec. It's real. Get your head out of your butt and focus. We're all going to die unless you learn to control the power inside you. Got that?"

Riley swallowed. What did Darius mean that their lives were dependent on Alec?

Alec took a step backwards. His eyes were blazing and his hands balled into fists. "Sometimes," he growled, "I hate you."

"Yes, I'm very aware of it. But what you fail to realize is that *that* is exactly what Rhozan is looking for. You're handing him his victory on a plate, Alec."

"What're you talking about? I'm trying to fight him," Alec yelled.

"Are you?" Darius took a step closer. "Really? You're in control of yourself, keeping your temper curbed, focusing on the task at hand? Or, are you so self-centred that your misery spills out of you like poison, and you burn with jealousy and hatred. Even though Anna warned you that your temper could destroy everything. Even though Logan planned to kill you because of it?" He took another step and Alec backed away. "Hatred, envy, self-pity – everything Rhozan wants and needs. How in the world will you fight him, Alec, when everything you think and feel feeds him and makes him stronger?"

Nearly an entire minute passed in tense silence before Alec stammered, "It's not, I mean, we won't. It's not up to me."

"It is." Darius drew himself up to his full height. Riley couldn't see his face, but his words had never been so hard. "It always has been. Grow up, Alec."

There was dead silence. Alec's fists tightened. His jaw clenched. Several heartbeats passed. Then he turned on his heel and faced the house. Riley felt her own eyes welling up as waves of his emotions slammed into her, and she turned away to focus on the mailbox at the end of the drive. By the time her vision cleared, Alec had jumped up into the cab. Wordlessly, he fastened his seatbelt before crossing his arms and staring out the windshield.

Darius slammed the door shut behind him and did up his own seatbelt as Riley turned over the engine and engaged first gear. Smiling slightly, she turned the truck around and headed back to the dirt road.

The next several hours passed without incident. Darius consulted a map found in the glove compartment and encouraged Riley to stay off the main thoroughfares. Alec slumped between them, sulking and silent. They passed through several small towns but saw very few people. Whoever was still around seemed to be obeying the government's orders to stay out of sight.

It was Riley who forced an eventual halt. Darius suggested stopping at the side of the road, but Riley was not squatting in the bushes while Alec laughed. They'd find a donut shop with a proper bathroom. There was one every two kilometres in Canada, she argued. Sure enough, they came across one within minutes. There were several cars in the parking lot, but no one in the store. And no donuts, either.

Riley had to move garbage out of her way to get into the ladies' room. The water was still running but the lights were broken. Swallowing her embarrassment, she left the door open a crack so she could see.

She was just washing her hands when she heard the noise. Her stomach dropped to her knees. Had Darius changed his mind and followed her in? As quietly as possible, she turned off the water and wiped her hands on her borrowed jeans. She peeked out.

Dressed in worn coveralls with "Al" embroidered on the breast pocket, the man wasn't much taller than Riley, but several times wider. Even from this distance, Riley could see his empty eyes. Prickles sprang to life all over her body. An Emissary.

Riley's hand plunged into her pocket for her orb. The only way out was straight past him.

She could hear his laboured wheezes. Maybe he'll keel over from a heart attack, she thought as she silently pulled the door closed and waited in the dark, heartbeats almost choking her. Nothing happened for ages. A sudden crash, somewhere near the kitchen, made her jump back from the door.

Truck.

The thought arrived suddenly. It took a moment to realize that Darius was sending instructions. Opening the door a crack, she peered out. The shop appeared empty. Pulling the door open wider, she tiptoed out into the tiny hall and leaned against the wall, looking around the corner as far as possible.

No one.

The store had two exit doors. If she headed for the more direct path to their vehicle, it meant crossing the wide expanse of the floor and being in direct view of anyone hiding in the food preparation area. If she chose the closer option, she'd have to run outside around the shop to reach the truck.

Riley bit her lip. Both choices sucked. She chose the exit closer to the truck.

Gathering her courage, she sprinted across the floor and dove at the door, jamming the unlocking bar down with both hands and pressing hard. It didn't move. She pressed again and again, but the door refused to open. Someone, and no need to guess who, had broken the locking mechanism.

Riley whirled around just as the Emissary approached the serving counter.

"Get away from me!" she shouted, yanking as hard as she could at the door. Shaking, she pulled out her orb and held it up so he could see it.

"I have a message for you," Al said.

"I have nothing to say to you," she panted. *Hurry up, Darius.*

"Rhozan wishes the suffering of this people to end." The monotone voice was incongruous with the little man and Riley wasn't sure if she was hearing his voice or Rhozan's. Did alien field marshals speak of themselves in the third person?

"Really? He's caused all this grief, you ass. He's *enjoying* it."

Al cocked his head to one side, as if listening to a voice far away. "Yes. The time for pretense is over."

Riley's heart hammered and doubled its speed. *That* was Rhozan. "So, what do you really want?" She had to find out the plan before Darius turned up and killed the little weasel. What did Rhozan want with Alec?

"The one who gave me access to this world," Al continued.

"And that would be who, exactly?"

"This one."

The sensation hit her broadside. Disoriented, she let go of the door handle. Clutching her head in her hands, she fought to repel the overwhelming sensation of Alec from her mind. Without realizing what she was doing, she tightened her grip on her orb and mentally *pushed* the Emissary away. There was a shuffling noise. Riley struggled to open her eyes. The Emissary had backed behind the counter.

"Drop the orb, Potential," Al croaked. "You do not have the power to fight me."

Riley held the orb out in front of her like a shield. *Hurry up, Darius.* "And what about the rest of us?" she croaked.

"Suffering. Hatred. Death."

"Oh, like that's a great choice."

"Give me Alec and I will spare your life."

"Sure you will," Riley said, leaning back against the door. "I bet you'll even promise."

There was a pause. Riley could almost sense Rhozan searching for the meaning of her words.

"I promise. Your life for Alec's."

She was about to make a scathing reply when Darius bounded into the room from behind the kitchen and knocked the Emissary to the ground in a flying tackle that would have won him awards in the CFL. Al hit the filthy ground with a pathetic grunt and was unconscious by the time Darius had landed the second blow. Riley ran over and grabbed at his arm to stop him from killing the man.

"He's out already," she shouted.

Heaving with exertion, Darius yanked his arm out of her hands and climbed off the Emissary's body. He brushed himself off. "Making bargains?" he snarled.

"Are you mental?" she shouted back. "As if."

"I heard," Darius began, pointing at the Emissary and uncharacteristically struggling for words, "what you said."

Anger flooded her. Without pause she stepped forward and grabbed hold of his shirt collar, pulling him almost off balance. "You absolute, total, insufferable *creep*," she exploded. "I'd never bargain for Alec's life. Ever. I was getting our enemy's plans, numbskull."

For a taut moment, she stared at him, anger and hurt pounding beneath her skin and mirrored in his eyes. She literally felt the rage drain from his body. "Sorry," he said. He reached up and covered her smaller hands with his. "I'm not thinking straight. Guess I'm not as regenerated as I thought. Forgive me?" He pulled her into his embrace and rested his lips against her forehead.

Alec ran into the kitchen and skidded to a halt. "I got rid of the woman but there are more," he gasped.

Riley abruptly wrenched her hands out of Darius'. She stepped back, avoiding Alec's narrowing eyes.

"Front or back?" Darius asked as he let her go.

"Back."

They spilled into the parking lot. Darius came to a screeching halt within a couple of steps and Riley barrelled into him. She looked around in horror. There were at least six of them at first glance, vacant-eyed, slack-jawed and armed with sticks and bottles. Alec shoved her between himself and Darius. Alec kept his back against her. She could feel him panting.

"Use your orb," Riley instructed. "Knock them out."

"And have Rhozan know exactly where we are and what we're up to? No thanks." Darius squared his shoulders. "I've managed to keep the power signal low enough to stay under the radar for the last two weeks. I'm not blowing that now, if I can help it."

"I think Rhozan knows we're—"

Darius interrupted. "How many do you think you could take, Alec?"

"Don't be ridiculous," Riley hissed. "He'll be killed."

"I'll take the goon with the Metallica shirt and the little one with the Mohawk. You keep the others busy until I've knocked them out." Alec flexed his muscles.

"No," Riley almost shouted.

"Head for the truck, Riley," Darius whispered. "We'll hold them off. Get it started and pick us up."

Riley caught sight of the half smile on his face and realized it was too late. She twisted around to see the same smile mirrored on Alec. "Oh for Pete's sake."

It was over in minutes. Darius bowled over three women in one flying tackle while Alec rushed the pot-bellied, heavy metal aficionado and knocked him out with a spinning hook kick to the temple that was close to poetry in motion. Riley mentally picked her jaw up off the ground as Alec parried, punched and kicked two more into submission. Where on earth had he learned that?

The truck. Riley gave herself a little shake and ran. She quickly shimmied into the driver's seat. The engine roared to life. Both Alec and Darius bolted from the melee and dove for the front seat. The instant the door slammed, Riley put the pickup into reverse and backed out of the parking spot, tires burning against asphalt. She ignored the high fives and whoops of bravado as she watched the last two Emissaries stumble out of the parking lot after them and disappear in a cloud of dust.

"Rhozan knows where we are now," she said once the other two had stopped congratulating each other.

Darius instantly sobered. "Keep your hands off your orbs from now on. He'll guess where we're heading but if we stay under his radar, we've got a chance of getting there without him knowing."

"He can't follow us without the orb signal?" Alec asked. He was rubbing the red and rapidly swelling knuckles of his right hand.

Darius gave a shrug. "I hope so."

There didn't seem to be anything to say to that. Riley bit the inside of her lip and concentrated on her driving.

It took several hours to get to the outskirts of Toronto. Abandoned cars and debris of all sorts littered the roadways. There wasn't a soul for miles. Nothing moved. As she slowed to steer around the carcass of a transport truck, Riley asked, "What are we going to do when we get to Alec's place? What if they don't want to come with us?"

"They will," Alec said. "I'll make them."

"You won't," Darius interrupted.

Alec twisted around in his seat. "Whaddya mean? We're going to save my parents. That's why we're going back to my place."

"Alec, you don't seem to understand this," Darius said

slowly, enunciating each word as if it pained him. "We can't just grab your parents and run. Where would we go? Rhozan is invading this world. He's turning the people against each other and they're doing the job for him. Look around you. This city is almost dead. Soon the entire country will be affected. Then the continent. Eventually, there will be no place to run."

"So, what are you saying? We're leaving my mom to die in some riot? Forget it, Darius. No way."

"Standing idly by while someone you love is in danger isn't in your DNA." Darius turned to give Riley a quick glance as he spoke. "We have two choices."

There was silence as the truck again slowed down to avoid a burned-out mail truck.

"So?" Alec challenged. "What are they?"

"One," Darius said, raising a finger into the air, "we keep running and hope we can hold out for as long as possible. Make for some uninhabited South Seas island and wait for Rhozan to come for us. Because he will. Riley and I both know it." He paused.

"Or two," Alec prompted.

"Or two, you take on Rhozan and close the rips."

For several seconds, Alec couldn't believe his ears. *Was he kidding?*

Riley reached over and shoved her hand under his chin, pushing his jaw back into place. "Flycatcher," she laughed, turning on the indicator light to change lanes, despite the complete lack of traffic.

Alec twisted around in his seat until the seatbelt was nearly strangling him. "I can't take on Rhozan."

Darius crossed his arms. He raised one eyebrow. "Got a better idea?"

"You're crazy. The guy's an alien. With like, superpowers. I'm just, uh, me."

"Sounds like your standard summer blockbuster, Alec. He may be the alien, but you have the home-world advantage. And as for powers, why do you think he wants *you?*"

Alec scrambled for something to say. "Riley, help me out here."

"No can do," Riley said. "Darius is right. Rhozan is after you. We won't be able to run forever."

"Yeah, but …" Alec couldn't believe this. "How do you know for sure?"

"He told me." She didn't take her eyes off the road.

"Who?"

"Rhozan."

"*What?*"

"'Fraid you're not the only one with connections, bud," Riley said. "'Al' was pretty clear about that back at the donut shop. Rhozan wants you to join him for world dominance et cetera, et cetera. I said you'd pass."

Alec laid his head back against the seat and closed his eyes. She was scared, too. He heard it in her voice and that rather pleased him. Maybe because it didn't make him feel so alone.

"Alec, we're with you in this," Darius said quietly.

"For sure," Riley chimed in. "I mean, it's not as if you're capable of winning without us, or anything."

"Thanks for the vote of confidence." He felt his lips turn up. He caught Riley's return grin out of the corner of his eye. "So just how am I supposed to stop him? Ask nicely? Threaten him with a 'time-out'?"

Riley giggled.

Even Darius cracked a smile. "What do we know about Rhozan? He's conquered other planets. He feeds off negative emotions. He can't control our minds. He's afraid of orbs. He's made contact through Alec's mind and is aware of what Alec is."

"We're screwed," Riley summarized.

"No, we're not." Darius leaned forward, giving her a pointed look. "There's something in that we can use. Some weakness we can exploit. I've been thinking it over, and–" He didn't get to finish as they drove into airspace that had radio reception. The car radio suddenly changed from quiet static to a man's frantic voice.

"Stop here," Alec ordered.

Riley slammed on the brakes and the pickup skidded to a halt.

"… And all highways are now closed, as of four o'clock today. Martial law has been declared. We repeat, all citizens are to remain home. Stay off the streets. Stay with your families …"

The signal faded. Riley turned the channel.

"Hey." Alec lurched forward. "That was important."

"Alec, it was *Chinese*. How the hell are you understanding all these languages?"

"I'm not, I'm just—" Alec stammered. He rubbed the back of his head, puzzled.

"You're in the right vicinity, just a bit lower and to your right," Darius advised.

"Huh?"

"The implant. That's its location." Darius pursed his lips at Alec's blank expression. "When you awoke in Med Ops, your head hurt, didn't it? Just there."

Alec took in a sharp breath as the memory resurfaced. "They put something in me?" he gasped, not sure whether to be thrilled or horrified or both.

"All Operatives have the implant." Darius was nonchalant. "It's a universal translator. Haven't you ever wondered how we know what everyone is saying? Think I spent about a hundred years boning up on Earth languages before taking this assignment?"

Alec paused. Actually, the thought hadn't occurred to him at all. He glanced at Riley and was surprised to see her mutinous expression.

"What's your problem?" he asked.

"I didn't get one," she snapped. "What's the matter, wasn't I good enough?"

"Potentials are usually implanted after they've been screened for aptitude and ability. We hadn't enough time to test all the Potentials, there was so much else going on. Alec was already unconscious and they had his scans available." He gave Alec a half-apologetic look. "We'd been monitoring you for a while." He turned back to Riley. "Sounds like we're in the middle of a curfew, Riley. Don't be surprised if we meet an armed convoy and they try to send us back."

"You mean the military? With guns and stuff?"

"Yup."

"What do we do if they do?" She stared straight ahead.

"Hope they're out of ammunition," Alec muttered.

Alec stared through the window without seeing anything. How on earth would he take on Rhozan and win? It was stupid, not to mention impossible. There had to be another solution.

"Cripes, speak of the Devil," Riley muttered under her breath. Up ahead, the highway narrowed as plywood barricades funnelled the several lanes into one. Numerous camouflage-coloured trucks and one tank were positioned at the end of the road. Soldiers were lined up behind the trucks, guns positioned and ready to fire. "Should I turn around?"

"Slow to a crawl," Darius advised Riley. "Don't do anything that spooks them."

"As if," Riley replied.

"And let me do the talking."

"Sure thing," she said as she brought the pickup to a complete stop.

A soldier carrying an assault rifle walked out from the barricade and waved at them. With the barrel pointed directly at the windshield, the soldier advanced.

"Put your hands in the air," Darius said quietly.

"I think the uniform makes her look fat," Riley muttered.

"Shut up," Alec whispered. He couldn't tear his eyes away from the soldier's rifle.

"Get out of the car!" the soldier yelled. "Keep your hands up at all times. Throw any weapons onto the ground."

Riley leaned out the window. "Can I turn the engine off?" she shouted.

The soldier nodded and Riley threw the gear into park and cut the engine.

"Take your time getting out," Darius advised. "No sudden movements."

Alec took a steadying breath, undid his seatbelt and stepped out into the stifling heat. He kept his hands up around his ears and hoped that the soldier couldn't see him shaking. All he could see was the ugly, open snout of the gun and it was way too close for comfort.

"On the ground," the soldier shouted, waving her weapon.

Alec couldn't hear Riley's comment, but he was sure it was scornful. He wished her nervousness didn't manifest itself as vitriol. He pulled the sleeves of his shirt over his hands, trying to protect the skin, and carefully lowered himself to the scorching concrete, keeping the soldier in sight. Whatever she was going to do, he wanted to see it coming.

He tensed as heavy, black boots surrounded him and the hot barrel of a gun pressed into the back of his neck. Harsh hands patted him down and he swallowed the retort on the tip of his tongue.

"Who are you and where are you going?" the female soldier demanded. Her eyes were dark and glittering. A sudden fear surged through Alec. Was she an Emissary?

"My name is Darius Finn," Darius began, his voice filled with Tyon *willingness*. "We'd been travelling across country when we heard the news about what is happening here. Alec's parents are frantic to be reunited with him. We must be allowed to pass."

Darius' words were *so* persuasive. The soldiers' faces gradually changed with each uttered word, from cold impersonality to uncertainty.

"Please let us pass. We are of no danger to you or any

person living within your boundaries. We wish to leave you in peace."

The soldiers holding Darius slackened their hold. The ones holding Riley let go of her completely. Riley caught Alec's eye and winked.

The soldier in charge seemed to be immune. "No one is allowed in or out of the city limits. The curfew remains in place. We cannot let you past."

"We *must* pass through. We are of no consequence. *Please* forget you have seen us," Darius urged.

The hands fell from Alec's body completely. Only the captain of the squad kept her gun, and her eyes, hard and unwavering, levelled at his chest.

Ever so slowly, Darius slipped his hand into his pocket. Alec fought not to smile.

"Let us pass," Darius said. The Tyon power was magnified ten times with his hand on his orb. Immediately all the soldiers backed up several steps. Two even started to walk back to their trucks as if they had already forgotten their presence. "Put your gun down," Darius directed his instructions towards the captain. "*Forget you met us.*"

The captain blinked several times. Her gun dropped to her side. Several of her comrades followed suit. The captain turned to follow them.

"We're not going to get very far in this pickup," Riley said as soon as the soldiers were out of earshot.

"Uh-huh," Darius nodded.

"One of those army trucks would attract a lot less attention, if there are more soldiers inside, and I bet there are," Riley continued.

"Uh-huh."

"So, I think you should ask really nicely and see if they'll let you borrow one."

Darius smiled. "You don't ask for much, do you?"

"If you don't ask, you don't get," Riley reminded him with a tight smile. "We're going to need every advantage. I'd take the tank if it had air conditioning."

Darius and Riley ducked under the barricade unchallenged and Alec followed. He found himself giving the tank a wide berth. He'd seen hundreds in his on-line games and he was pretty familiar with them as artillery, but playing pretend had never relayed just how fearsome a weapon they were. Darius headed directly for the smaller truck. He stopped at the cab and peered up at the driver, a young man who'd barely begun to shave and looked like he'd rather be anywhere else.

"I need your truck," Darius said with a gentle, disarming grin.

"Uh," the boy soldier moaned. His eyes widened. His jaw went slack.

"Let us have your truck," Riley said pleasantly.

A frisson rolled down Alec's back. Where had she learned to do *that*?

The soldier handed the keys out the window.

"Make sure you stop anyone trying to come after us," Riley added as she pulled the door open and put one foot up onto the step. She leaned over his nametag. "Do anything you have to, Jeff."

From the other side, Alec climbed up into the stifling heat of the truck's cab. Fuzzy dice swung from the rearview mirror. Darius got in beside him and closed the door.

"Leave, before he changes his mind," Darius advised.

"He'll throw himself in front of a train before he lets anyone come after us," Riley said smugly as Jeff walked away as fast as his legs would take him. "You know it."

"And *you* know that wasn't necessary. Don't let this power corrupt you, Riley. We have to be kind to lesser beings, not play with them. With great power comes great responsibility."

"Yeah, yeah, Superman," Riley muttered as she put the truck into gear.

"Spiderman, know-it-all," Alec corrected.

211

Riley stuck her nose in the air and steered the lumbering vehicle down the wide multi-lane highway. They manoeuvred carefully around the worst of the debris and crunched over the smaller stuff that couldn't be missed. They passed under multiple overpasses, all empty of life. It was the eeriest thing Alec had ever seen. A post-apocalyptic world, straight from the games he loved to play. Except this was real. And, somewhere inside this hell, his mom was hiding.

Riley pulled off the highway and entered the city. It was late afternoon and the trip, which normally would take forty minutes, had stretched into hours. There had been several other checkpoints to pass through and several detours because of burned-out vehicles blocking the road. So far they hadn't found anything to eat: every fast food joint was either empty or destroyed. Alec was getting progressively grumpier with every minute and even Darius' stomach was growling. They ought to rest too, she decided, before engaging in any combat with Rhozan.

36

She steered the truck down the wide thoroughfare that changed from industrial to retail in a matter of a couple of blocks. She slowed as she spotted a possibility: a pizza joint on the other side of the street. A latticed metal blind still completely covered both the window and the door. Riley made a U-turn and pulled up onto the sidewalk, leaving minimal space between the side of the truck and the storefront. She cut the engine. Darius hopped out and jimmied the padlock open with a bit of wire.

Inside, the little take-out was in surprisingly good shape. The smell of yeast and pepperoni still clung to the air. Riley washed her hands and splashed water over her face at the kitchen sink. The humidity was stifling. Not wanting to overload any circuits, Riley turned on the ovens, left the air conditioning alone and forced herself to ignore the heat. She ordered Darius to take a seat in the front room and keep an eye out for trouble. She gave him a cold can of cola and a clean glass and gave a rueful shake of her head at his overly pleased expression.

She and Alec worked side-by-side, rolling out the dough that was in the freezer until it had thawed enough to form the correct shape. Alec had proven himself unacceptably dangerous with the vegetable peeler, so she gave him the bacon to fry.

She watched him out of the corner of her eye. The way his hair flopped over his forehead and he kept having to push it back with the back of his hand was kind of endearing. She watched him eyeing the telephone as he finished with the meat and sprinkled the last generous handful of cheese over what she had labelled "his pizza."

"Thinking of calling your folks?"

Alec picked up his overloaded extra-extra large and slid it easily into the wide-mouthed oven. He closed the door and shrugged. "As soon as we find one that works."

"Better ask Darius first. Just in case."

"In case what? I doubt Rhozan's listening in."

"You can't be sure. You don't know what Rhozan's capable of."

"Do you?"

"Well no. I don't," Riley conceded. Why did every conversation with this boy turn into an argument?

"Maybe you ought to phone your own parents. Won't they be worried about you?"

Riley turned away and grabbed at a cloth. She began wiping down the counter. "My dad'll be at the hospital. There're probably lots of injured people flooding the wards and every doctor and nurse will be on duty. He'll be too busy to worry about me."

Alec stood in her way, blocking her from rinsing out the cloth under the faucet. "What about your mom?"

"Move, Alec." Riley gave him a little shove. It was

like shoving a mountain. She took a shocked step back as something fluttered inside her and slipped away.

"You do have a mom, don't you?" he pushed.

"Yes, I do. She just isn't around."

"Where is she?"

"Africa," Riley snapped. "Somewhere in Africa. Doing relief work. I don't know where, exactly. It's been at least five months since I've had a letter."

"Whoa," Alec breathed. "I'm sorry."

Riley blinked back the tears that threatened. She wished she didn't always start to cry when she thought about her mom; it had been four years since she'd left. Surely it shouldn't still hurt so much?

She was about to turn away when Alec's arms encircled her and he pulled her into a warm and rather awkward hug. He rested his chin on the top of her head. For a long moment, Riley didn't pull away. It felt so comfortable, so comforting and so *right*.

Good grief, what on earth was she doing? He was just a *kid*.

Gathering all her resolve, she pushed her hands against his chest, shoving him away. "Get off me," she snapped, her face flooding with a telltale burning.

"Jeez, no need to take a fit," Alec snapped back, his own cheeks now on fire.

"If I wanted to be mauled by some kid, I'd ask for it." The words were out of her mouth before she could stop herself. "Keep your damn hands off me from now on, you hear me? Stick to babies your own age." She whirled around, catching a glimpse of his stricken face, and ran out of the room.

Alec didn't follow.

Darius was standing at the side of the window, staring out past the bulk of the truck to the road. "He's trying to be nice to you," he said quietly. "Why do you insist on hurting him every time he does?"

Riley picked up a cloth and began furiously wiping the counter.

"I should make you walk back in there and apologize," Darius began, holding up his hand at her sharp intake of breath to stall her reply. "But I won't. You'll decide how and when you'll tell him how you really feel. You're not a child any longer and neither is he. Work this out between you with the minimum of wounds, Riley. Life is fleeting and unpredictable. Don't waste time on pride."

Tears spilled down her cheeks and she angrily wiped them away. Without a word, she dumped the cloth next to the cash register, yanked open the glass door of the drinks cooler and helped herself. The gas hissed as she popped the tab. She swallowed eagerly, the cold fizz soothing the burning in her throat but not easing the lump that had lodged there.

Alec licked the last of the pizza sauce from his fingers and sighed with contentment. He couldn't remember ever eating a better meal. Riley might be unpredictable and beyond annoying, but he had to admit she could really cook.

He was trying very hard to ignore her, but it wasn't easy. Darius sat between them at the counter that faced the window and all three of them hardly spoke while they ate. Darius kept giving the two of them intent looks, and Alec had the feeling that he was trying to impart some telepathic message to him. Too bad he didn't have the skill to pick up on it.

Darius apparently had never eaten pizza before and had mooched pieces from both Riley's and his pie as "experiments in cultural appreciation." It had been worth losing the food to see his expression as he bit into the overburdened crust with every single topping available in the store. He'd stifled a laugh as Darius picked off the remaining anchovies before finishing the slice.

37

Now, replete and bordering on uncomfortable, Alec wondered what they were going to do. Confronting Rhozan and closing the rips was not an option. He didn't know how to do it and would only get himself killed. Running was a far better option. Head over to his apartment, tell his folks the truth (Hi Mom, guess what I did?) and convince them to take off into the unknown with the three of them.

He remembered the dead phone in the back. "Darius—"

"No," Darius cut him off. "No phone calls."

"Why not?" Alec exploded. "One call. Just to check that they're okay. If they're not at home, I need to know it."

"Alec, we're not going back to your apartment to pay a social call. We're going to close the rips and send Rhozan packing. It's not going to be pretty. You'd better hope your parents *aren't* at home. You don't want them in the way. I certainly don't."

"Yeah, but ..." Alec almost turned to Riley for support before he remembered that he was mad at her. "Darius," he pleaded, trying as hard as he could to infuse the Tyon power into his voice, "my mom will be frantic. I've been missing for weeks. The city is under siege. I just want to tell her I'm all right. *Please.*"

Darius said nothing, but wiped both his hands on his napkin before standing up and embracing Alec in a tight hug. Alec was so shocked he didn't move. He didn't see Riley get up and head to the kitchen.

"Please, trust me. I have good reason for not permitting this contact now. I'm sorry." He let Alec go and took a step back.

No one ever hugged him but his mom. Alec turned away. He was *not* going to blubber like a little kid.

A bright flash, somewhere in the distance, momentarily lit the room. Alec whirled around to see out the window. A moment later the entire room rumbled with thunder. The first raindrops hit the hood of the truck with sharp pings, then the deluge began.

Darius stood with his hands on his hips, staring out at the torrent. Alec stalked over to the counter and started rummaging, the need to be moving and doing something almost overwhelming. The till was empty, but the tip jar still held a few bills and coins. He'd automatically emptied it into his hand before he realized what he'd done. He hesitated for a moment before he dumped the money back.

Rain drummed on the roof, louder and louder as the

heavens heaped their wrath upon the city. There were two more brilliant flashes of lightning and the echoing thunder, then, as quickly as it had started, the storm was over. It was only as the constant roar of the rain ceased that Alec heard the voices.

Darius was under the counter in a flash and into the kitchen before Alec could make a sound. Alec dashed through the swinging doors. He skidded to a halt, almost dizzy in his relief that she was okay. Riley had found and set up a small portable television on the counter, with its aerial pointing towards the high, narrow ventilation window. She was perched on the opposite counter, her back against the wall and her arms crossed.

The picture was grainy and the sound less than pristine, but it was the news and more than welcome. Alec moved forward until he stood next to Darius.

A pale and unshaven anchor sat in shirtsleeves at a desk covered with piles of paper.

"What channel is this?" Alec asked.

"CNN," Riley replied in a small and trembling voice. "New York is in big trouble and several spots in California. It's spreading."

"That's the usual course of things," Darius sighed. "The more negative emotions, the stronger the Others get, and the more they can manipulate naturally occurring rips for their own use. It's a vicious spiral."

The anchor pulled one sheet from the pile to his left. His voice was hoarse. "As of midnight tonight, this channel will cease broadcasting from our headquarters here in Atlanta. Evacuation of this city has begun and is expected to continue throughout the night. The president enacted martial law as of noon today in the list of states you see on the screen beside me." A long list ran down the screen beside the anchor's ear. The screen was too fuzzy to read clearly, but the list was pretty long.

There was a sudden fizzing sound and the power went

off. The little TV screen glowed eerily for a minute then faded. Darius hopped onto the counter and peered out the small window to the alleyway behind. "Alec, run to the front and see if there are any other lights on."

"Sure." Alec turned around in the darkness and felt his way along the counter to the doors. He pushed them open and walked into the front room. He stubbed his toe and banged his hip on the counter, making his way to the window, but it was a useless venture. The entire street was dark. He made his way back. "Nothing. The whole street is out."

"Might be city-wide," Darius mused. "We'll stay here tonight. It's too dangerous to try and drive anywhere in the dark. Don't open the fridge until morning. If we're lucky, the food will be fine." He hopped down. "I'm going out to the truck to see if there's anything in the back we don't want stolen. Then we'll pull down the metal blind thing and lock ourselves in for the night."

They made beds out of the jackets Darius found in a rucksack and lay in the middle of the restaurant floor, but Alec couldn't rest. The news had hit him harder than he expected. The world really was falling apart – it wasn't just his own country. No one, other than Darius, seemed to think they could stop it worsening. Tomorrow he was going to face the instigator of this whole mess and he didn't have a clue what he was going to do. Did Rhozan know how scared he was? Was the Other laughing his head off right now? Did Darius actually have a plan or was he just trying to keep their spirits up until it was too late?

For a long time there was only the sound of their breathing and the soft moaning of the wind through the lattice of the metal curtain. Alec was pretty sure that Darius and Riley were awake, too. How could anyone sleep knowing that tomorrow all of them might die?

The light woke Riley. Bright, glaring beams, boring straight into her eyes. She started to sit up. Her brain scrambled to make sense of what she was seeing.

The glass from the huge plate-glass window blew in with a roaring crack as the metal curtain slammed into it. The wooden countertop splintered and fell to the floor in a sharp crash as the long, wicked snout and the hull of a tank broke through the flimsy barrier with a dull screech. The rumble of the engine and the rolling of the caterpillar track were ear-splitting even as the tank came to an abrupt stop just inside the wall of the restaurant. Debris rained onto the tiled floor.

Riley barely managed to shield her face.

Darius moved so fast she almost didn't see him. One second he was sleeping on the makeshift bedroll next to her, his warm breath on her shoulder, his arm flung across her stomach. The next he was on his feet, orb glowing in one hand. He reached down, grabbed her, threw her over his shoulder and leapt towards the tank at the same time he yelled at Alec, "Get up!"

Riley had a brief glimpse of Alec, hand shading his eyes from the glare of the turret lights, his face a mixture of disbelief and horror, before Darius began to climb up onto the closest track of the tank. Wait a second; he was climbing *onto* the tank.

Darius pushed his way through the broken metallic curtain and dangling bits of plywood and

38

metal to get outside. A particularly large hunk of wood caught Riley unaware. "Ow!"

"Keep your head down," Darius advised too late. "*Alec!*"

Alec scrambled up onto the hull of the tank so quickly he passed the both of them. He jumped onto the sidewalk beside the remains of their truck. Darius and Riley landed beside him. Riley had the wind knocked out of her as she tumbled off Darius' shoulder to the wet pavement. She wasn't able to take a breath in to shout as the tank recoiled towards them at the same time as a deafening *bang* nearly burst her eardrums.

The pizza shop blew up: glass, wood, tile, ceramic counter, everything in tiny pieces and flying towards them like missiles. Darius flung himself over Riley to protect her from the worst of the airborne danger. She heard Alec, several metres ahead of them, cry out sharply.

"Move," Darius yelled, as he yanked her to her feet. She had a glimpse of the gutted pizza store and the turret of the tank turning slowly in their direction before Darius pushed her away.

Her feet slipped on the cluttered sidewalk as she took off after Darius. He was already at Alec's side and helping him up. A trickle of blood ran down Alec's forehead and across his pale face. There wasn't time to ask if he was hurt elsewhere.

"Follow me," Darius yelled as he ducked down an alley between two storefronts and headed for the service lane behind.

Riley and Alec pounded behind him. Once out of the tank's spotlights, the darkness was complete and treacherous. Riley slipped twice. Instantly Alec was at her side, pulling her upright, and urging her onwards. His hand clasped hers tightly.

The entranceway to the alley exploded as another shell detonated. A hail of brick particles rained down. Riley yelped and ran harder.

They ran down the alley and turned left. This new lane was wide enough to permit delivery trucks. Huge trash bins reeking of refuse jutted out into the roadway, looming out of the dark like monsters. The central gutter was still ankle-deep in rainwater. Riley splashed into the puddle before she could stop herself.

They were halfway down, Darius ahead by several metres, when headlights from the far end of the alley blazed into a blinding glare. Instantly they skidded to a stop. Alec raised a hand to shield his eyes and Riley ducked behind him. The truck's engine roared to life and its tires squealed against the pavement as it leapt towards them.

Darius' orb flashed brightly, the beam heading for the fire escape high up on the wall to his right. The mechanism unlatched and the ladder dropped to the ground.

"Get onto the roof. Cross to the other side of the building," Darius hurriedly instructed as he lifted Riley up so she could grasp the lowest rung.

Shimmying up the metal rungs like a monkey, she headed for the top. Alec was right behind her and, in his hurry, almost climbing the same rungs as she was. The second she was up and over the rooftop edge, Alec was right behind her. He stopped and peered downward.

"Darius, hurry," he yelled.

The resounding clang of metal hitting metal reverberated through the alley. The upper brackets of the fire escape strained and partially lifted as the lower ladder was hit by the truck and pulled apart. Alec bent forward over the ledge. Riley grabbed onto the back of his jeans and yanked as hard as she could.

"Riley, stop. I'm trying to reach him," Alec grunted.

Riley immediately let go. She leaned over his shoulder. The truck had plowed into a dumpster the next store over, but its headlights were still lighting up the alley. Below her, the fire escape abruptly ended six rungs from the roof. On the fifth rung, hanging by one hand, was Darius. He

223

still had his glowing orb in the other.

Riley watched as he popped his orb into his mouth, swung his now free hand up onto the rung and pulled his feet up enough to hook his knees over the rung. He rearranged himself and began to climb. He was over the wall in a second. Riley continued to watch the alley below. The truck's engine was still running, but no one had opened any of the doors or gotten out of the vehicle.

"Come on," Darius said as he dropped his orb into his pocket. He wasn't even out of breath. He led them across the roof to the other side of the building. Crouching down, they surveyed the street below.

The heavy cloud cover obscured whatever moonlight there might have been. The street lamps were dead. The air was clammy, cool and heavy. Nothing moved below them. Other than the fire in the pizza joint, the place was silent.

"How'd they find us?" Riley whispered. "We haven't used our orbs."

"Good question." Darius frowned. "Maybe Rhozan doesn't need an orb signal any more."

There was an uncomfortable silence as they pondered the implications.

"Why aren't they following us?" Alec hissed. "It's obvious where we've gone."

"Hmm, it is, isn't it?" Darius replied quietly.

"So?"

"Maybe whoever is in the tank can't think any more." Darius let that unpleasant idea sink in for a moment.

Riley was leaning against Alec and she felt him shudder. "What?" she asked. "What is it? What's he thinking of, Dare?"

There was a moment of hesitation before Alec answered for him. "Zombies."

"Are you kidding me?" Riley rolled her eyes. Of all the stupid ideas.

"Not so stupid," Darius sighed. "He's familiar with the

kind of games Alec plays, knows what scares him and what doesn't. He's toying with us now."

Riley rounded on Alec. "Are you telling me that Rhozan has read your mind and knows all the games you play? Is that where he's getting his ideas?"

"Yeah, I think so."

"Please tell me you love games with little bunnies and hopscotch. Please."

She felt his stifled chuckle through his shoulder, which was pressing into hers. "No such luck."

Riley cursed beneath her breath. She knew damn well what kind of games he played. The same ultra-violent, horror-filled blood fests that all boys his age seemed to be obsessed with. She'd sat next to boys on the bus who ranted and raved over the latest version of *Flesh Eating Ninja Warlords from Mars* or *Ultra Total Mega Battle Destruction IV* until they were blue in the face. Alec's memories coursed across her mind, unbidden. He loved those things. Other than soccer, it was the only time he felt in control. She sighed. "What do we do now?"

"It's too far to walk to Alec's and far too dangerous to travel around in the dark. I have no idea what else is out there," Darius murmured. "I think we're going to have to stay put for the moment and wait for the sun to come up."

"Here?" Riley looked around with distaste. Why hadn't she grabbed a couple of the jackets in their headlong flight for safety?

"Fraid so. Huddle together and try to keep warm. I'll stay awake and keep an eye out."

There was nothing else to do. Little puddles of rainwater dotted the stone-and-tarred roof. There was no shelter, but the enclosed stairwell near the centre provided something to lean against and some protection for their backs. Riley scrunched herself against the rough brickwork and watched, mildly stung, as Alec purposely walked around Darius to sit on his other side. She leaned against the warmth of Darius' shoulder and closed her eyes.

If Alec was right, Rhozan was using corpses to hunt them. Rhozan might be able to track them without an orb signal, too. Who knew what else this creepy alien would do next? Would this nightmare ever end?

Riley did nothing more than doze intermittently. It was uncomfortable on the rooftop with the pebbles under her butt digging in every time she moved and a post-rain fog swirling around like a convention of ghosts. The eerie silence didn't help either. What was going on down on the ground, out of sight? Was an army of mad, obsessed killers amassing right now, just below the ramparts of the building?

Riley shifted position and sighed. In some ways, she just wished tomorrow would never come.

"Can't sleep?" Darius whispered.

"Too cold," she lied. The temperature had nothing on her fear.

"Here." He shifted slightly, lifting his arm and wrapping it around her shoulders.

She smiled in the darkness. There was something about him that made her feel special and cared for. And attractive. She gave herself a mental shake. He seemed to make everyone feel that way. She changed the subject before he could pick up on her thoughts. "There are a few things bothering me. Feel like talking?" she whispered, not wanting to wake Alec who had slid down until curled up with his head resting on Darius' leg.

"Sure. Fire away."

"There was the guy in the donut shop and the soldiers, but no one else. I mean, this is a city of what, three million? Where is everyone?"

"The ones that are still alive and in this dimension are mostly hiding. If you hold your orb and open your mind, you'll feel them. Just out of sight. Frightened and not knowing what to do."

"And what about those rip thingies? Like on the house-boat. I haven't seen any of them. Have they all gone?"

"I wish," Darius sighed. "I feel about two dozen in this neighbourhood alone. They're pretty small and hard to see until you're right up next to one. I haven't drawn your attention to any because we've been far enough away. But it's a good idea to keep your eyes open. The closer we get to Alec's apartment, the more there'll be."

Riley let this unsettling news sink in. "Well, you know we had that spot of trouble leaving the Base?" she began carefully.

"Hmm hmm."

"Well, are they coming after us? I mean, could we turn some corner to find a bunch of your Guardian pals standing there, waiting to take us out?"

"Riley, the Tyon Collective doesn't believe in revenge. It's not logical. None of them are out there, hunting us down. Were you worried about that?"

"Sort of," she replied. She hesitated, not really wanting to hear the answer to her next question. "And, will they, you know, be around if we, you know, fail with Rhozan?"

"You mean, come to our rescue?"

"Well, yeah."

"No."

The silence after this bombshell stretched for ages, while Riley considered the news. She had figured as much. Rhozan wanted them dead. The Tyon organization wouldn't bother to save them. And the *entire world* was falling into disarray.

"I'm not even sure if they've left yet," Darius murmured into her hair.

"Who?"

"The Collective. Regrouping would have finished by now. Logan's plan was to leave as soon as everyone was at Home Base. They've probably left the planet."

Riley couldn't help raising her eyes heavenward. Was there a spaceship blasting off right now and circling her world at this very minute? She thought of all the devoted scientists, living their lives in anticipation of extraterrestrial contact, and the irony that aliens had already been here and no one had noticed. It just showed that Fate had a twisted sense of humour.

Darius' voice grew bleaker. "That's all they do, you see? Introduce the resistor gene, train those who acquire it to resist the Others' mind control, and if that works, eliminate any witnesses. They don't actually fight anyone themselves. Sometimes, they just pick up the Potentials and leave. Like here." Darius shifted and pulled Riley closer until her head was resting under his chin.

"What do you mean, eliminate witnesses?"

"We're actually not supposed to be doing this at all." He sighed. "It's a long story."

"It's a long night."

"Fair enough." She heard the smile in his voice. "Okay. The prime mandate of the Intergalactic Council is to permit the growth and natural evolution of all cultures, so attacking one group of beings just because they are overly aggressive was politically unpalatable. There's a lot of jockeying for power and control on the Council, as you might imagine, and some pretty powerful lobbies made it clear that the Others were to be ignored. So some members of the Council secretly formed the Tyon Collective and sent them out to do what, legally, they couldn't."

"Sneaky."

"Hmm. The trouble of course is that the Collective has been doing the Council's dirty work illegally for so long now that the secret is pretty much out. There has been pressure for the Collective to be dissolved. Of course, all this is pretty high-level stuff. I'm not supposed to even know about it."

"So, how do you?" Riley asked with a good idea of the answer.

"Anna told me." Darius paused and Riley worried for a moment if he was going to cry or something. She was relieved when he started to speak again. "Anna was second in command at Home Base and privy to a lot of what was going on because of her relationship with Logan."

"What relationship? I thought she was your girlfriend?"

"She was to be partnered with Logan after they were retired from the Collective. Pair bonds are often pre-arranged by the Council in order to ensure maximum continuation of the genetic Tyon ability."

"She agreed to an arranged marriage to Logan?" Riley sat up. "But she loved you."

"Love is a pretty strong word, Riley. I'm not sure if Anna actually knew what that meant or if she felt it. Attraction, yes; desire, yes; willingness to break rules on my behalf, maybe. But love? She isn't like us, Riley. Orions are raised in a world where emotions are dangerous to their survival. I loved her. But did she love me? I don't know."

Riley thought it over. Heaven knows the woman was strong enough with Tyon power, and her skill combined with Dean's would probably have been more than enough to kill the three of them. But she *hadn't*. She'd literally kept her orb at her side and had let Dean's killing force bounce back towards her. What else, other than love for Darius, could have caused her to do that?

For a long time neither spoke. Riley was caught up in the thoughts swirling like a vortex around her mind. The mandate of the Collective, the danger they were in, Darius' love for Anna. She thought about Darius growing up amongst the Collective, his need to love and be loved not understood or sanctioned and resulting, she realized with sudden insight, into a need to flirt and provoke everyone around him, just to be acknowledged.

"Are you sorry?" Darius' voice startled her.

"Sorry for what?"

"Sorry you're involved. That we ever met."

Was she? Days ago the answer would have been an unqualified "yes." But now, she wasn't quite so sure. If Darius hadn't invited her for coffee in order to separate her from the crowd, if those Emissaries hadn't tried to kill her, if she hadn't the gift the Tyons were looking for, then what? Right now she'd probably be in Vancouver, at Deborah's, dealing with her hysterical, incapable older sister while the world fell apart around her and she would have been helpless to do anything. Not only helpless, but ignorant.

Here, now, she had a fighting chance to make a difference. There was power inside her that might make Rhozan sit up and pay attention. She was going to be of help.

"No," she answered.

"That's my girl."

Off to their right, several streets away, a flash of light lit the darkness. The echoing recoil of sound bouncing between the buildings indicated the tank was momentarily in operation. Alec didn't move beside them.

"He's really exhausted," Riley noted with worry.

"And today is going to be a hell of a day," Darius sighed.

They got up as the first faint rays of light slid over the rooftop. Alec was sore all over from a combination of a miserable night of nightmares and sleeping with his neck in an awkward position. They kept mostly to the shadows as they jogged towards the high-rises in the distance. An uncomfortable sensation built inside Alec's stomach with every step closer to his home and what waited for him there. He couldn't stop the worrying thoughts that spun around in his brain: his mom, Peter, zombies, Rhozan, the list was endless. How on earth would he fix the mess he'd started?

40

Darius spotted a convenience store that hadn't been looted and called a temporary halt midmorning. Between them they pried the locks off the doors and raised the metal shutters. Darius pulled the glass doors open and they advanced into the gloom. The power was still off, but otherwise the store looked and smelled normal. There were three small aisles loaded with snack foods and a bank of refrigerated coolers along the back wall.

"Grab something healthy," Darius reminded them as Alec reached for a bag of chips.

Alec dropped the bag back onto the rack and surreptitiously grabbed a chocolate bar, shoving the whole thing in his mouth before Darius could notice. Alec gave the magazine rack an interested look, his eyes straying to the girlie magazines on the top shelf. No one would know if he ...

"You don't need those either." Darius' voice

came from the other end of the store.

Rolling his eyes, Alec wandered down the aisle.

"Do you like chocolate chips?" Riley was looking at something on a lower shelf.

"Cover slugs with chocolate and I'll eat them. That and carbonated liquids were the things I missed the most while I was off planet." Darius reached down and pulled up a box. "Grab a bag, Alec," he instructed.

Alec sighed and turned around to head for the cashier desk. He circled it, and reached under the counter for a stack of neatly folded plastic bags. Then his heart stopped.

Sparkles.

"They're still cold. Do you want chocolate milk or regular?" Darius shouted to him from the back of the store.

Alec couldn't answer. The sparkles were an inch from his hand. If they moved …

"Alec?"

Goosebumps rose all over his body. Alec pulled his hand back carefully and looked around, terrified. Sure enough, there, by his feet. Between him and safety.

"Darius," Alec said softly, almost afraid the rips could hear him and would zero in on him once they did. "I can't move."

Darius didn't hear because his head was inside the cooler, but Riley did. Her arms were filled with milk cartons and granola bar boxes. She walked up to the cashier and looked down her nose. "What's the matter with you?" she asked, her mouth full of granola.

"Watch where you're walking. This place is filled with rips."

Riley blanched. She peered over the cartons at her shoes. "Are you sure?"

"There are two right here," Alec whispered. "I can't move."

Riley dumped the milk onto the counter. "I'll get Dare." She headed towards the cooler, watching her feet with every step.

A carton of granola bars slid off the counter. Alec watched in horrified fascination, only stopping his automatic urge to grab it in time. The box fell straight into the sparkles. It vanished. Alec's guts clenched. *Just like Peter.* He forced himself to take a long, deep breath, trying to keep his eyes on the sparkles at his feet and those by his hip at the same time.

Darius was suddenly at the counter. "Where?" he demanded.

Alec pointed.

"You're going to have to jump over them. How're your high jump skills?"

"Normally, I get a bit of a run first," Alec said. If Riley could fake nonchalance in the face of danger, so could he.

"Yeah, well, sorry." Darius leaned over the counter. "Could you climb over the register instead?"

Alec twisted around. The cash register was huge and the flimsy shelves might not hold his weight. "Looks okay."

Darius kept one hand hovering over his pocket but didn't actually touch his orb. "Go for it."

Alec pivoted carefully. Then, reaching up with one foot to balance on the thin shelf, he grabbed Darius' outstretched hand. He pulled himself up.

He was halfway there, poised over the cash register, one leg lifting up to step onto the narrow space on the counter, when the shelf broke. Darius yanked. Alec fell over the counter, knocking Darius backwards onto the floor. The cash register fell beside them with a crash. He landed on top of Darius with a grunt. He was just about to apologize when he saw them. Sparkles. Less than a hand-span away from Darius' right ear. And *moving.*

Without thinking, he leapt to his feet, pulling Darius' hand as hard as he could, hauling him upright. "Look out!" he yelled.

Almost immediately Darius shouted, "Don't move."

Riley halted in mid-step towards them. She looked

down at her feet and then nervously around the room. She opened her mouth to speak, but Darius laid a finger across his lips and shook his head slightly. He pointed to the closed-circuit camera system over the cash counter. Its red light was on. Slowly the camera tracked in their direction.

A decidedly clammy sensation ran down Alec's spine. No one was watching that camera. No one alive, that was. He turned to keep the closest cluster of hovering sparkles in sight while he kept one eye on the moving camera. They had drifted a few inches closer and now were still just above the dirty floor, next to a display of motor oil. In the bright light from the overhead fluorescents, they were almost impossible to see. How many more were there?

Riley screamed. Alec whirled around.

Just like a scene from a movie, anything not tied down became airborne. Cans, bags of chips, greeting cards: everything sailed through the air directly at them. A can of ravioli hit Alec squarely in the middle of the forehead. He staggered, and would have stepped right back into the rip had Darius not grabbed him.

"Get out of here," Darius yelled.

Hands around their heads to protect from the sharpest of items, they ran to the door. Darius reached it first. There were sparkles hovering over the door handle. Darius braced his hands on the glass to stop from falling into the rip as Riley and Alec barrelled into him.

"Oof," Alec grunted, as his chin made painful contact with Darius' shoulder blade.

Darius shoved them both backwards. A hail of canned goods hit the door and smashed the glass. Riley cried out in pain.

235

"Get your orb out, Riley. See if you can put up a shield," Darius shouted.

"I can do it," Alec gasped as he fended off a flying bottle of cola.

"No." Darius' tone brooked no argument.

Riley struggled to reach her orb. She grasped it and held it out towards the store, eyes shut tight with concentration. Alec tried to shelter her. Darius turned back to the door. He kicked at the glass several times, but despite the multiple cracks, the door seemed to have a mind of its own and refused to open.

Another onslaught of cans and bottles headed their way, sailing through the air as if thrown. A bottle of orange soda hit Alec on the side of his head as he ducked to miss several cans of soup.

"Get the barrier up," Alec yelled at Riley.

Tears streaming down her cheek, Riley shook her head mutely.

Darius hit the glass again. It bulged outwards, the thin wire mesh inside the glass holding it in place. He reached for his orb.

Alec looked up just in time to see the heavy glass doors of the wall coolers pull off their hinges and start to fly towards him. Thoughts flew even faster. Darius wasn't looking; he was focused on the door. Riley wasn't looking; her attention was on the orb. The barrier wasn't up. Those doors were heavy and would kill them if they struck them.

There was only one thing to do.

Alec reached out, grabbed Riley's hand around her orb and yelled at the top of his lungs.

"Stop."

T he power came alive the instant Alec's fingers touched Riley's orb. In him, through him, around him.

The barrier Riley'd been trying so infuriatingly hard to put in place winked into existence the very second Alec willed it so. A wave of satisfaction flooded him. *This* was what he was made for. The door bounced off the invisible barrier and fell with a resounding clatter to the floor. The second and third door did the same.

"Good job," Darius cheered as he turned around for a moment to look. "Alec, no!" he shouted as he took in who exactly was protecting them. "Let go," he ordered.

"Get the door open first," Alec panted. His eyes were blazing and a thin beading of sweat lined his upper lip. Rhozan was throwing more things at them and the power, which initially had come so easily, was now starting to tire him. At the back of his mind a strange touching sensation was oozing in.

Alec saw Darius' fury for only a second until he turned, and, with renewed purpose, smashed open the door with a well-aimed kick. The door swung open, protesting on its hinges. Alec focused on the hordes of things still flying at them: the shelving, the ceiling tiles, the cash register, the safe. Wait a minute. *The safe?*

He doubled his effort.

"Alec, get out of here," Riley yelled as Darius eased around the rip and ran outside.

41

The safe hit the barrier and fell with a heavy thud to the floor at his feet, cracking the linoleum.

Alec dropped his arm, let go of the orb and ran out the door in one smooth move, just remembering in time to avoid the rip. He pushed at the foreign presence inside his mind and it dissolved the second his fingers left the orb's crystal surface. He couldn't help but grin despite his exhaustion. That had been so *cool*.

Alec's pleasure turned to dust the moment he was outside. Darius was waiting for them in the middle of the street and he looked furious. Before either of them could speak, the sound of a truck engine revving shattered the silence. Several blocks down the street, a heavy army transport turned onto the road and began to advance.

No one needed any orders. Darius led them down the sidewalk as fast as they could go, towards a narrow opening between two demolished storefronts. They rounded the corner, feet pounding into puddles and garbage alike, down the rank alley and out into the wide secondary street behind. All three skidded to a stop.

"Get your hands up."

A small squad of soldiers, their truck nowhere to be seen, stood together in a tight formation, their rifles raised and levelled directly at them. Their uniforms were filthy and bloodstained, their faces coldly pale and grimly determined.

For a second no one moved. Then Riley stumbled against Darius, grabbed him around the waist and wailed loudly, "No, no, don't let them hurt me." She buried her face against his chest. Her muffled sobs could be heard in the next street.

238   All the soldiers visibly tensed. Alec's heart zoomed up into his throat. What the hell was she *doing*?

That was before he noticed her hands. Out of the corner of his eye, he watched as one small hand surreptitiously reached into Darius' pocket. He tensed all over, trying to keep his facial expression neutral.

"Stand back from him, or I'll shoot," yelled a rapidly blinking soldier, hefting his gun directly at Riley.

With remarkable speed, Riley pulled out Darius' orb and thrust it upwards into his hand. Darius grabbed it and held on with her. A bright flash of light emanated from the orb towards the soldiers. Instantly they fell to the ground. There was a stunned moment of silence.

"Guess that's one time you wanted me to read your mind," Darius said.

"Guess so," Riley replied shakily. She walked over to the soldiers who had collapsed into an ungainly heap. "I hate guns." Riley yanked the rifle from the limp fingers of the closest soldier. "I can't stand them. Especially when someone is pointing one at *me*." She whirled around to face Alec, the weapon still dangling dangerously from her trembling fingers.

Darius was at her side in an instant. He deftly pulled out the magazine clip and threw it away in a display that would have garnered him an award in the baseball hall of fame. "Well done," he praised her.

She flushed. "I won awards for drama at school."

"Darius." Alec ground his teeth together. "I really need an orb. I could have saved the both of you, right then. Riley took a huge chance. Someone might have shot her for the over-acting alone."

"Piss off," muttered Riley.

"No orb." Darius's expression hardened. "That's final. I'm not taking a chance on you hurting anyone with it. Riley, that means under *no* circumstances do you ever give an orb to Alec, again. Ever. *No matter what*."

"You'd both be dead if I hadn't helped," Alec hotly protested. Was a simple "thank you" too much to ask?

"Did I tell you not to touch an orb, Alec?" Darius began. Fury stained his cheeks. "Did I?"

"Yeah, but–"

Darius advanced quickly towards him. "Nothing, no

excuses. If we die, we die. You *cannot* touch one again, do you hear me?"

"Nothing happened." Alec barely resisted the desire to stamp his foot in rage. "He can't control me."

"And you're an expert on Rhozan, are you?" Darius leaned in. He was only a foot away and the laser blue of his eyes was razor sharp. "Know exactly when he's with you and when he's not, do you? Keeping track, are you?"

"Well, I–"

"I, nothing," Darius spat. "He's been around on and off all day. He got into your head while you were sleeping. Or didn't you notice?"

"You don't worry about Riley. Can't he get to *her*?" Alec sputtered.

"If Riley touches her orb, he doesn't seem to care. If Riley kills someone, it won't affect her. If you do, it will." Darius turned his back. He bent down and began removing the soldiers' guns with sharp, angry movements and throwing them as far away as he could. He didn't look up.

"I'm not going to fall apart." Alec kicked at the ground with annoyance and looked everywhere but at Riley or Darius. "If I feel him, I can force him out."

"That's not what I'm worried about," said Darius, unearthing a wicked-looking knife from the waistband of one soldier and tossing it up onto the nearest roof.

"So? What is it?"

"Death will corrupt *you*. Killing will corrupt *you*. Revenge, hatred, anger, all of it. It'll destroy your soul. And with the kind of power you've got, you'll destroy the world. So I'm stopping that before it can get started." Darius pulled a grenade from another soldier, expertly pulled the pin and lobbed it well out of sight. A loud bang echoed from two streets away a moment later. Riley flinched but Darius didn't.

"I caused the rips, didn't I? The night I got into a fight with my dad." There, he had said it out loud. The whole thing was his fault. He waited for the confirmation.

Darius released a long sigh, ran his hands through his messy hair and finally, after what seemed like forever, nodded. "You don't do anything by halves, do you?" he said quietly, the anger seeming to drain out of him, replaced by something that looked a bit like sorrow.

"I didn't mean to," Alec said.

"No, of course not. And, Alec, Rhozan was waiting for it. Rips open all the time, and generally nothing happens. The rips aren't connected to any place or time, they're just weird anomalies in the fabric of the universe. Sometimes, someone is really unlucky and trips into one."

"I've never heard about them," Riley piped up. "I watch the news all the time and I've never heard about these."

"Terran science hasn't gotten around to believing they exist. But you have heard about them. Hikers who disappear into thin air, sailboats discovered with no one on them, the Bermuda Triangle. All rips. It's just your planet's bad luck that this time someone was waiting at the other end, using the rips as a conduit between when/where they are and here."

Alec shuffled his feet. It wasn't an easy thing to know that the mass destruction around you was singularly your fault. Even if it were an accident.

"All you did was let him in a bit early, Alec. That's all. He was waiting for a natural rip to appear and one would have, eventually. Don't beat yourself up over it."

"But Logan–" Alec started.

"Logan's been wrong about me for years. He didn't know Anna very well and they were pair-bonded for after duty. Don't take Logan's word as absolute truth."

The three of them looked at each other, while the words hung heavy in the air. Overhead, the sky was a dull pewter grey. A slight breeze sprung up, surrounding them with the stench of death and smoke.

Riley wrinkled her nose. "How much farther?"

Darius raised his eyebrow and looked at Alec.

"Ten kilometres at least," Alec said, squinting off into the distance. "You can't see my building yet."

"Then we're going to need transportation," Darius decided. "There was a truck in the last street. Let's see if we can find it."

"Aren't we going to take one of these guns?" Riley placed her hands on her hips and stared back and forth between Darius and Alec as if they were playing a fast game of tennis.

"No," said Darius, shaking his head. "No guns. Rhozan can control inanimate objects, as we've just seen. We're better off without a gun. Your orb is a better weapon."

"But I don't know how to use it without you," Riley wailed to Darius' back. He was already heading down the street at a smooth run. Riley gave Alec an exasperated look and took off after Darius.

Alec took a deep breath and followed.

The sunlight was already dimming, despite the early hour. Riley stopped the military vehicle they'd acquired at the three-way intersection and waited for Alec's directions. She glanced over at him. He was very pale and staring straight ahead. Riley allowed several silent seconds to pass before she smacked him across the upper arm. "Hey, quit your dreaming. Which way, left or right?"

"Cut it out," Alec flared, pulling his arm away from her and giving her a dark look. "Ask nicely."

"By the time you wake up and get with the program, Rhozan'll have South America destroyed. Hurry up."

"Piss off, Cohen."

"Yeah, eat dung, Anderson," Riley fired back.

"Hey, hey!" Darius shouted. "Leave him alone."

"He's not going to morph into Darth Vader just because he gets pissed, Darius. Relax."

"Yeah." Alec added his insulted voice to hers. "I'm not."

"Which way, Alec?" Darius sighed deeply and looked out at the cityscape as if too frustrated to look at either one of them.

"Left," Alec instructed. The truck rolled forward, picking up speed once onto the newer road. "Is that what you think will happen to me?"

"What?" Darius asked, frowning.

"I'll turn into Darth Vader."

"Who?"

"A character in a popular movie from the

42

eighties," Riley butted in. Alec would take all day to explain, and to be frank, she was just as curious. Not that she thought Alec would. He was a really sweet kid, underneath the bravado. "He had, like, evil tendencies and got pushed over the edge, turning into the ultimate bad guy. But then he turned good, in the end, when his son saved him."

Darius peered around Alec to look intently at Riley. She spared a quick glance before focusing on the road again.

"I'm not familiar with the reference," Darius began, "but the idea is relatively similar. Anger, despair, vengeance – all these can lead anyone into a hopeless state where their reason becomes clouded, their sense of themselves gets lost. I'm not just talking about Rhozan, although he's the main problem. Kids who lose their sense of moral direction, act out, and never find their way back. Alec has the added complication that he's susceptible to Rhozan because he's entered his mind when he was sleeping and vulnerable. I have no idea what he's planted inside your head, Alec, what might already be there to turn you away from us. So I need you to stay as calm as possible, keeping the anger at bay as much as you can. Do both of you understand?"

Riley nodded. Beside her Alec muttered something that sounded like "whatever" under his breath and slouched down in his seat, his shoulder rubbing up against hers in the tight space. With her own shoulder, she gave him a little shove of encouragement before focusing entirely on the road again.

Up ahead, several cars were piled up together in the middle of the road, and only passing over the sidewalk on the left would give them access to the road ahead. The sidewalk was blocked with several shopping carts, piled into a tangle. Riley came to a stop. She pointed at the carts with a finger. "You two'll have to move those."

"No problem," Darius said, already opening his door. "Alec?"

Riley shifted the truck into park and took her feet off the pedals with relief. She was a bit too short to drive the truck, which consequently put a strain on her neck. She rubbed her shoulders for a moment, watching Alec and Darius as they tackled the massive heap of carts.

The knife poked her throat, just enough to get her attention.

"Don't move," a hoarse voice whispered in her ear.

Riley's heart zoomed up into her throat and began a wild tattoo, so loud she barely heard the man's next instructions. "Turn off the engine."

She couldn't see him. He was outside the truck, his dirty sleeve winding through the open window towards her. Turning her head slightly, she glanced in the side-view mirror. The young man was dishevelled, dirty and grimacing. Slowly and carefully, she reached forward, the knifepoint never leaving her skin, and flicked her wrist. The engine died.

Suddenly there were dozens of them. Swirling out from the buildings around them, sliding out from the pile of cars in the accident, dropping down from the roof next to the sidewalk. Darius and Alec were instantly engaged in a vicious battle.

"Get out of the truck," the hoarse voice instructed.

Riley eased herself off the seat and opened the door. There was a second in which the knife was gone from her throat but she couldn't act fast enough. The door was wrenched open, hands reached in to grab her and she was yanked out. She fell in a heap to the ground, bruising her hands and knees.

"Leave her alone."

She heard Alec's voice break in his fury. *Don't get angry,* she mentally pleaded with him.

A pair of booted feet walked into Riley's view and stopped next to her nose. Hands pulled her upright. Her heart sank.

"We meet again, Potential," said the Emissary. He was young, around Darius' age, and stinking of sweat and hatred. He wore a wedding ring and expensive shoes. His voice was deeper than she might have expected and was probably Rhozan's. She peered closely and a thousand shivers coursed down her back. *He wasn't breathing.*

With lightning speed, the man slapped her hard across the face. She heard Alec's shout and opened her mouth to tell him to shut up when the pain hit.

"Search them," the Emissary said. "Take everything out of their pockets and give it to me."

Oh no, not her orb.

She glimpsed Alec and Darius over the shoulder of the Emissary who had dragged her from the truck. Alec's arms were cruelly pulled up behind his back and his nose was bleeding. Darius was on the ground, unconscious, the rapid swellings indicative of the beating he had taken. His orb, and Alec's, were handed to the leader, who said nothing as he deposited them, along with hers, into his jacket pocket. "Put them in the back of the truck," the Emissary ordered.

She was dumped onto the floor. Alec was tossed up beside her.

"You okay?" Alec grunted just as someone's booted foot kicked his back. Angry, he twisted around. "Cut it out."

"Shut up," the Emissary instructed as he climbed aboard and settled onto the bench that ran down both sides of the truck-bed walls. "Both of you."

Riley sat up and clasped Alec's hand. Darius was lifted up over the tailgate and dropped onto the floor. He didn't move. Without hesitation, Riley shimmied forward and lifted his head into her lap. She smoothed away his hair from his forehead and willed herself to touch his mind. Nothing. She raised her eyes to Alec's.

246 The truck engine roared to life and the vehicle lurched forward. Riley swallowed her sob as she swayed with the movement. Heaven only knew where the Emissary was taking them, and heaven help them when he got them there.

Anger pounded through Alec's veins. He'd used that very same ambush scenario hundreds of times in *Attack of the Zombie Warlords from Pluto* and it hadn't even occurred to him for *one second* that Rhozan might use it on him. How incredibly stupid. Problem was, he had no idea what to do now. Rhozan clearly knew all the game strategies he did and that meant the Other would be aware of any possible attempt at escape Alec might choose. Maybe Darius had some idea of Rhozan's weaknesses, but he'd never discussed it with them and if he had a plan, Alec didn't know it and Darius was in no shape to tell him now.

With Darius out of the equation, at least for now, the responsibility fell to him. Sure Riley was older and infinitely bossier, but her skill with an orb was sorely lacking, not to mention her penchant for annoying the hell out of her captors. If he could get her to somehow understand his plan, she might be of help. That was, when he had a plan. Right now he was finding it a bit hard even to think straight. All he wanted to do was hit someone. Preferably Rhozan.

Rhozan. Alec tried to suppress the shudder. The alien field commander had been in his head, knew what he knew, and had powers Alec couldn't begin to match. The world around him was falling to

43

pieces. If he didn't figure out what Darius considered to be Rhozan's weakness, they were all doomed. Him, Riley, his parents. Everyone.

There *had* to be a weakness. He just had to figure out what it was.

And fast.

R iley shuddered as the truck jerked to a halt and stopped. Alec's arm tightened around her for a moment, then let go as the tailgate of the truck dropped open. The Emissary clambered down awkwardly as if not used to the body he in-habited. When both feet were on the ground, he turned and faced them.

"You will follow me," he ordered.

"And if we don't want to?" Riley asked.

"We can beat you into submission. Is that preferable?"

"Well, no, duh."

"Then follow me."

"So, why'd we need to come back to my old apartment building? Is this your secret base?" Alec asked.

44

"The conduit here is open far wider and stronger than elsewhere," the Emissary said. "As you suspect, Alec. Get down off the truck. Carry Finn."

Riley grimaced but before she could make a scathing reply, an invisible energy yanked her hands off Darius and pulled her across the tailgate, dumping her onto the ground with enough force to knock the wind out of her. She lay in the mud, gasping for breath.

"Leave her alone," Alec growled.

"Silence," said the Emissary, turning his back to them. "Carry the Tyon."

They were in front of a tall multi-storey apartment building that even before the looting and rioting would have had no street appeal whatsoever. The cement walkway was cracked and weed-choked, the metal balconies rusted and the paint around the windows blistered and peeled. People didn't move here by choice, Riley decided.

"I'll take his shoulders," Alec said quietly, "you take his feet."

It took a moment to manoeuvre Darius into their arms and pull him from the truck. Groaning slightly with the weight, she and Alec carried their swinging cargo up the front path, Alec walking backwards.

The security doors were off their hinges and piled in the corner of the otherwise empty lobby. Someone had spray-painted obscenities all over the walls and the smell was unbelievable. They waited by the elevator doors, trying as hard as they could to hold their breath. Surprisingly, the doors immediately slid back with a faint *ding*, permitting them entry. The Emissary came in with them, followed by several of the group who had attacked them, crowding her and Alec against the back wall.

There was a faint lurch, then they began to climb. Riley had the unsettling sensation of the space beneath her feet and the ground increasing, a thin and rapidly uncoiling wire the only thing between life and death. Rapidly she forced the thought from her mind. Rhozan didn't need any ideas.

A louder *ding* and the elevator came to a shuddering stop. The second the doors opened and the Emissaries got out of the way, Riley scuttled out.

The long, dingy hallway was barely lit. Broken glass littered the floor and spray paint adorned the cement brick 250 walls. Alec didn't look up. He started to back down the hallway, shuffling slowly, his shoulders hunched. He looked different, Riley observed, as she struggled to keep hold of Darius' ankles in her small hands. Defeated. Worry increasing, she glanced back. The Emissary in charge was smiling.

Alec stopped only a few steps down the hall. He nodded towards a door to their left. Number twenty-seven. The seven was loose and lopsided.

The door unlatched and opened of its own accord. A bright, overpowering yellow light flooded the hallway. Riley blinked furiously. Her eyes began to tear. Her skin crawled. She felt ill. A dull pounding started at the back of her head.

"Enter," said the Emissary.

Riley swallowed the lump in her throat. She glanced at Alec, but he was staring downward.

The Emissary shoved her.

"Cut it out, creep," she snapped as she fought to regain her balance. "We're moving."

There was nothing else for it. Surrounded and seriously outnumbered, there was no way to stall, no place to run, and no method of escape.

She took a deep breath. The power hit her broadside as she stepped into the doorway.

The massive rip hovered in the middle of the room, just in front of the sliding glass doors to the balcony. It undulated and pulsed with a sickly light as the outline shifted constantly. Sparkles meandered and twinkled inside. Darkness, misery, fear, terror – all emanated from inside, flowing outward in almost visible waves.

Alec shuddered violently as the thoughts settled into his mind. This was horribly familiar. It was the dreams he'd been having ever since the fight with his dad. The dreams were Rhozan's, after all. Darius had been right all along.

Wordlessly, he and Riley lay Darius on the floor. Riley rubbed her neck with relief. Behind them, the Emissary dropped silently to the ground, like a puppet whose strings were cut. The other Emissaries lay in the hallway, dead or unconscious. Alec knew the instant he or Riley made a run for it, they would spring to attention and there were too many of them for him to fight alone.

Alec turned back to look around his former home. A stack of mail, opened and read, lay on the side table next to his father's chair, and his father's newspaper was folded into sections on the coffee table. His mother's favourite shawl hung over the back of a chair, as if she'd laid it aside just for a moment while she went to get her purse. There was no sign of panic or struggle or terror. It was as if they'd gotten ready for the day and stepped out. Alec shuddered. It all looked so …

"At last." The lights inside the undulating rip

pulsed brighter for a moment then dimmed. The words rolled around inside Alec's head.

"Rhozan?"

"Come closer. Join me."

The voice was enticing, but not strong enough to force him. Alec crossed his arms.

"I demand you obey."

"No," Alec said. "And you can't make me." He tapped the side of his head. "I have it. The genetic gift. I can resist you. So, piss off."

For a split second Alec thought it was ridiculously easy. But just as his brain reasoned that it couldn't be that simple, Rhozan retaliated.

The sound was so loud Alec fell to his knees. Riley screamed and dropped to the worn carpet, her hands clasped over her ears and her knees pulled up to her chest. The lights inside the rip grew to unbelievable proportions. Alec shut his eyes tightly, but the sickly yellow blazed into his retinas. It hurt. Badly. He curled into a ball. There was a sudden pain as something large and heavy slammed into his back.

"Riley," Alec yelled, trying desperately to concentrate despite the pain and the howling inside his head. "Watch out."

Something else hit him, this time across the forehead. He didn't need to shove it away. The object moved by itself as a sudden category-five hurricane-strength wind tore through the living room. Papers flung themselves into the air. The furniture upturned and slid across the floor. Alec squinted into the maelstrom. Riley had flung herself over Darius, protecting his face with her body.

A vase sailed across the room and smashed into the wall. The sofa slid several feet towards them.

"Do something!" Riley yelled.

What on earth could he do? He didn't have an orb. He didn't know how to stop Rhozan.

"You will obey me," Rhozan's voice thundered through Alec's mind.

Riley held onto Darius as tightly as she could, but it was a losing battle. The wind was impossibly strong and, inexorably, pulled Darius away. Something hit her shoulder and she grunted at the impact. The newspaper fluttered through the air and came to rest over her face, momentarily blinding her. She shook her head to dislodge the sheets. They flew across the room and directly into the rip. Then they were gone.

If the wind got stronger ...

The Emissary sprawled lifelessly near the front door and Alec was only a few feet away. He was curled up in a ball and rocking back and forth, moaning. Only Darius knew how to overcome Rhozan and she couldn't get through to him. The aliens' weakness, the power of the orbs, the skill and knowledge of the Tyon Collective who had done this before, were all Darius' knowledge, not hers. If she couldn't wake him ...

She shook him again, ignoring the lamp that bounced off her shoulder and towards the rip. "Darius, wake up." She leaned over his face, pressing her ear next to his lips. *Please, let him wake up.* He was barely breathing.

The words formed inside her head with the beating of the rip's light. "Come to me."

For a split second she actually wanted to, the voice was so commanding. Then she remembered. "I won't."

"Come to me or the Guardian dies."

46

Riley clutched Darius' shoulders even tighter as the demand grew stronger. Without Darius they were goners. "No."

"Then he dies."

Darius' body jerked beneath her fingers. He was yanked forward, just a handspan, but closer to the rip. Icicles ran down Riley's spine. She grabbed him harder and pulled back, but the force was almost unbeatable.

"He's mine," Rhozan said. The words rattled off the inside of her skull, over and over. "You can't save him unless you come to me."

Darius slid another few inches.

There was nothing to brace against. The carpet gave only the slightest traction. She rammed her feet against it and braced for Rhozan's next onslaught.

It was worse. Darius slid closer to the rip, pulling her with him.

"Darius, wake up. Help me!" Riley screamed. They were only about two metres from the sparkling cloud. She couldn't let go. But if she didn't, they'd both get sucked in. "Alec!"

Across the room, Alec didn't even seem to notice her plight.

"Your choice, Riley." Rhozan sounded pleased. "Either you let him go or you continue this feeble attempt to save him and I get you both."

The wind picked up in strength. Riley was nearly flattened to the floor. Her hair whipped into her eyes. The sofa overturned and slid across the floor straight into the rip. She ducked her head again as the contents of the closet near the front door emptied into the air and *whooshed* into Rhozan's world. The lifeless body of the Emissary rolled along the floor and stopped abruptly as it came up against her back. She suppressed a scream.

Darius was pulled another foot closer. The Emissary's arms flung up with a sideways gust. She kicked at the body, desperately trying to shove it free. The wind pushed the corpse closer to her, wrapping the torso around her. Horrified, she twisted wildly and kicked again. She couldn't suppress the scream that tore from her lips.

The wind tore brutally at her, this time from the side, knocking her face-down onto Darius' stomach. The corpse, its obstruction removed, slipped free and tumbled towards the rip.

Wait. The Emissary had the orbs. He'd put them in his jacket pocket. With only seconds to spare, Riley leapt into action. She let go of Darius and lunged towards the corpse as it rolled towards the rip.

She caught the edge of its jacket in her right hand. She held on as tightly as she could.

Freed, Darius began to slide towards the rip.

Heart in her mouth, Riley clawed for a better grip. The material of the Emissary's suit began to tear.

"No," she cried in horror. Scrambling with an almost Herculean effort, she grabbed again.

Something firm and round clinked under her fingers. The orbs. She almost had them.

Darius' shoulders slid past her.

Another metre and Rhozan would have him.

She tugged and pulled. Where was the opening to the pocket? Why couldn't she find it?

The wind rolled Darius over. Another foot closer. He slammed into the coffee table.

She clawed at the suit jacket, but the wind was so wild it tossed the material around. She couldn't get a proper grip. The corpse was about to be pulled into the rip. She couldn't stop it.

256   Only the overturned coffee table lodged against the kitchen doorway blocked Darius' path into Rhozan's world.

"Darius!" she screamed. "Wake up."

The Emissary opened his eyes.

The wind stopped. Everything airborne fell to the ground.

The Emissary lunged at Riley. His filthy hands scrabbled at her. His fingers grabbed her neck.

Get the orbs. They were the only things that mattered.

His hands tightened. She couldn't breathe.

The orbs.

Her fingers found the edge of the pocket opening and plunged inside. She touched the warm glass. *Yes.*

Tighter still. Glittering lights of asphyxiation under her eyelids. Desperate to breathe.

Another inch and an orb slipped into her palm. The two other orbs clinked together. She grabbed at a second one, barely managing to clasp two in her small fingers.

Could. Not. Breathe.

Get lost, she thought with the last of her strength.

The Emissary jerked away as if hooked by an invisible cord. His eyes closed, his body fell limply to the floor. Then, as the wind restarted with a vengeance, it took him and pulled him into the rip.

Riley flattened herself to the carpet. The wind blew over her. She tightened her grip on the orbs. *Hold me still*, she instructed the Tyon power inside her.

Darius, she aimed whatever power she had in his direction. *Wake up. NOW.*

47

Darius groaned. He raised a shaky hand to his forehead.

"Darius, we're in trouble!" Riley yelled, her voice barely audible above the tempest.

Darius tried to sit up but was flattened by the wind. The gusts changed direction. Darius just grabbed onto the kitchen doorframe in time. His body swung around as, feet first, the wind pulled him towards the rip. The coffee table swung around and, now free of the door frame, slid straight for the rip.

"Orb," Darius gasped.

Riley transferred one orb to the arm closest to Darius. His hand grasped the smooth glass.

"STOP!" Darius yelled.

Yellow lightning burst out of the rip. It hit the ceiling, slammed into the walls, pierced the floor. The carpet, only inches from Riley, burst into flame.

She screamed.

"You are mine." Rhozan's voice shook the walls.

"No." Darius panted. Fingers white, he could barely hold onto the doorframe, the hand aiming the orb at the rip. His body was pulled off the ground.

Lightning barely missed him.

"Alec," Darius called. "We need you. For god's sake, fight."

Rhozan was inside Alec's head. Alec had the smothering impression of something without boundaries. There was a towering intelligence, too, but it seemed strangely limited to Alec's way of thinking. Glorified memories of games he'd played swirled around inside Rhozan, too. War, torture, winning, destruction: a veritable feast. Alec had never realized just how violent his beloved games were.

He felt sickened.

Rhozan thought the games were real. The first touch of Alec's mind had stimulated a desire to attack, born of the belief that this planet was a banquet of violence. Alec's own anger and sullen temperament had tipped the balance in favour of staying to invade.

48

It was his fault. His temper, his predilection for violent games, his belief that he could solve his problems with his fists.

It was overwhelming. Regrettable. Shameful.

He sunk deeper.

Rhozan's presence grew stronger.

Something sharp hit him across his temple. Again. And again. Penetrating his despair. He opened his eyes.

Darius was gripping the door frame to the kitchen with one arm and in his free hand was a ceramic mug. Darius lobbed the mug in Alec's direction and yelled.

"Alec, fight him."

The porcelain smashed into shards inches from Alec's face.

"It's my fault." Alec could barely get the words past his lips.

Regret. Wishful longing.

"Change it," Darius gasped. "He thinks it's a game. Change the rules."

Alec mutely shook his head.

Rhozan was pulsing now inside him. His skin burned with the assault. Soon it would be all over.

"Step into the portal," Rhozan instructed. "Come to me."

If he did, it would be over. Rhozan didn't want anyone but him. The wild unhappiness inside him would feed Rhozan for ages. He deserved to die. It was all his fault.

Despair. Shame.

Riley screamed. "You can still win, you idiot. Don't give up now."

"Ignore her," said Rhozan. "I command it."

Riley's face screwed up with anger. "I have an orb. Take it. Blow this sucker to kingdom come."

"No," yelled Darius. "He's too angry."

Could he? Was it possible to make up for all he'd done?

Rhozan's voice rumbled through him. "It is all your fault. You can change nothing. The game cannot start again."

Riley reached out as far as she was able. The orb glistened.

"Take it," she yelled against the screaming wind. "There's no more time."

Time. Alec's heart stood still. He knew. *He knew.*

Doubt vanished. Without thought, he swung out his hand and connected with hers. Fingers wet with sweat scrabbled for the orb. For a horrible second he thought she'd dropped it.

His fingers closed around hers as he pulled the orb free.

Riley's eyes widened in fear. "No," she shouted, "Alec, don't."

"No," Darius shouted. "Don't. You don't know what you'll start. Alec, *please.*"

"Stop. I command you!" Rhozan roared.

Riley screamed as the wind pulled her the last few feet before the rip. Darius let go of the doorjamb to reach her. Alec saw their hands connect in the split second before Darius was pulled inside the rip.

Riley was sucked in after.

They vanished.

No!

Alec had no choice. He couldn't let Riley and Darius die.

He threw himself into the rip before he could change his mind. Gripping the orb tight enough to almost break his knuckles, he focused every molecule of concentration on the task. He didn't know how to make it happen, but he'd done it before. *Take me back to when it started*, he thought desperately, *take me back.*

The howling inside his head increased in volume the moment he crossed over. Sensations unfamiliar and repulsive flowed over him. He kept his eyes closed. Whatever was in here he didn't want to see. *Concentrate.*

Rhozan was yelling "No" over and over, increasing in volume with every beat of Alec's heart.

Take me back to the beginning.

Colours danced and swirled inside his eyes. Souls touched and flitted away. Peter, then gone. Strangers, then gone. Their essence mingled with his and left. Too many souls. Too many thoughts. Overpowering. Nauseating. 261

Darius and Riley, his mom and dad, his brother, the kids from the bunker, everyone. He could save them all. Despite Darius' concerns.

Take me back.

The power grew. The electric charge was building under

his skin. Wild, uncontrolled power. His. He forced himself to stay focused. Felt his body begin to dissolve.

Take me back.

Someone grabbed his leg and didn't let go. He paid no attention. Focused.

The power increased. Just a bit more.

Take me back ... Make it work.

The power hurt. Burned through him like a live electrical charge. His mind boiled.

Rhozan's scream rose to an impossible pitch.

His resolve wavered for an instant with the enormous pain of it.

Suddenly, the power exploded. In him, through him, outside of him. A conflagration of possibility and force, destroying him in one all-consuming instant of *being*.

Then nothing.

Alec gave a massive shudder as his present self slammed into his previous self, merged and became one. Awareness hit him broadside. He was out of the rip. Back in his old apartment. But *when?* The vertigo hit the same time as nausea drowned him, a hundred times worse than the transport to Halifax. He groaned.

He hardly noticed Darius and Riley winking into existence beside him; he was too busy retching and reeling. He barely had time to register the thought that he must have really done a number on the time-travel thing to feel this incredibly awful when a sudden stunning blow across his chin momentarily focused his attention on something other than his churning stomach.

He spun around with the force of the strike, his shoulder slamming into the hallway wall an instant before his forehead made contact. Temporarily stunned, he began to slide to the carpet, all thought momentarily stalled. Someone grabbed his upper arm in a biting grip and halted his descent. What the *hell?*

A woman screamed.

A familiar male voice yelled, "Stop it, *now.*"

Alec was dimly aware of shouting, but the burst of pain in his chin drowned out any interest in what was going on around him. It took a moment before his brain began to function again. Who had hit him? Who was yelling? He blinked several times, trying to clear his fuzzy vision. The familiar tingle of Tyon *willingness* flitted across his skin.

49

"*Stand still.*"

The grip on Alec's arm lessened somewhat and Alec braced against the wall to hold himself up. Man, did that hurt. He squinted into the semi-gloom of early evening in the dimly lit hallway of his apartment.

Darius moved between Alec and his father, letting Alec's arm go completely. Alec had never seen him so angry. The air crackled with tension.

"There is *never* an excuse for a man to hit his child or his wife." Darius took another step towards Alec's dad. Despite the fact that Darius was a couple of inches shorter and slimmer, the bigger man stepped backwards, both hands in the air in front of his chest in an acknowledgment of defeat. The stench of sweat and booze oozed from Alec's dad and tainted the hallway in a miasma of failure and misery. "You're a coward," Darius spat. "Just a stinking coward."

Alec shook his head to clear it. The sharp pain was already fading, although a steady throbbing was taking its place. The sickness persisted, but he pushed that forcibly out of his mind. He had to pay attention.

Alec was suddenly pushed farther down the hallway as his mother shoved in front of him, barging her way between Darius and Alec's father.

"Stay out of the way, Marina," Darius said firmly. His eyes never left Alec's father. His muscles visibly tensed.

"I don't know who you are or how you got into my home," Alec's mom gasped, reaching out to grab Darius by the arm. "But please leave."

"Yeah," Alec's father snarled. "Get out. Whoever you are."

264

Alec took a shaky breath. There was no reasoning with his dad when he was like this. And besides, his dad had boxed in university and had a wicked left hook as well as at least twenty kilos on Darius. He had to stop this and fast.

"Dad," he began, his voice far wobblier than he would

have liked. "This is Darius Finn. He's a friend of mine and—" He didn't get any further.

"Wipe that grin off your face, you worthless little—" His father swung again, reaching for Alec with a closed fist that would have knocked him unconscious had it landed. Darius pivoted and twisted simultaneously with feline grace. He grabbed the moving arm and, using the momentum, flipped Alec's father around and down. He landed on the ground at Alec's feet. There was a distinctly horrible crack. His father gave a sharp cry. Darius let go.

Alec's mom gave a shriek and dropped to her knees beside him. She touched his shoulder tentatively. Alec's father muttered something foul under his breath as he shoved at her. His left arm was clearly bent the wrong way.

"How dare you?" Alec's mother flared. Tears streamed down her cheeks. Her eyes flashed with anger as her voice rose. "You come in my house uninvited. You assault my husband."

"Your husband belted your son, you stupid cow." Riley was almost hidden in the shadows. She was on her hands and knees on the floor farther down the hall, almost in the living room. Her eyes were huge in her unnaturally pale face. She stared at Alec's mom, a look of disgust momentarily flashing across her features.

"Don't talk to my mom like that," Alec said automatically. He couldn't meet her eyes. His face burned with embarrassment and anger.

"Get them out of my house." Alec's mom pointed an unsteady finger at him. "I don't care who they are. And get out with them."

Alec swallowed bile. This was all wrong. He was supposed to come back and turn everything around. He was supposed to save them all. Now, Darius had broken his father's arm, his mother was screaming at him to leave and Riley was convinced his entire family was a bunch of losers. Why on earth had he picked *this* moment to return to? Any minute a neighbour was going to call the police. He had to stop this.

"Mom," he yelled. "Listen to me for a minute."

His father groaned as he pulled his useless arm closer to his body. He swore loudly and pointedly at Alec's mother.

"That's enough." Alec's jaw clamped shut. White-hot anger surged through his blood at the profanity. This was the last time his father was going to bully his mother. The last time she cowered and took it to save their skins. "Leave. Her. Alone." He pulled the orb out of his pocket. It pulsed with brilliance as Alec's power flowed through it. The entire hallway lit up. "Be *still*."

Both his parents froze in position.

"Once you've used it you can never go back," Darius said with a deep and shuddering sigh. He moved to Alec's side and leaned against the wall, closing his eyes with profound fatigue. His blistering fury was replaced by an expression of utmost sadness.

Alec looked away. He faced his parents. He had to think this through. He had the power literally in his hands to change everything. He could make his father behave. He could end the drinking, the rages, the *pain*. He could make his mother stronger and less dependent. He could wipe her memory of all the sadness. His father's, too. Darius could heal the broken arm. Neither parent would ever know.

Alec glanced at Riley. Did she understand what he could do?

"We can't use the orbs, Alec," Riley said hesitantly, as if the words were forming in her mind at the same speed as her understanding. "There's no place for it now. In this time."

Alec gave his head a brief shake. She was wrong. He could fix it.

"The orb gives you an edge, Alec, and not just in time," Darius explained. "It's a power to rule the world if you want to. An uncontrollable, unpredictable power. Once you've chosen to use it, you've chosen a life with me. With the Tyon Collective. You cannot remain untrained."

"No. I'm not. I'm just going to …" Alec trailed off. He was just going to what? Wipe the last few minutes or days or even months, from his parents' lives as if it had never happened?

"We're not meant to have this kind of power," Riley whispered. "How will you give it up once you've used it here? Now? What'll happen when you get angry the next time? What if you do something in your sleep?"

Could he tap into the Tyon power when unconscious?

"The fact you've reached for your orb tells me just how much you've come to rely on it," Darius said wearily. "It's become a part of you, just like it's a part of me. You may have changed time, Alec, brought us back to before the first rip, but you haven't changed yourself. The power is still inside you and you know how to use it. Going back won't undo what you know."

"I'll give my orb back," Alec said, cringing at the pleading tone in his own voice. But his hand didn't move and his grip didn't lessen even as the words left his mouth. He couldn't pull his eyes away from his parents.

"It doesn't matter," Darius sighed. "Once it's awoken inside you, not having an orb won't make much difference. You'll still be able to do a fair bit of damage without one. You have done. Remember?"

Alec's heart was pounding. He didn't want to hear this. It wasn't fair. After all the sacrifice and hard work they were back to the same place again. A feeling of inevitability surged through him. He tried another desperate appeal. "You can stick around. Teach me to keep it under control."

Darius shook his head. "And that's gonna work? You're going to stay beside me, day and night, week after week, pretending to the world you're just some ordinary kid while focusing every ounce of attention on keeping the tiger inside you asleep?"

"We've changed." Riley took a deep shaky breath. "I can't go home, either."

"There really isn't a choice, Alec. We have to wipe their memories and let them go," Darius added.

Alec mutely shook his head. Darius didn't know what he was asking.

"There was never any real choice," Darius continued, speaking to Riley now as much as Alec. "I didn't want you to shift us in time for lots of reasons, Alec, but mostly this one. Giving up this future is harder now that you've seen it. But you can't stay here. None of us can."

"I can learn to control it." Alec could barely get the words past his numb lips. He couldn't stay. He had to stay.

"We don't have time," Darius said. "They'll be on to us any minute now. We might have the edge on them for a couple of days, max, but a shift this big won't go unnoticed. Even if I wanted to let you stay here and now, I couldn't. They won't let you, even if I would."

"Who are they?" Riley climbed to her feet. She swayed for a moment until her hand braced against the wall. "Who's gonna notice?"

Darius moved to her side and put an arm around her waist to steady her. She leaned into him with obvious relief. Darius stared at Alec across the narrow expanse of hallway, Alec's immobile parents between them. "The Collective. There are monitors at Home Base that are blaring right now. Trust me: Logan's trying to pinpoint the source of this as we stand here." Darius took a deep breath. "But the Council's the bigger problem. They're dead serious about controlling time. They'll be after you, Alec, the second they figure out who did it. And it's putting it mildly to say they hate a shifter."

Alec stared at his father's face. The anger was dissipating from his blood, and fear was taking its place. He felt it in his bones. Darius was right. He'd urged him not to move them in time, warned him the consequences would be dire, but he hadn't listened. He'd been too desperate. Too willing to damn the consequences. Even when he hadn't known what they were.

"It was the only thing I could think of to save us." Alec spoke almost to himself.

"They'll be after your family if you stay, Alec." Darius reached out and touched his shoulder for a moment, but Alec flinched away. Kindness was worse. "You love them. I know you do. So protect them, keep them out of the way of the Collective and the Council. Leave now, with me."

"I …" There was nothing to say. All the arguments died on the tip of his tongue. He was a danger to the people he loved. There was no way he could be sure he'd never use the power to hurt someone in a moment of anger. A huge knot formed in his throat.

"If Alec goes with us now, can't you, you know, fix this?" Riley pointed her finger at Alec's parents, both still frozen on their knees. "I mean," she waggled her hand meaningfully, "put things right. Alec can't leave knowing his father might beat the living crap out of his mom and stuff. You could help them."

"Changing people's personalities is seriously against the rules, Riley." Darius' voice was gruff.

"Yeah, like we haven't broken any rules so far." Riley rolled her eyes. "Get real, Dare. The guy's only gonna mope about his folks for the next twenty years unless you give their attitudes a major adjustment. Cut him some slack. He's had a rough day."

Alec could barely meet their eyes. Deep inside he knew Darius was right. Tyon power surged through his blood with every beat of his heart. There was no way he could turn it off now, and controlling it was harder than he wanted to acknowledge. It was only childlike thinking to believe that he could return to the boy he'd been a few weeks ago.

Alec stared at the immobile faces of his parents. Sadness, regret, love and longing surged through his heart. He couldn't turn his back on them and never see them again, no matter what Darius said. He just couldn't.

"I can help them both." Darius' orb pulsed and mixed with Alec's own. "Start the process of healing. I can't guarantee your dad will give up the booze, but I can work on the depression. If his mind is clearer, he can fight his own demons."

"And my mom?" The words barely made a sound.

"She's stronger than you realize, Alec. But yes, I can help her, too. With Riley's assistance."

Riley pulled away from his embrace a bit to stare up at Darius' face. "Are you yanking my chain?"

Darius' smile was brief. "I wouldn't dare. You have the healing gift. Same as me."

"Cool." Riley raised an eyebrow. For a moment her eyes met with Alec's before she turned back to face his parents, the faintest blush tinging her cheeks.

"You'd better get started." Alec gave a curt nod. He launched himself from the wall and brushed past them, heading quickly to the living room.

Riley opened her mouth to say something but Alec ignored her. He was too distracted as he trudged down the hallway towards the living room. His mind was reeling. It was all over. In fact, it had never happened. Rhozan hadn't arrived yet. The world was not destroyed. Peter was in his bedroom, not floating around Rhozan's rip. His parents were alive and safe and shortly would be in a better state than they'd been for over a year.

270 He was leaving the life he'd known for something completely unexpected. The sustaining dream of fixing Rhozan's invasion and living happily ever after was over. What the future held, heaven only knew.

He ignored the faint tingle of excitement in the base of his stomach. The incredible possibilities of a life with

Darius Finn and Riley were nowhere near the forefront of his mind. There was lots of time to get used to that idea, even embrace it. But not now.

It never occurred to him to look back towards the hall closet where the first rip he'd created had once sat, waiting. It never occurred to him that the wild anger he'd briefly expended had had any results. He didn't see the sparkles.

About the Author

Susan M. MacDonald lives
in Newfoundland. She is
married, has two children,
two dogs and a fluctuating
number of goldfish.

www.susan-macdonald.com <http://www.susan-macdonald.com>